I0762055

TREE OF MATCHSTICKS

PART THREE OF THE HOUSE OF MATCHSTICKS SERIES

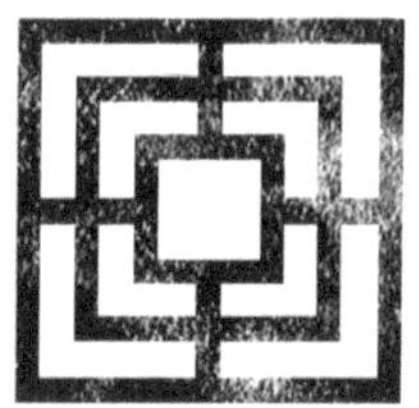

ELISA DOWNING

ISBN: 978-1-7778857-0-0 (Hardcover)

ISBN: 978-1-7773305-9-0 (Electronic Book)

ISBN: 978-1-7773305-8-3 (Paperback)

Cover Art by Merilliza Chan

First edition, 2021

For content warnings, visit Elisa's website at elisadowning.com/content-warnings.

For Bennett

Let's do something somewhere, sometime, maybe.

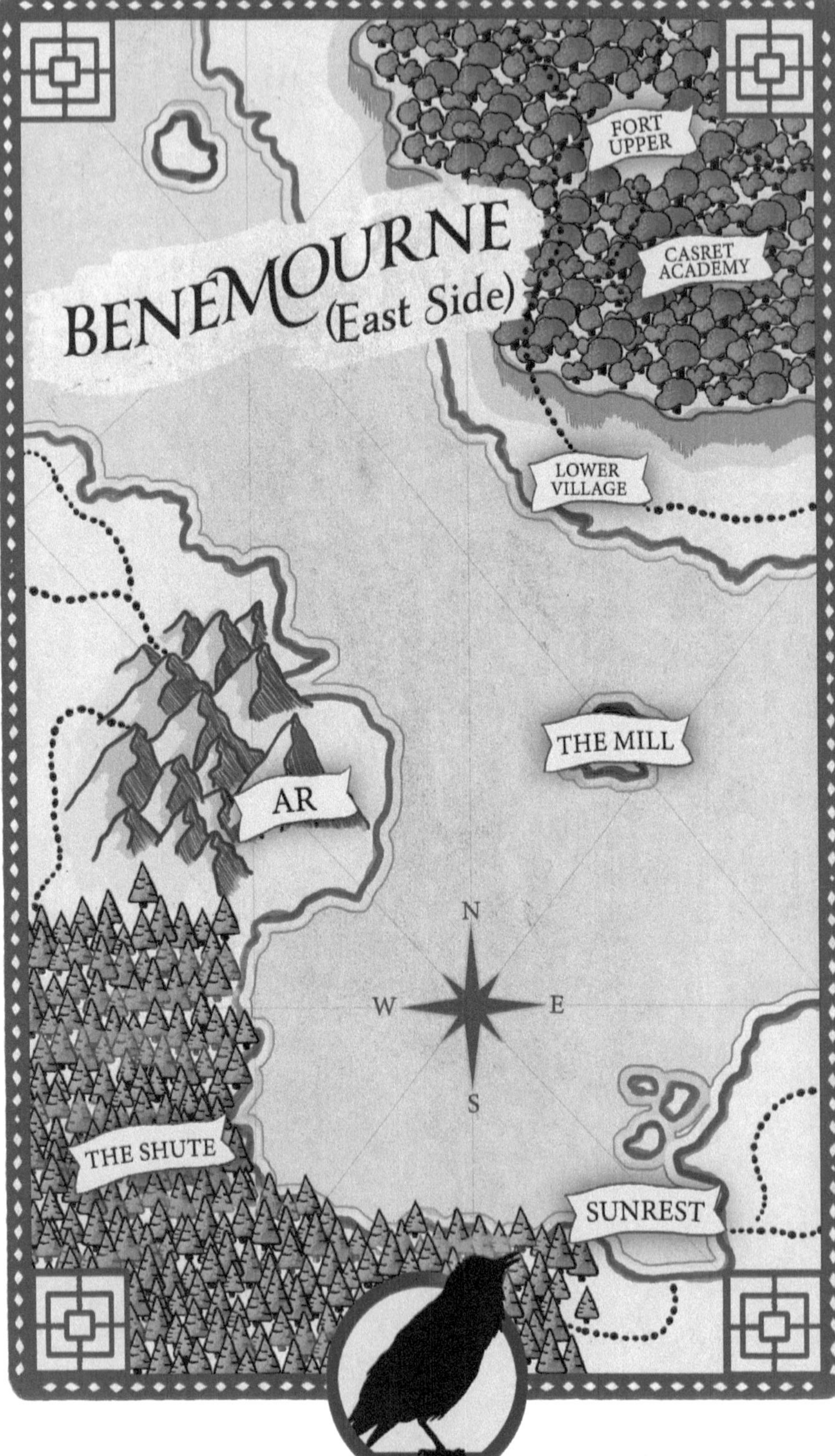
BENEMOURNE
(East Side)
FORT UPPER
CASRET ACADEMY
LOWER VILLAGE
THE MILL
AR
N
W
E
S
THE SHUTE
SUNREST

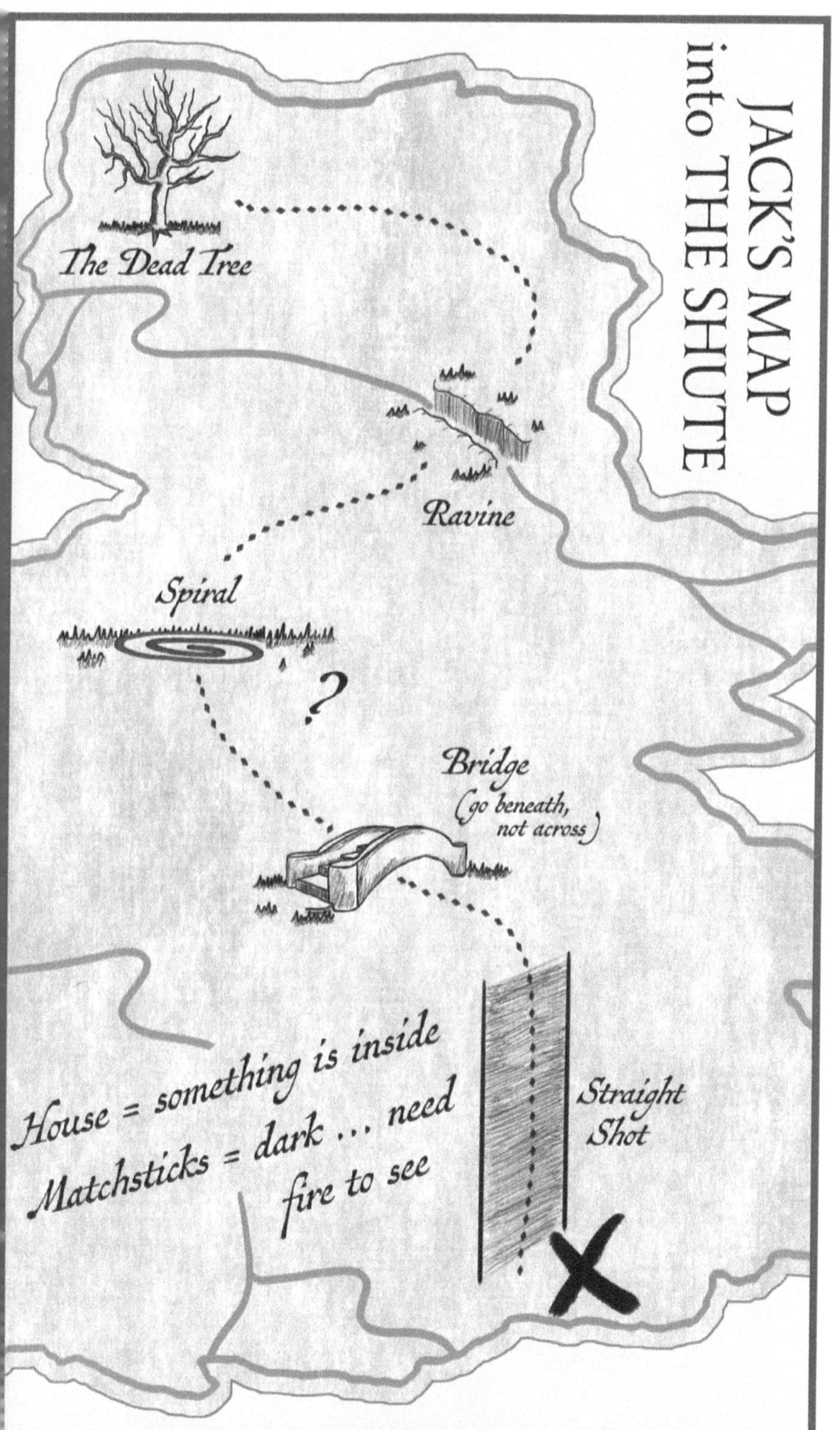

JACK'S MAP
into THE SHUTE
The Dead Tree
Ravine
Spiral
?
Bridge
(go beneath,
not across)
Straight
Shot
House = something is inside
Matchsticks = dark … need
fire to see
X

TABLE OF CONTENTS

PRONUNCIATION GUIDE

Adrises → a-DRY-sees
Adrudian → a-DREW-dee-an
Agustin → Ah-GUST-in
Caladrius → cal-AH-dree-us
Fael → FYE-ell
Faraday → fair-AH-day
Isaline → ee-SAH-leen
Jame → JAY-m
Minna → MEEN-ah
Nalissa - nah-LISS-ah
Neave → NEEV
Purpesia → perp-EZ-ee-ah
Rhody → RO-dee
Shute → SHOOT

TREE OF MATCH STICKS

PART THREE OF THE HOUSE OF MATCHSTICKS SERIES

1

UNSEEN
THE COLLECTOR

That night, the Collector left for the mill too late. He stepped from the edge of Ar's white sand shores and walked toward the cold rock island that held the mill. The sea air rushing into his sleeves and the waves lapping at his ankles were welcome feelings. He was going somewhere. Movement was what made him feel alive.

Or, the Collector corrected himself, *whatever I am that passes for being alive.*

Despite the relief of making a journey, his body was heavy. Halfway to the island, the Collector changed his composition and stood on the surface of the dark sea. There was nothing but silence and the churn of water. No moon or stars lit the plain of the black sky. Only a swathe of blue light emanating from the Jar of Lights forced back the night.

On instinct, the Collector scanned the horizon for Caladrius, and for a second, he thought he saw a tiny, bird-shaped bunch of stars soaring against the clouds. Of course, it was nothing. His eyes were playing tricks on him.

He gathered his fingers on the handle of his lantern and walked on.

Two nights prior, the Collector and Caladrius had escaped King Faraday's palace. The Collector had stumbled over the palace square, a wide stretch of black tile occupied only by a line of clockwork guards and the King's massive, crimson-sailed warship. Free of the shadow of the palace, he lurched into an alley after Caladrius. It took him a second to realize this was the same length of alleyway they had followed Cameron Agustin into on the day Lillian and Philip Just were executed. The day this all began.

Caladrius, squawking, had led the Collector to the little alcove where Cameron had sat waiting for Winn Just. The alcove was empty, a brick closet with a thin, slimy pipe sticking out the base of one wall. The Collector had run inside and pressed his back to the knobby bricks, setting the Jar of Lights down by his ankles with a shaking hand.

He'd passed his palms over his chest, his arms, and his

legs, searching for wounds as if the King's gaze could bore him full of holes. But there were no holes; simply the starry, insubstantial fabric of his coat, the ends of his sleeves, and the tops of his boots.

Having judged himself unharmed, he'd hurriedly upturned a cupped palm. "Caladrius ..."

She'd landed in the bowl of his hand. Her feathers were ruffled, spread every which way as if she'd been caught in a thunderstorm. The Collector had passed his fingertips gently over her wings. She was okay, too.

"What happened?" the Collector had rasped. He sank back against the wall. "He looked right at us, Cal. He talked to us."

Caladrius had shaken out her feathers, making a barely-audible twittering sound. The message was clear: She didn't know. Whatever she'd expected to happen when she led the Collector into the palace tonight, being seen by the King was a surprise.

"It's wrong." The Collector had lifted her to his shoulder, then rubbed his hands over his face. "We never should have been here."

Caladrius had chirped, squeezing his coat in her claws.

"He *saw* us, Cal. And I—I took a breath. I needed to take a breath."

Through his fingers, he'd stared at the souls bobbing in the Jar of Lights. He recalled the urge to breathe, the feeling of drowning in the throne room. His lips parting and a stream of air filling his lungs. And with the air ...

A memory.

"I saw myself," the Collector had murmured. The world wobbled, and he stared ahead in silence before continuing. "I was walking around the Dead Tree at the entrance of the Shute. And there were people waving goodbye to me. A woman, and a child. A daughter. My—" A quake began in his shoulders. He slid down to the ground, pulling his knees to his chest. "I was human."

The sensation of existence was still with him. Would he ever forget being stuck down in the world, living as bones and flesh? Or worse, maybe he had never forgotten in the first place. Maybe humanity had always been written into his shadow, hiding behind the breeze of his limbs, and lurking within the deep, invisible layer of reality he stepped through.

The Collector had shuddered. Caladrius made a whistling noise, far louder than he would have expected, and jumped into the air. He'd lifted his head from his hands, watching her soar around the alcove.

"What is it?"

She'd swooped and nudged the top of his head with her claws. The Collector had grabbed the brim of his hat before it could drop from his head. His mouth fell open—he couldn't believe his ears. Caladrius was singing, circling in the air as she had done that night in the forest at Casret Academy, with hundreds of starlings in murmuration.

A horrified shiver had gone through the Collector. "You're happy?"

Caladrius had fluttered onto his outstretched hand. He'd brought her to his face, and she'd pressed the top of her head to his brow. Her feathers were warm, but the breath puffing from her beak chilled him, dunking his heart in ice. How could she react this way? They had been thrown from their purpose. They had been *seen*.

The Collector had an abrupt thought. He pulled his hand from his face and stared at Caladrius.

"You wanted this to happen. You wanted me to remember."

She'd offered a quiet response. A low coo.

"That's what this is about." He'd paused, another realization dropping into his head like a stone. "The Justs told you."

Her bird's eyes had flashed, glittering within the shadow of her silhouette. The Collector's gaze slid down to the Jar of Lights. There had been a moment, after the executions, when he'd sensed the souls of Lillian and Philip Just communicating with Caladrius. As if soul and starling shared a language.

Caladrius hadn't been herself since that day. She'd led him across the sea and back again, only sometimes to souls that needed collecting, and always after that girl. Isaline. He'd thought it was because Caladrius wanted to help Isaline and her friends—maybe that was part of it, still—

but she'd had another intention, too. Trying to remember who they had been.

Memory had consequences. He and Caladrius had a purpose, clear-cut. They were a gateway, helping humans get to wherever they went after they died. If the Collector breathed the same air, remembered a human life, what was to keep him from becoming human? From dying?

The thought opened a pit in his stomach. He wanted things to go back to normal. He had told Caladrius that, over and over.

She'd nuzzled the tip of his nose with her feathers, then hopped to perch on his knee. The Collector drew back, his face twisting into a grimace.

"No. You didn't say anything about this part."

Caladrius had chirped at him, as if to say, *I tried.*

He'd balled his hands into fists. The murmuration. Hundreds of birds flying in tandem, each connected to the other, affecting the other, until they were one being with many parts, bound by existence. She'd been trying to show him how he might fit into such a puzzle. How *she* might.

"Leave this be, Cal." The Collector had hugged one arm around himself, drawing his coat closer to him. "We never should have followed them. We should have left this alone, like we're supposed to."

He hadn't wanted it to sound like an accusation, but it did. She fixed him with a stare, stretching her light-flecked wings.

"It isn't our place to see any of this. Pushing that boat

was wrong—helping her was wrong." As the Collector spoke, something tight in his chest had relaxed; this was the truth, finally. He tapped two fingers to his shoulder, gesturing for Caladrius to hop on. "It's time for us to walk away."

She'd made a long, deep, unhappy sound. He tapped his shoulder again, but she'd just stared, her claws digging into his knee. His face warmed.

"I told you before. We are apart. This—" He'd gestured to the alcove around them, the darkness of the alley and the city beyond. "—isn't for us. I've been foolish. I've entertained this for too long. Come now."

She'd bitten his finger. The sharp stab of pain made him yelp. He gawked, and she whistled loudly.

"I don't care if the King knows where they're going."

She'd whistled a second time.

"I don't care if I started it."

He had seen enough of Caladrius' expressions to know she was glaring at him. "I don't care if you want to help. Aren't you listening to me?" His voice was rising, but he was powerless to stop it. "*We are not part of them!*"

Caladrius had flinched, hopping backward a few inches. The Collector tried to swallow, but found his throat tight and dry.

"Go, then, if you care so much. About those humans. About remembering. Go after them and see what you can do."

He pressed his elbows to his sides. The Collector and

Caladrius had never disagreed. There had never been anything to argue about. She led him to the dead, and he collected souls until they were ready to move on. It was how their lives were supposed to be.

Caladrius had gathered the fabric of his trousers into her claws and flapped her wings, tugging as if she could pull him with her.

"I'm not going," he'd whispered. "I won't die, or disappear, just to know who I was before."

She let go of his trousers and went still. There was a look in her eyes that he had never seen before. Something desolate, like after a century of walking she'd found herself in the same place as she'd begun. The Collector fixed his eyes on the ground.

After a long minute, her weight had lifted off his knee and she'd taken to the air. The Collector had sat in silence for a while longer, fuming, before glancing up.

"Caladrius," he'd said.

But she was gone, lost to the sleeping city.

HE'D SPENT two days on his own, wandering the streets of Ar, before deciding to go find her.

The sun was mercilessly hot and the streets thick with the dust of thousands of people traveling shoulder-to-shoulder. On the first morning, the Collector lingered at the mouth of a side street, then approached the nearest sales stand. An old, wrinkled man sat behind the makeshift wooden table, next to an Adrudian-heated stove roasting nuts and vegetables. He was hunched over in his chair, head propped in one hand, staring at the hordes of passerby.

The Collector wedged himself in front of the table. The old man's expression didn't change.

"Hello?" The Collector said, feeling ridiculous.

The man didn't respond. The Collector waved his arms in front of his face. Nothing. The old man's gaze slipped over the Collector in the way he was used to, like river water over a rock.

A trickle of relief ran through the Collector. Faraday was the only person—if he could be called a person—that could see the Collector and Caladrius. And, the Collector reminded himself, the King only spotted him when he'd taken a breath. Maybe the act of breathing, a human gesture, made the Collector visible.

No problem, then. The Collector planned to never take another breath.

He made his way up to Ar's red-tiled rooftops, avoiding the crowd. Walking through humans made his insides sludgy and slow, and he was annoyed by his tendency to notice what each person was saying.

"Damned Thieves got ahold of my money, if I don't find a way to ..."

"City Watch are around the next corner. Tell your friends to double back and go through the alleys."

"Are they stealing Adrudian, now? Why in the world wouldn't you have any, Drinker?"

This last statement worked its way under the Collector's skin, nagging at him as he strode across the rooftops, watching the crowd mill. He didn't know what he had expected. The Adrudian shortage wouldn't happen all at once. It would grow by degrees: the world getting darker little by little until they were all frozen, night-blind, and dying.

If Isaline and her friends couldn't stop the King, all of Benemourne would suffer.

"They better know what they're doing," he said, but there was no one to listen.

Aloneness settled on his back as hours on the rooftops stretched on. He ignored it and focused on the sky instead —perfect blue, unmarred by clouds. Tiers of buildings stretched beneath him in a vast spread. They were jumbled against the white marble of the Watch Wall as if they had slid down the side of the mountain in tandem, coming to rest steps from the sea.

Day turned to night, then morning again. The Collector's heart grew stormy. Without Caladrius, he was a boat without a steersman, unable to find any souls to collect. He considered leaving the city, but when Caladrius came back, how would she find him?

On the second day, he drifted, his mind a jumble. The lives of the humans around him pressed against his ears and eyes, making it difficult to think. He tried to steel himself against them, but with Caladrius gone, he couldn't help but observe. He stood in a corner, watching a group of Quandary Thieves pick the pocket of a pompous man in a suit. He slunk in the shadows, listening as a young woman pleaded with an Adrudian Drinker to tell her the fate of her vanished friend. He gazed at families, couples, and groups walking hand-in-hand at the edge of the ocean.

As the light grew blue and the sun began to set once more, he perched at the end of the Watch Wall, staring while a woman and her son pointed to the first flickers of stars. The wonder on the boy's face made the Collector's chest ache.

Dragging his eyes away, he turned the Jar of Lights over in his hands. The souls inside swirled, silent balls of light that belonged to each of the dead humans he'd met over the last week. He waited until the souls of Lillian and Philip Just floated close, then leaned down, bringing his face to the lantern's bulb.

"Why haven't you left yet?" he said. "You're supposed to move on."

They made no response, just bobbed in the way that souls did. The Collector pursed his lips, glowering at the three of them: Lillian, Philip, and the dead girl from the dorm room at Casret Academy.

He should never have pushed that rowboat.

He tightened his fingers around the Jar of Lights' sides. Sixteen years had been spent avoiding thinking about why he had helped Isaline. Pushing the boat had been impulsive and foolish, yes, but he was starting to worry that there had been something else, too. A longing to give Isaline the chance to experience life—a human life that he had once known.

Take a breath.

Groaning, the Collector turned the Jar of Lights and shook it upside down.

"Go! Leave! Fly away! I want nothing to do with you."

The souls inside the lantern rotated in place. The Collector tossed the Jar of Lights to his side with a frustrated growl.

"Have it your way."

But night fell, the sky and the sea darkened, and the stars came out in earnest. Clouds rolled in from the horizon. The stars wouldn't be visible for long, yet the boy and his mother kept pointing. This one, to this one, to this one; drawing lines with the tips of their index fingers, stars connecting as if they were birds, flying at the nexus of each point, hinting at the vast constellation Caladrius had tried to get the Collector to see.

The Collector couldn't see the constellation. He wouldn't. But maybe he could still convince her.

As the clouds thickened, blotting out the night sky, the Collector glanced at the souls in the lantern. They had gathered at one side, facing him.

"Stop looking at me like that," he said to them.

He stood, slowly, and stretched. Then he grabbed the brass handle of the Jar of Lights and headed out to sea.

The Collector had walked nearly to the island when he was arrested by a strange sound. The murky, orange-splattered silhouette of the mill had come into view, still small on the horizon, but the waves close to him were splashing against something solid. He looked around, and a shape appeared from the night: a ferry, tossing darkly on the cold ocean. Its onboard lanterns had been closed.

The Collector hesitated, peering at the misshapen figure. This had to be the ferry Isaline, Jame, and the rest of them had taken to the mill. He recognized the scorch marks on the hull and the weathered grooves coating its sides. But the Collector was traveling two days after them. Plenty of time for Captain Knots' ferry to make it back to Ar or Lower Village. Why was it here, sitting motionless on the ocean, not even halfway back home?

Casting a look at the mill, the Collector strode toward the ferry and lifted the Jar of Lights. Blue light washed over the dilapidated steel hull. Nerves skittered along the Collector's shoulders. Something wasn't right.

He rose up the side of the ship and onto the deck. The wood was damp but sturdy beneath his boots, the air chilly and silent. There was no one in sight, just empty steel benches and closed iron lanterns creaking on their lines.

"Caladrius?" he called.

No response. The back of his neck tingled.

The Collector did a quick search of the deck, but found nothing that told him why the ferry had stopped. Small, sealed drums of Adrudian lined the interior, pressed up against crates of cork life jackets, stockpiled in the likely case of the ferry's sinking. A long streak of glistening seawater was splashed from the side of the boat to a hatch that led below deck.

The Collector approached the hatch. It was sitting propped open on its hinges, a sheet of empty darkness beyond. Crouching, he lowered the Jar of Lights and illuminated an iron ladder.

"Hello?" he said. "Caladrius?"

The ferry groaned, but there were no answering sounds. Forcing down his unease, the Collector dropped through the opening, using the lantern to guide his way.

Below deck, the ferry was as dark and silent as it had been above. The Collector sidestepped stacks of wooden boxes crammed with fireworks. Each firework was ornately designed with a long, white fuse hanging from the end. The Collector winced. A spare flame would set the whole boat alight.

He turned from the fireworks and spun in a circle, swinging the Jar of Lights in a wide arc.

"Cal?" he murmured into the silence.

Nothing responded, but a glint of light caught his attention in the far corner. The Collector froze. An eye? No—the sparkle was near the ground, sitting on a pile of something he couldn't make out. The glinting object was round and shiny. A button.

The Collector slowly crossed the cabin, passing around wooden crates and bunches of fireworks. As he went, the pile of shadows turned into a big overcoat lined with buttons. Then the overcoat became a figure, which became a man. Or what was left of a man.

Swallowing, the Collector kneeled next to the body. He reached to touch it, then pulled his hand away. Captain Knots' eyes stared up at nothing, two silver coins. He was laid limply on the ground on his back. The Jar of Lights' blue glow illuminated his normally round, pink cheeks, now sallow and greenish.

Seeing his expression, the Collector's head jerked back. Captain Knots' face was stretched in horror. His jaw hung open, revealing dry, blackened gums.

The man-snake.

It had come onto the ship. The streak of seawater across the deck was its trail. The Collector shivered. He recalled the brown-haired girl in the dorm room at Casret Academy. She had been slouched against the wall, her skin greened in death, her eyes wide and staring.

Her soul swirled in the Jar of Lights at his side. The Collector chewed his bottom lip, looking at the body. He had tried for two days to find a soul in need of collecting, but now he hesitated. Could he do this without Caladrius? *Should* he?

He didn't see another option. The Collector pressed

his hand to Captain Knots' chest and *pulled*. Bright light pooled beneath his palm. He led the soul into the Jar of Lights, watching as it fell from his fingers in a radiant mist that made him think of the sea.

When it was done, the Collector straightened and slid through the side of the ferry onto the water again. In the fresh air, he shook his arms. His heart thumped in his ears. If the man-snake had been on the ferry, it wasn't there now. Which meant there was only one place it could be.

The Collector skimmed over the water and touched down on the rocky shore of the mill's island.

"Caladrius, it's me," he called, hoping against hope she was near enough to hear him.

Nothing moved. Just that unending stillness.

He pushed his hat firmly onto his head and walked to the mill, dread blooming in his chest. The massive brick building was a giant crouched against the black sky. The Collector was tiny compared to the mill—and Caladrius even tinier. He could hardly think she was alone inside. How could he have let her go by herself? His stomach clenched.

As he approached the building, he lifted the Jar of Lights to examine the front door. Blue light slid over the brick wall and illuminated only a dark hole where the door should have been. Someone had torn the huge sliding door clean out of the wall. The Collector changed his composition and felt around with the toe of his boot. There it was, just inside the mill: a heavy sheet of metal lying dented on the concrete ground.

Bracing himself, the Collector stepped inside the building. He didn't get far before he had to stop, his mouth thinning in surprise. The interior of the mill was wrecked: whole machines had been knocked down and broken into pieces; discarded metal and Adrudian blanketed the dust-ridden floor; the mottled limbs of clockwork pickaxers were strewn everywhere. The Collector bent and turned over a featureless, wooden head that had been ripped from a mechanical neck.

What happened here?

The mill's floorspace, though clearly the site of some violent brawl, was now still and silent. The King's voice came back to him: *I'll send orders for the mill to be closed. We'll give them a little head start, shall we?* No one had been here since Isaline and her friends.

The Collector drifted from wall to wall, finding his voice and calling out to Caladrius. She was nowhere to be found.

Eventually he came upon another body: the mill warden, slumped against a wheelbarrow near the double doors to the mine shaft. Her matted yellow hair hung in tangles, obscuring her face. In the crook of her neck was a large black rat, curled against her shoulder with its whiskers trembling. The Collector didn't bother to reach past the rat to see if the mill warden's eyes were wide and her face tinged green. He already knew they would be.

Rhody Charlotte's soul was a bright, pinkish hue. It fell into the Jar of Lights and joined the others.

The Collector stood, eyeing the doors to the mine shaft. They were wrenched open, the thick metal rippled on either side, leaving a patch of darkness between.

Take a breath.

The urge to inhale scraped at his ribcage. He ignored it and walked the few steps to the mine shaft. Raising the Jar of Lights, he stuck his head through the space between the doors. The shaft beyond was small and empty. A series of robust metal cables reached from a pulley mechanism on the ceiling. He followed the cables with his eyes until they descended out of sight.

"Cal?" the Collector ventured. "Caladrius?"

No response. An upwards flow of air kissed his face. He imagined the creature—*Richard*, the Collector reminded himself—winding down the cables like a snake, following Isaline deep underground. Following *Caladrius* deep underground.

The Collector's hands started to tremble. She was on her own down there. This mine was no place for a starling. For his friend.

He urged himself to step into the mine shaft, to find her and convince her to come back with him, but his feet were frozen. He couldn't help but imagine his last visit to the mines, collecting the souls of human pickaxers burned to ashes. How many times had he glanced down the tunnel and imagined a coiled thing in the dark? Staring at him. Waiting to reach out with its claws and drag him screaming to a place he'd promised himself he'd never see again.

No. The Collector shook his head, trying to clear it. *Not* again. *For the first time.*

Take a breath.

His vision blurred, the mine shaft warping. The urge to breathe was only going to get stronger if he went into the mines. He might get lost, and the urge would grow so intense he wouldn't be able to stand it. He would open his airways, fill his lungs, and a memory would come to him, down there in the dark. He'd be alone, remembering the life he'd forgotten. Changing in ways he couldn't understand.

Meanwhile, Caladrius would be roaming in the blackness with those humans. She wasn't afraid to remember, not like him. But the more she breathed, the more fragile she became. What was to keep her from getting hurt, the way a bird did? What was to keep her from dying?

The Collector dug the fingers of one hand into his chest. Caladrius was his friend—she was his only friend, and she was in danger. He couldn't leave her alone.

But he *was* going to leave her alone.

He knew it even before he backed away from the mine shaft, treading on shards of broken machines and piles of unprocessed Adrudian. He pressed the Jar of Lights to his hip and rushed from the mill and onto the rock-scattered shore. There, he sank to the ground behind the concrete retaining wall, afraid to stand lest he draw a breath.

Had he been a coward when he was human? Had he been afraid, senselessly afraid as he was now?

The sea crashed, invisible behind a barrier of solid night. The Collector remained still as the clouds above churned, as the tide pulled in. And then, later, he remained still as the drumming of an engine pierced the air. Giant, crimson sails appeared on the horizon—the warship, flown from its place in Ar's palace square.

The Collector didn't peek from behind the retaining wall as the warship came to land on the island. He didn't dare look as King Faraday disembarked, enormous feet clanking on the concrete, brass limbs grinding, engine-heart pounding.

The King cocked a pistol, the same type he'd used to try to kill a baby in a rowboat sixteen years ago. He entered the mill and disappeared down the mine shaft, in pursuit of Isaline and her friends.

When it started to rain, the Collector changed his composition and let the drops fall through him to the rocks below, as if he'd never been there at all.

2

THE TUNNEL

ISALINE

Isaline told herself she could envision the sky. If she looked up, the orange beam of her headlamp illuminated nothing but the tunnel ceiling, a strip of rough rock scattered with sparkling flakes Cameron called *mica*. But if she unfocused her eyes, her imagination transposed a sky on the rock, making the tunnel expand.

In the hours after they left the mine shaft, her dream-sky was bright blue with bunches of wispy clouds. It matched her memory of the sky in the forest at Casret Academy, sunlight filtering through the rustling canopies of trees. Now, as they entered their fourth hour of walking through the tunnel, she imagined a night sky instead. Violet layers of clouds drifted across a big moon, two times its usual size, nothing but air between her and its shining face.

A drop of sweat ran down the center of her back. She

shifted, uncomfortable. She'd taken off her Milk-drenched blazer and hooked it beneath one of the straps on her backpack, but she was still too warm. Her top was sleeveless, at least, but she'd had to get used to seeing her bruised and mottled arms. Purple against beige—a constant reminder that she'd almost been buried alive.

The tunnel was stuffy and suffocating, and it never stopped. Just miles and miles of bare rock held up by thick wooden supports. Partway through their journey, Neave had taken a pot of glowing orange paste from her backpack and started drawing crossed lines on the wall to mark every ten minutes of walking.

"Adrudian paint," she said, flashing one of her lupine grins. "In case we lose our lights."

"I thought an *X* marked your destination, not your progress," Winn said from the head of their procession. The coils of her hair were escaping her bun, her dark brown skin shining with sweat.

"On our way back, they will." Neave rubbed her hand on a square of fabric from her weapons belt. "These'll help us find our way home."

Isaline hadn't realized how soon Neave's words would come true. After five hours of walking, the tunnel they'd been following came to an abrupt dead end. The path simply tapered to a close as if the rock were clay pinched together with a giant hand. The six of them faced the featureless wall.

"That doesn't make any sense," Cameron said to

Isaline's side. He had taken off his jacket and draped it over the back of his neck. The ends of his golden hair were beginning to tangle. "Why would it end here?"

Isaline ran her hand over the wall, half-expecting the rock to be some kind of illusion. They had walked down a straight tunnel—there hadn't been anywhere to turn. Was this all there was?

She looked around to each of them: Cameron's handsome, angular face was streaked with dirt; Neave's fitted shirt had come untucked; Jame had looked pale and shaken since they'd left the mill; Winn's rounded lips had hardened into a frown; and Jack was nearly as soaked in Adrudian Milk as she was, the veins on his cheeks a severe blue in the harsh light. They were exhausted. The tunnel *couldn't* end.

The back of Isaline's arms prickled. She had an irrational thought: what if they turned and the path had closed behind them? What if they were trapped?

She whipped around, looking down the tunnel. Her headlamp illuminated a stretch of empty path, nothing more. Isaline let out her breath.

Stop jumping at shadows.

As she turned back to the dead end, the beam of her headlamp ran over Jack, who was leaning against the opposite wall with his arms crossed. Their eyes met, and Isaline could tell he knew precisely why she had spun to look down the tunnel. Her face flushed. She didn't want him to think she was losing it.

Jack's sharp blue eyes studied her a moment before traveling to the others. "We should be keeping our hands on the walls. That way we won't miss a passageway."

"But we couldn't have missed another path, right?" Neave had started running her hands over the dead end, her black-tipped fingers poking between grooves of rock. "It would have been obvious."

Winn tugged on the straps of her backpack, adjusting the buckles across her waist. "He's right. We should go back." Her posture was straight and perfect—the posture of a member of the Seven Thrones—but her eyes were bloodshot. She was as tired as the rest of them. "We'll be more careful."

"Not one of my natural traits," Cameron muttered.

They walked the way they had come, three of them skimming their hands over one side of the tunnel, the rest taking the other. Isaline stood to the left, between Neave and Jame. Their surroundings were so empty that it seemed they hadn't turned around at all.

Three of Neave's glowing orange Xs came and went before they found a passageway they had missed. Jame felt it first; he stopped without warning, causing a small pileup as Isaline bumped into him, then Neave into her.

"Whoops," Isaline said, at the same time as Jame said, "Sorry."

They smiled at each other. Neave patted Isaline on the shoulder and peered inside the tunnel branch. The entrance was only a few feet wide, but it was big enough they should have caught it the first time. Her headlamp illuminated another path carved into the rock.

"It's an obvious fork," Neave said, leaning against the wall on one hand. "How did we miss this?"

"Does it matter?" Cameron took a drink from his water bottle and rubbed his mouth on the shoulder of his jacket. His arms were soaked in coppery Milk from the Adrudian vat. "Maybe it leads to a lake. I could use a bath."

That makes two of us, Isaline thought. Her entire body was stiff with dried Adrudian Milk. When she turned to the side, her whole head of hair went with her, as if she were wearing a hat.

Neave took a moment to draw an *X* on the wall with her orange paint, and they continued into the new tunnel. This passage was much like the last: a stretch of vacant rock, narrower than the previous tunnel had been, but still the same perpetual hole in the ground. Eventually they came to another fork, one path heading to the right, the other to the left. Winn waved for them to stop, peering into the halved blackness.

"Which way do we go?" Jame asked.

"Well, they both look the same, so ..." Neave pointed her headlamp down each path. "It shouldn't make a difference. This is a mine, not a cave system. If there's tunnels, we're bound to hit the King's workshop eventually. It's a matter of taking the right route."

Next to her, Jack had slipped a book from the inside of

his jacket and was scribbling onto a page with a pen. Isaline ducked her head to read the book's title: *Gravel and Lode: Rocks and Gemstones of the Shute.*

"We need to be able to find our way back," Jack said. He pointed past Cameron with his pen. "Let's go to the left. I'm keeping track."

There was a round of agreement, and they set off down the left tunnel. When they came to a second fork, Jack marked it in his book, and they kept on. But that path came to a dead end, like the first one, and they needed to double back and take the other tunnel. *That* tunnel led to another fork, and another, and then a third dead end.

Isaline's feet were heavy as concrete. A blister was forming on her right heel, warm and stinging. How long had they been walking for? Six hours? Seven?

When the tunnel widened into yet another fork, this one with three different passages, she had to fight back frustrated tears. Cameron slumped against the wall, letting out a heavy sigh.

"We've got to stop," he said. "This place is huge. How are we going to find anything, at this rate?"

Winn leaned on a wooden support, one finger pushing into the bridge of her nose. Her grease-coated hand left a smudge between her brows. "Let's take a break. Decide on a direction." She slid open one eye. "Maybe one of us will have a feeling."

Was it Isaline's imagination, or did Winn look directly at her?

They sat on the rock floor, drinking water and stretching their aching muscles. Jame offered Isaline a biscuit from his backpack. She had a package of her own, but she was too tired to tell him, so she took the biscuit and bit into the dry disc. He watched her chew, one side of his mouth pulled into a smile.

"Better?" he asked. "You've got to be hungry."

The biscuit had turned to dust on her tongue, but she nodded. She hadn't eaten since before their ferry ride to the mill, which seemed a lifetime ago. "Much better," she said, gulping the crumbs down with a sip of water.

Jame smiled, satisfied, and retrieved a ball of yarn and needles from his pocket.

Across from them, Neave ate four biscuits in a row, her head hanging between bent knees. Jack and Cameron sat next to her, studying the map Jack had been drawing in *Rocks and Gemstones of the Shute*. They looked tired enough to fall asleep with their eyes open.

Winn was the only member of their party to stay standing. She had wandered to the head of the tunnel and was gazing down each passageway, fiddling with the cover of her matchbox.

Isaline examined the ceiling of the passage. There had been a thought nagging at her since she'd woken up slumped over Jame's back, being carried through the mines. Part of her had expected the interior of the mine to look familiar, a kind of déjà vu.

Ignoring her aching calf muscles, Isaline got to her feet

and joined Winn at the head of the tunnel. The Princess looked at her askance, chewing on the wooden end of a matchstick.

"Which direction would you have us go?" she asked. She was shorter than Isaline, but still Isaline felt she had to look up to meet her eyes.

"I'm not sure." Isaline played with the collar of her shirt. Both she and Winn had closed their headlamps, so the three passages before them were nothing but dark holes. "They're all the same. It's impossible to choose."

"Maybe impossible. Maybe not." Winn tipped her chin toward Isaline's neck. "You know what I'm thinking."

Isaline dug a finger beneath the bronze chain inside her collar, uncovering the pendant. She knew. The Princess had said as much in Little Space: *The King found this ritual site, the House of Matchsticks. He stole the keystone—the pendant. Somehow it ended up with your roommate.*

The thought of Nalissa made Isaline's heart twinge. The lock hadn't ended up with her roommate. It was Isaline. Just Isaline.

The girl with the pendant.

"You think I've been here before?" Isaline asked, the words hardly daring to escape her mouth.

"It's not out of the question," Winn said. Her face was unreadable, a semi-frown beneath her high, defined cheekbones. "You were named on the recording, were you not?"

It is with the girl. In a Watch Academy. She doesn't know ... the wearer forgets.

"And if not you, then the pendant. It will know." Winn passed the match to the other side of her lips. Her hand came to rest on her belt, next to a series of wrenches, screwdrivers, and other tools Isaline didn't recognize. "It somehow deals in memories. Perhaps it will allow you to recall events from a young age ... events you otherwise wouldn't be able to access."

"I thought you didn't believe in magic," Isaline said.

"I don't," Winn replied. "But I saw the eye, same as you. I'm not skeptical enough to waste time." She set her palm on the small of Isaline's back, pushing her closer to the forked passages. "Try. Look for a feeling."

Isaline hesitated, examining the entrance to each passageway. They were identical: the same width, the same height, all human-made rather than natural openings in the rock. Without a map, no one would be able to tell one tunnel from the next, let alone which direction would lead to King Faraday's workshop and the House of Matchsticks.

But what if I don't need a map? What if I already know?

Isaline closed her fingers around the pendant, squeezing. Wishing on the pendant was nothing new—she'd done it hundreds of times without any luck. But then, she had been praying to whoever had given her the necklace. Maybe she was looking in the wrong direction.

Casting a cursory glance at Winn, Isaline shut her eyes and turned her awareness inside, to her lost memories.

For three breaths, nothing happened. She stared at the backside of her eyelids. The wet, earthy odor of unprocessed Adrudian made her nose scrunch. Her mind's eye offered a progression of images: a spot, round and obsidian, staring from a projection of the pendant; Jame's hand, reaching to brush her hair behind her ear; and, intruding with a painful clarity, the memory of sitting in a leafy alcove at the base of her dormitory with Nalissa on the first night they'd met.

A sound distracted her, coming on the trail of her image of Nalissa. Isaline furrowed her brows. The noise was unmistakable, but it was displaced. A bird's twittering, in a mine? It came from straight ahead of her, from the middle tunnel.

Isaline opened her eyes, facing the three empty passages. She was hearing things. If it were a true message, wouldn't a voice speak to her? Wouldn't there be a sign that it wasn't just a mistake, her brain conjuring sounds for no reason? She was fooling herself.

"Anything?" Winn asked. She had come to stand at Isaline's side, eyes trained on her face.

"No." Isaline's voice was small. She dropped the pendant into her shirt. "The middle, maybe, but that's ..." She shook her head, her feelings too complicated to describe. "I'm standing right in front of it."

Winn let out a sigh, her posture drooping the tiniest fraction. "Worth a try."

The disappointment on her face made Isaline's stomach sink. She'd let down the Princess. A *Just*. Worse, Isaline's heart was a traitor. She didn't want to hope—for a history, for a destiny, for something to be extraordinary about her—but she did anyway.

After a few seconds, she couldn't stand to be alone with Winn anymore. She turned from the passageways and headed toward her spot beside Jame, who was busy knitting something that looked like a mitten.

Ba-bump-bump.

She stopped in her tracks. Jame froze, a length of yarn swinging beneath his knitting needles. Jack, Cameron, and Neave went still, raising their heads to look down the tunnel from which they'd emerged.

"What was that?" Isaline murmured, but Cameron held out a hand to silence her.

Ba-bump-bump. Again, issuing from the darkness of the tunnel. Her arms broke out in goosebumps. The sound was strange, off-rhythm, but there was no misinterpreting it.

Footsteps. Someone was coming.

NEAVE WAS the first of them to jump into action. She shot to her feet and slid a long dagger from her belt, her rope-like braid swinging at her waist. Cameron and Jack were next, Jack pushing his book into the folds of his jacket while Cameron's fingers hovered over the Flash Camera in his weapons belt.

"Who could it be?" Isaline whispered to Winn, who had dropped her match and ground it under her heel as if it were a cigar.

"No one good," the Princess replied, rolling her sleeves to her elbows. She crossed to the other side of the tunnel and squinted into the gloom, gesturing at the others to keep to the shadows.

Isaline's heart pounded. The footsteps were growing louder. *Ba-bump-bump, ba-bump-bump.* She couldn't figure out what kind of feet might make that sound. A person loping down the tunnel with a walking stick or injured leg? Or two people? Neither of those ideas rang true.

"Should we run?" Jame asked in a hushed tone, looking around at the rest of them.

"No time." Winn had unclipped a pair of brass binoculars from her toolbelt. She spun a dial on the eyepiece, adjusting the focus and looking down the tunnel. "It's a clockwork pickaxer, and it's coming fast. Stay still and don't make a sound. It won't see you, but it can sense you."

Adrenaline made Isaline's head swim. She didn't know if she was ready to face a clockwork again. The last machine she'd fought had been cracked in half under a mechanical wheel, the very wheel that had buried her in Adrudian.

Ba-bump-bump. Ba-bump-bump. Ba-bump-bump.

The clockwork emerged from the darkness. It lurched into the light on three claw-like legs—the source of its strange-sounding stride—and interlinking joints of wood, metal, and rubber. Groaning arms swayed beneath the weight of its shoulders and head. A round patch of Adrudian shone from its torso. She fixed her eyes on the light to avoid looking at the rest of its body.

Creaking, the clockwork lurched down the center of the tunnel, past their frozen, breathless party on either side. Isaline cringed as it passed her, a whisper's space between her shoulder and its odd, faceless head. A moment later, it had scuttled away from them, going directly into one of the passageways.

Isaline blinked. It had gone into the middle tunnel.

As the sound of its footsteps faded, they all looked at each other, eyes round.

"Well?" Neave reached up and opened her headlamp, releasing a bright beam of light. "What are we waiting for? Let's follow it."

Winn confirmed the idea with a nod. She swung her backpack over her shoulders. "Walk quietly and don't make a sound."

They gathered their things and set off down the middle tunnel. Isaline could hardly hear beneath her heartbeat pulsing in her ears. Her instinct had been *correct*

—the clockwork had taken the middle tunnel. Could the bird sound really have been her intuition? Was it her own memory, unearthed years later? Or something else?

The clockwork's glowing belly led them through a maze of passageways, taking turns and navigating fork after fork. Their path sloped downward, and the air thickened to the consistency of syrup, making Isaline's lungs heave.

I was right. I was right.

The tunnel widened and a bend appeared, supported by a series of moldering wooden posts. The clockwork scuttled around the bend, disappearing into a fold of rock while the rest of them followed. Neave crept forward and peeked through the fold.

"That's ..." She trailed off, astonished. "Wow."

She waved the rest of them through. Isaline's mouth fell open as she stepped from the tunnel. They were in a cavern that must have been twice the size of the mill. Three or four times, if she counted the ceiling, which soared away beneath a nest of stalactites.

Isaline opened her flashlight and swept it in an arc. The cavern was expansive, and as the clockwork moved into the distance, its belly illuminated the edge of an underground canyon. A split in the ground had opened up, a sheer drop on either side creating a broad gorge.

"Water," Jame breathed. "Listen."

They came to a stop, Isaline tilting her head to the side. The roar of rushing water met her ears. Her chest opened at the sound, making it easier to breathe despite the heat.

Cameron shone his flashlight into the gorge. His face broke into a smile. "It's a river."

"Your wish came true." Neave joined him at the edge, the pointed toes of her boots inching toward the drop. A moment later she barked a laugh. "Now wish for an airship. That's a long way down, even for a bath."

Ahead, the clockwork's shining belly had shrunk to a pinprick of orange in the dark. It was lurching across what looked like the metal panels of a bridge. Winn strode after it, coming to a stop near the lip of the canyon, and shone her flashlight over a dusty iron crank at the bridge's edge.

"This is old technology," she said, rifling through her tool belt and donning a pair of thick gloves. "Hand-operated. Faraday didn't build this."

She wrapped both hands around the crank's handle. Neave made a startled noise.

"Shouldn't we—" she said, but Winn was already rotating the crank.

A metallic squeal sounded, the grinding of metal against metal. Isaline's eyes widened as a long line of lanterns opened at once, dimly lighting an iron footbridge leading across the gorge and into the darkness. The clockwork had disappeared over the other side.

Cameron whistled, joining Winn at the edge of the bridge. "Sixteen years, and the Adrudian in those lanterns still has some light."

"Only some," Winn said, clapping dust from her gloves. "But Adrudian lasts a long time, if you don't burn it for fuel. Or waste it in other ways." She glanced at Jack over her shoulder. "No offense."

Jack's lips thinned. He was scribbling on the pages of his book again, making note of the cavern on the map he'd been drawing. His blue veins were inky streaks on his jawline.

"None taken," he said flatly.

They began to discuss whether to camp on the clifftop or in the tunnel. Isaline drifted toward the edge of the gorge. She got farther than she thought she would—only a few paces from the drop—before a familiar shudder made her stop. She let herself sink to the ground, sitting cross-legged on the cavern floor.

How many times had she sat like this while Nalissa danced at the edge of the rooftop at Casret Academy? She had just been a Watchling, then.

Now, I'm ... Isaline tapped the pendant beneath her shirt. *Something else. Something more.*

A pair of boots came to stand beside her. Isaline craned to see Jame, the underside of his chin sprinkled with the beginnings of a traveler's beard, one finger running beneath the strap of his headlamp.

"Want to look at the river?" he asked.

Isaline made a strangled sound, something between a snort and a cough. The light from her flashlight cut through the dark and cascaded over the brink of the gorge.

Jame grinned. The dusting of freckles over his pointed nose was concealed beneath a layer of soot from the mill, from when they'd hidden under the wheel machine. "I'll describe it to you, if you want."

The thought of fighting clockwork guards, almost being buried alive, and walking for hours through tunnels only to have Jame describe a river to her was utterly ridiculous. She couldn't help it—a bubble of laughter escaped her chest.

Jame's grin widened. "What? I'll do it for free."

"For *free?*" The words came out with more laughter. "What do you usually charge?"

"Nothing expensive," Jame said. He strode to the edge, perfectly relaxed. His hand wandered into the open air, waving above the crook of his elbow, where he'd rolled his sleeve into a neat fold. "A couple gold pieces. A good meal." He stretched, craning to look at the stalactites above them. "A few seconds of sunshine."

Isaline gazed at him. "Okay, then. What do you see?"

He leaned over to peer into the gorge, putting his weight on one foot. Isaline's stomach flipped. Were all Quandary Thieves like this? Eager to fall to their deaths over a cliff or rooftop? It was a miracle none of them had suspected she wasn't a Thief. Not yet, anyway.

Jame looked at her from the corner of his eye. "Last chance to come see for yourself."

She glared at him, the strap of her headlamp digging into her brow.

"All right, all right," Jame said, chuckling. The beam of his flashlight swung into the gorge. "There's a river running beneath the bridge. It's a long way away, but it's fairly big. It reminds me of the river in the forest at your school."

Nalissa's school, too, Isaline thought. Even if she wasn't Nalissa to him then, when they were at the river, Jame was under the impression she had always been the Quandary Spy from his letters. The girl he *actually* had a crush on.

Isaline resolved to remember that during moments like this, when his voice made a flutter travel up her arms.

"There's a lot of rocks." Jame shrugged, scratching a hand through his hair. "A little like your forest, too."

Nalissa's forest.

"And then there's the bridge." He gestured at the footbridge with a limp hand, his smile starting to fade to a cringe. "It's also kind of like the one at ..." Laughing, he shook his head. "Turns out I'm not very good at this."

"I can't believe you charge for this service," Isaline said, folding her arms.

Jame lifted his hands in a gesture of defeat. "Well, it's only a couple—wait." He stopped, his headlamp pointed past his feet, over to the right. His head cocked to the side.

"Jame?" she said.

He didn't respond, just stared over the edge. His outline was shadowed by the pitch-dark, swallowed in the rest of the cavern.

Isaline's hands tightened on her sore arms. "Jame? What is it?"

Adjusting his headlamp, he backed away from the gorge and turned to address the others. "I think I found somewhere to camp. There's a ledge down here, with a cave." He offered Isaline a hand to stand up, eyes twinkling. "Something's glowing."

ISALINE DIDN'T SEE the cave until she was inside, on account of the fact that Jame and Cameron had to guide her down to the ledge with her eyes shut.

"Jame wasn't kidding," Cameron said cheerfully, helping her down from the lip of the gorge. "You really are afraid of heights."

She didn't know how to respond to that, so she was thankful when Jame said, "We're all afraid of something." He released her hand, clearing his throat. "For example, I'm afraid of whatever *this* is."

Isaline cracked open an eye. They were in a large cliff-side cave with a smooth interior, as if the rock had been hollowed out with a spoon. Clusters of luminescent fungi blanketed the walls, a vast spread of glowing green caps on long stalks.

She squinted into the far corner, at something Neave was gathering into her arms.

"It's a blanket," Isaline said, her brows lifting.

"A few of them," Neave corrected. She nudged a pile of old coverlets that had been pushed to one side of the cave. Coughing, she shook the dust from the aging fabric. "Someone was staying in this cave. Pickaxers, maybe? Before the fire?"

"If it was, they were storing things here, too," came Jack's voice from the other side of the cave. Isaline turned to see him kneeling beside a worn wooden chest locked with a padlock.

Cameron turned to Jame. "You think you can get that open?"

"Undoubtedly," Jame replied, rolling down his sleeve and shaking out his thin, bronze unlocking tool.

Isaline knew she should be comforted by signs of humans, but a cold feeling washed down her spine instead. This cave was meant to be a secret. Whoever had been staying here hadn't wanted to be seen by others using the bridge on the clifftop—and what pickaxer decided to spend the night in the mines? Winn had said human pickaxers would have used carts to travel before the fire. There was no reason to stay in the mines overnight.

Shivering, Isaline wandered to the back wall of the cave, drawn to the luminescent fungi. The caps were yellow underneath, with strands of hair-like filaments stretching from stalk to end. She closed her headlamp and let her eyes adjust to their light, the orange in her vision turning to a cool blue-green.

"Nalissa," Jame called from across the cave. "You have to see this."

She turned to find them all gathered around Jack, who had a bundle of papers in his lap. The lid of the wooden chest was propped open, the padlock on the ground. They were staring at a rectangular, yellowing paper Jack had held up to the light.

"It can't be him," Neave said, one hand clenched around the end of her braid.

"Of course it's him," Winn replied. She stood and walked from the group, staring down the cliff and to the rushing river below. Her face was grave. "Look at the eyes."

Apprehension licked at Isaline's ribs. She walked toward them and looked over Jack's shoulder.

What she had thought was a paper was actually a photograph, old enough to have turned yellow. The picture showed five people in pickaxer uniforms: two women and three men, standing in a line with their arms around each other. At the end of the line was a lean man with muted gray hair, his hand resting on top of the head of the woman next to him, who was short with a friendly smile and a close-cropped head of curls. Next to her was another woman, a pickaxe slung over her shoulder, its point hidden in her long, ash brown hair. Isaline couldn't see her face because it was playfully pushed into the shoulder of the next man, who had an athletic build and a striking, mischievous smile.

The final pickaxer was the man at the end of the line on the right side. He was taller than the man with the athletic build, and his face was only half-smiling. The whites of his eyes shone from the photo as if someone had painted them on.

Handwritten text on the bottom of the photo read:

Mining Team 5.

From left to right: Richard Gray, Mio Morgan, Theresa Lurell, Haris Panan, Johannes Faraday.

Isaline's eyes had been drawn to the woman with the long hair—was she familiar, or was Isaline's exhausted mind mistaken?—but when she read the final name, her eyes snapped back to the man at the end of the line.

Johannes Faraday.

She was looking at the King.

3

PUZZLE BOX

JACK

Jack's next vision began where the last had ended. On the lost expedition, after climbing from the ravine, he and Cameron walked all night in search of the House of Matchsticks.

THEY MADE a brief stop to build a fire and dry their boots, which were soaked with river water. The night had deepened, the Shute's ancient trees creaking and moonlight gathering in silver pools on the ground. To Jack's dismay, as soon as they had settled, Cameron curled his bootless feet beneath him and started talking, keen on conversation. He began telling the story of his latest expedition, and was still recounting the details when Jack doused the fire, pulled on his boots, and headed through the forest again.

"We didn't know where we were," Cameron said, trailing across the forest floor behind Jack. It was sometime later and dawn light was sneaking through the trees. "But there was a door ahead of me, so I just pushed it open, and you'll never guess what was on the other side."

Jack ran a hand down his veinless face, rubbing his fingers into the corners of his eyes. "I'd never dare."

"Mivnia's ring!" Cameron exclaimed. He had found a branch on the ground and was using it as a walking stick. For some reason, Jack found this more annoying than the endless story. "There it was, sitting in the open. Neave wanted to grab it right away, but I'd read Mivnia's diary—it was so old I had to spend three nights deciphering one passage—and Mivnia was obsessed with keeping the ring hidden. It couldn't be that easy."

"Couldn't it?" Jack muttered. The muscles in his legs burned. Their path had slanted up the side of a steep hill, weaving through trees like towers, branches misty in the growing light. He was out of breath—but Cameron seemed to have enough air for the both of them.

"Well, a quick survey of the ring revealed ..."

Jack tuned him out, focusing on keeping his balance in the damp grass. He knew the end of the story. Cameron's discovery of Mivnia's ring had been gossip for weeks, one of the many tales Jack had heard about Cameron Agustin, Treasurehunting's famous golden boy.

He reached into his jacket and pulled out his map, shaking the folded parchment open in his palm. If he had his bearings, they would be coming to a landmark at the top of the hill—a plateau. Jack ran his fingertip over a hand-drawn spiral on the map, tucked between a cluster of trees and what looked like a winding path. The closer they came, the more his insides hummed, the familiar anticipation of discovery.

They crested the hill as the sun peeked in earnest from the horizon, casting the crisp air in pinkish yellow. Jack stepped from a line of trees onto a large, rocky plateau. The far edge of the plateau offered an extraordinary view of the Shute and the mountains beyond, but Jack was far more interested in what was lying at his feet: a large stone platform, twenty paces across and raised from the ground by two stone steps.

"Oh, neat," Cameron said, emerging from the trees behind him.

Jack pressed the toe of his boot to the first step, wary of traps. There were deep grooves in the platform's surface, as if someone had carved into the stone with a giant knife. The design showed three concentric squares—a small square inside a larger square, and that square inside one even larger.

He did a quick study of the entire platform, then pulled out his map. The parchment crinkled as he tapped the spiral with his forefinger. Concentric squares weren't the spiral he had imagined, but he could have mistranslated the text he'd found.

Stowing the map, Jack strode across the platform and

took a step onto the smallest center square. The press of his foot made a hollow sound.

"Hey, look at this," Cameron said from the other side of the plateau. He had one hand threaded in his hair, the other digging in a patch of overgrown vegetation. In the new light, his shadow was tall enough to reach Jack's toes. "There's a pile of tiles here."

Jack was only half-listening. He tapped the ground with the flat of his boot again, in the center of the platform. The hollow echo sounded out a second time.

A trap door.

That's interesting.

"There's eighteen of them." Cameron had picked up a handful of square, palm-sized tiles. He turned them in his hands, colorful light playing over his face. "Nine red, nine blue. You thinking what I'm thinking?"

Jack kneeled and drew his dagger, digging the blade around the edge of the trap door. "Probably not."

"The platform—it's a game board," Cameron said, arranging the red and blue tiles in stacks of three. "It's Nine Men's Morris."

"It's what?"

"Nine Men's Morris," Cameron repeated, as if that clarified anything. Jack lifted his head, giving him a confused look, and Cameron raised his eyebrows. "The board game. You've never played Nine Men's Morris?"

Jack clenched his jaw, returning to the trap door. He

couldn't open it. His dagger wasn't strong enough to dig beneath the stone.

"Wait." Across the platform, Cameron made a horrified face. "You've never played a board game."

It was a statement, not a question. Jack shifted, unwilling to meet Cameron's eyes. It wasn't that he had no interest in board games—it was that there had been no one to teach him how to play. His parents had disappeared at sea when he was young. Now, in his mid-twenties, there had been no one to challenge him, beyond the various men he'd spent time with over the years. But he'd sooner set his hand on fire than tell Cameron about his failed romances.

"Well, that won't do." Cameron picked up the nine blue tiles and deposited them on the ground beside Jack. "Here's how the game is played: you need to get three in a row. That's called a mill. You can put tiles here ..." He walked around the platform, nudging the corners of each square with his foot, as well as the middle points of each line. "We take turns, and if you get a mill, you get to take one of my pieces. And vice versa."

Curious, Jack pressed his thumb to the corners of the trap door. There were tiny, barely visible slots in the stone, perfect size for the tiles Cameron had discovered at the edge of the board.

Stars. *Cameron was right. They needed to play to get through the door.*

Jack rubbed a hand over his forehead, sighing. The sun

was visible now, bathing the plateau in warm light. He could use a meal and some sleep—and a strong drink.

Cameron's eyes sparkled, seeing the change in Jack's expression. "You've figured it out, then?"

"How to play the game?"

"No, that we need to play the game to keep on."

Jack made a concerted effort not to gawk at him. "You figured it out already?"

"As soon as I saw the board." Cameron stacked the tiles in his left hand and used his right to arrange the fleece collar of his jacket. "But I didn't want to spoil it for you."

Scowling, Jack stood and picked up the blue tiles. He didn't know whether to be annoyed or impressed. What would he have done if Cameron wasn't on the expedition? Played against himself? But he wouldn't have known the platform was a game board, or how to play. He would have had to take a shovel to the trap door. Not that he had a shovel.

Cameron flashed Jack a dazzling, white-toothed smile. "You're lucky I'm here, it seems."

Jack didn't feel like agreeing, so he just said, "Let's play."

The game took all of ten minutes. Jack quickly caught onto the rules; he was soon in the lead with three mills near the left side of the board. And he was enjoying himself. Every time he got a mill, Cameron made a frustrated sound in the back of his throat that made him want to smile.

By the end of the game, Jack had stolen all but two of Cameron's tiles.

"Does this mean I win?" he asked, eyeing the trap door at the center of the platform.

"As soon as you take the last tile, I think." Cameron abandoned his own tiles at the edge of the board, adjusting his collar. "Beginner's luck, by the way."

Smirking, Jack bent and pulled his last stolen tile from the ground.

The effect was immediate. A groaning sound issued from under their feet, as if a stone giant were standing up beneath the hill. Jack's stomach lurched. He stepped with one foot onto the trap door, and to his surprise, the stone sank an inch into the platform, as if it were a button.

A trap, *he thought, a split-second too late.*

With a deafening crack, *the ground split, a rip appearing and curving across the platform. Great chunks of stone moved, revealing a pit that had opened up beneath the plateau, a hole so deep the bottom was shrouded in darkness despite the morning sunlight. Cameron, who was standing at the outskirts of the platform, cried out and jumped aside.*

An image flashed into Jack's mind: the platform, as seen from above, stone sliding open in a spiral pattern, all the way to the center.

The center.

"This way!" he cried, stretching out a hand to Cameron, who gaped for only a moment before leaping across the widening gap and breaking into a sprint. Jack stepped onto

the square he had thought was a trap door. Solid. The earlier echo had been some kind of auditory illusion; this center square was the only part of the platform that wasn't *a trap door.*

Cameron staggered across the heaving ground, knees wobbling over shifting stone, careening one way and the next. He was close, almost close enough to grab Jack's outstretched hand. The ancient stone mechanism coughed up dust that clouded the air.

"Here," Jack called into the fray. "Here!"

A flash of hands appeared, followed by the rest of Cameron rushing toward the center of the platform. Jack's heart dropped as a piece of rock gave way at Cameron's ankle, upsetting his balance and sending him slipping backward. The pit yawned, opening like a grinning mouth, light vanishing into the blackness.

Jack huffed a breath, reached to his arm's limit, and grasped the end of Cameron's sleeve. He yanked Cameron onto the square of stone with him as the last of the platform gave way.

A moment passed before the sound of moving stone faded. Silence swept in. Cameron's side was pressed into Jack's chest, his breath coming in gasps.

"I take it back," he said, pushing two fingers into his temples as if checking to make sure he had really survived.

Jack's head was spinning a little. "Take what back?"

"About the beginner's luck."

Something like a laugh escaped Jack. He peered into

the pit, arm brushing Cameron's side. He thought he had read about a trap like this before, but he couldn't remember. The faint smell of beeswax coming from Cameron's jacket distracted him.

"Well, that tells us one thing," Cameron said, looking down at Jack from the corner of his eye.

"What's that?"

"This is an elaborate trap. So ... the ritual-makers who hid the House of Matchsticks. They were engineers."

The square of stone started to descend, a mechanical click-click-click *carrying them into the pit. Cameron hooked an elbow around Jack's side, making sure neither of them fell, and they rode the lift all the way down*

down

down ...

JACK OPENED HIS EYES.

He was on his back in the hazy glow of the cliffside cave. Soft snores punctuated the sound of rushing water from the bottom of the gorge. Caps of luminescent fungi were clusters of light beyond his eyelashes.

Swallowing a groan, Jack lifted his head. They had made camp in the center of the cave, haphazardly laying their bedrolls and closing their headlamps, flashlights, and lanterns. The sleeping forms of his companions were lumps in the darkness, shadowy in the glow from the fungi coating the walls. *Lantern mushrooms*, Jack thought they were called, but he didn't have the books to confirm it.

Something heavy was weighing down his left hand. He drummed his fingers on its edges. Cool metal. Rounded. His flask of Adrudian Milk.

The hours before they had gone to sleep returned in gradual images. Jack had sifted through the items in the wooden chest, searching for clues. He'd found more photos, but none of Mining Team 5. Instead, there were shots of tunnels, rocks, and the interior of the cliffside cave. Neave had guessed one of the pickaxers on Mining Team 5 had fancied themselves a photographer.

Beneath the photos had been a leather-bound mining ledger. Mining Team 5 had used it to sign in and out of work. Their scribbled signatures went back three years before the fire, becoming sporadic near the end, then stopping altogether.

His most interesting discovery was hidden beneath the ledger, pushed into the corner of the chest. Jack had rummaged it out from the stacks of photos and set it on the palm of his bandaged hand: a wooden cube covered with a series of bronze dials on each side. A puzzle box. Faraday's handiwork.

Winn had taken one look at the box and walked to the other side of the cave, pulling her bedroll from her pack.

"It does seem a bit like yours, you have to admit," Jack had said.

"That's not one of my Spiders." Winn's voice was flat

and hard. She set out her bedroll, keeping her back turned. "Our inventions are nothing alike."

Cameron and Neave exchanged glances, but nothing more was said about the box. The six of them had eaten in silence and gone to bed.

Now, as Jack's eyes adjusted to the dim, he sat up on his bedroll and cradled his head. The flask rolled onto his lap, sloshing. He had waited until the others were sleeping before taking a swig of Adrudian Milk, but the vision had arrived too quickly for him to hide the flask. He could only hope Cameron hadn't noticed it during the night. Their conversation at the Harper and Cup was clear in Jack's mind.

Say you won't Drink Adrudian. Not a drop.

We don't know what she *wants, not really.*

Cameron had referenced the woman from Jack's visions. The round-eyed, ivory-skinned woman who had asked Jack to bring Nalissa into the mines and offered to show him the lost expedition in return.

Jack scratched his nails over the back of his neck. Dangerous or not, the woman was keeping her part of the bargain.

A soft sleep noise issued from his right. Slipping the flask into his pocket, Jack squinted over the domed bedrolls in their camp. The dark was too thick to tell who was who, but one bedroll was empty, its blanket neatly folded. He thought he remembered who had been sleeping there.

Jack glanced over his shoulder, toward the far end of the cave. Cameron was alone, sitting cross-legged near a bright cluster of lantern mushrooms. He had taken off his jacket and folded it beneath him, the bandage around his cut arm fraying at the edges. The puzzle box was in his hands, making a gentle clacking sound as he fiddled with the dials, trying to solve it.

Jack exhaled through his teeth. He could go back to sleep. He was tired enough. But before his mind had made the decision, his legs had pushed him up and he was walking across the cave, gathering his unruly hair into a knot behind his head.

Cameron smiled slightly at his approach. "Did I wake you?"

"No," Jack whispered. He sat on the rough ground, drawing his knees to his chest. "I woke myself."

Having an Adrudian spell didn't count as sleep, but it wasn't exactly a lie. Cameron just nodded, spinning the box between his palms. He was pressing dials at random, as if he'd given up trying to find the right pattern.

"You don't want to sleep?" Jack asked after a moment, looking at the bags beneath Cameron's eyes. In the light, they were a deep gray against his blue-tinged skin.

"I don't sleep much." Cameron pressed a tired hand to his jaw, scrunching one side of his face. He yawned. "Have you checked your watch?"

Jack rolled up his sleeve and stared at the smooth face

of his wristwatch. Eleven o'clock at night. He bit back a gasp. Ten hours since they'd made camp.

"Exactly," Cameron said, as if reading Jack's thoughts. "The dark makes time feel ... weird."

Despite yesterday's journey through winding, suffocating tunnels, Jack hadn't keenly felt the absence of the sun until now. He lifted his chin, peering into the blackness of the cave ceiling. It could have been a void, an inversion of the pit that had opened up beneath the Nine Men's Morris board in Jack's vision. He wondered if Cameron would have made the same association if his memory hadn't been lost.

"I was going to wake everyone up," Cameron continued, spinning a dial on the box with his index finger, "but it seemed like a good time to do this instead."

"The puzzle?"

"Yes, while ..." He cast a meaningful glance at the sleeping silhouettes across the cave.

Jack understood. "While Winn is asleep," he said. He rubbed the bandage wrapping his palm, careful to watch Cameron's expression. "You're hiding it from her."

Cameron gave the box a fierce shake, then heaved a sigh and set it on his knee, pressing his fingers into his temples. He looked so much like he had in Jack's vision, massaging his head after escaping the pit trap. Jack had to remind himself it was a year later.

"Winn's grieving," Cameron said. "Lillian and Philip —it hasn't been long."

"She chose to come here."

"Doesn't mean she has to suffer."

Jack stared at him through the dark. He was right, of course, but Jack couldn't shake the feeling Cameron had misjudged Winn. Yes, the Seven Thrones had been overthrown, forced into hiding, and executed—and she had taken on the responsibility of rebuilding the Thrones with only weeks of experience—but none of it changed the fact she was keeping secrets. Jack could read it plainly on her face.

He bit his tongue, as he had done every time Cameron and Winn bent their heads in conversation. It was obvious they liked each other, but that was the problem with liking: it made you blind.

"There's going to be more of Faraday's inventions," Jack said. He paused, then took the puzzle box from Cameron's knee. The cube was heavy in his hand, intricately crafted, an eerie resemblance to Winn's Listening Spider. "You can't protect her."

Cameron watched as Jack started spinning dials in a simple sequence. He patted his pocket, touching his ring of keys, as if making sure it was still there. "I can try. It's what friends do. They protect each other." His voice lowered. "They talk to each other."

The weight of his last sentence settled on Jack's shoulders. He glanced up from the box to see Cameron scrutinizing him, his chin propped in his hand. The look made Jack's throat tighten. Winn might not be telling the truth, but neither was Jack. Even after Cameron had asked him to be honest.

If you have any more visions, you can tell me.

"I—" Jack's fingers slipped from the side of the puzzle box, disrupting the sequence he'd been trying. He gritted his teeth and started over. "How'd you know?"

"You're not exactly subtle. You have visions with your eyes open."

Jack swore under his breath. He should have been more careful. This expedition could be his only opportunity to find the House of Matchsticks. But he couldn't just stop trying to uncover his memories because Cameron thought it was dangerous. He couldn't start trusting Winn simply because she was their leader. Jack's fingers tensed on the puzzle box. If it hadn't been for Nalissa, he could have ...

"Jack," Cameron said, hiding a grin beneath the heel of his hand. He let out an airy laugh. "Relax."

Jack exhaled. The flask of Adrudian Milk hung heavy in his pocket, and his shoulders rounded. He had slept far too long to be this tired.

"The vision wasn't interesting, anyway." He looked briefly at Cameron before fixing his gaze on the puzzle box, restarting the sequence a third time.

"Was it from the lost expedition?"

"Yes. We had to play a game to get past a trap."

Cameron's head perked, his chin lifting from his hand. "What game?"

"Nine Men's Morris."

"Ah! I'm an expert." His voice was dreamy, as if imagining years of victories. "Don't leave me in suspense. Who won?"

Jack didn't reply, letting silence speak for him. Realization passed over Cameron's face.

"Sounds like beginner's luck, to me," he grumbled, and Jack simultaneously smiled and had an intense feeling of *sameness*, as if time were folding in on itself. Something about the feeling nagged at him, but there was no time to investigate it; the puzzle box in his hands made a series of snapping noises and divided in half, falling open in his fingers.

Cameron's lips parted in a silent gasp. "How'd you do that?"

"Beginner's luck," Jack said, peering into the box. There was a tiny, metallic switch nestled inside. "Interesting."

He reached in and flipped the switch with his middle finger.

A grinding noise pierced the silence, stone scraping against stone. The tall cluster of lantern mushrooms behind Cameron began to shake, as if they were at the epicenter of a tiny, concentrated earthquake. Cameron made a face and scooted forward, twisting to watch as a portion of the wall slid to the side, revealing a hidden passageway.

No matter how many times he saw it, Jack never got

used to how Faraday's technology worked. It *shouldn't* have worked. A little switch powered by Adrudian shouldn't be able to control a door mechanism across the room. The incongruity of it made his hair stand on end.

Cameron seemed unfazed. He turned to Jack, his eyes alight. "You're kind of brilliant."

"Sure," was all Jack could say. The words skated over his skin in a peculiar way, the prickle at the beginning of goosebumps. He pulled his sleeves over his wrists and stood. Behind him, numerous bedrolls were shuffling, and a sleepy voice issued from the dark.

"What was that?" Neave said, yawning.

Cameron got to his feet, brushed off his jacket, and broke into a sunny smile. "The way forward. Time to wake up."

After breakfast, they packed their bedrolls and strapped on their headlamps. Jack stowed the photo of Mining Team 5 on his person, pressed between the pages of *Gravel and Lode: Rocks and Gemstones of the Shute*. It bookmarked the map he had been drawing and the notes he'd taken on their journey to the cavern.

Within the hidden passageway was a steep set of stairs, carved into the stone with treads overlaid by split wood. Lanterns hung from the walls at intervals, their Adrudian long dead. Jack's insides hummed. Whatever was beyond the passageway, Faraday didn't want it found.

Winn led them down the stairs in a single-file line. Her flashlight swept through the darkness, light catching sparkling motes of dust. The path zig-zagged down at a steep height, and the close quarters made the going slow and difficult.

Eventually, the sound of rushing water traveled up the passageway, much louder than it had been in the cave. Jack wiped a hand over his moist forehead. The air was stuffy and humid, the air so thick he felt he could squeeze it like a sponge.

"Here we are," Winn said from the front of their line.

The passage had led onto a rocky shore. Noises of relief escaped each of them as they spread out, picking their way across the rocks toward a strip of clear, flowing water. The river. They were at the bottom of the gorge. Jack craned and adjusted his headlamp, shining light into the space above him. The iron footbridge at the top of the cliff twinkled, a tiny row of dim lanterns in the distance.

"It's warm," Neave said, bending and swishing her hands in the river. The tip of her braid skimmed the surface of the water, snapping with the current. "You'll get your bath, Cameron."

Cameron dunked his head in the water as Jack stepped across rocks and stood at the river's edge, letting his eyes follow the current's broad curve. Piles of multicolored stones tumbled over the riverbed. He selected a palm-sized rock near his boots and tossed it underhand into the river. Its splash was lost beneath the din of the rushing water.

What could Faraday be hiding here?

He slid *Gravel and Lode* from his jacket and made note of the hidden passageway and the river on his map. Ink blotted the page as he pressed his pen to the corner. The map was sparse: merely a long, straight line to indicate the mine shaft, then a series of branching scribbles to signify the tunnels, and finally the bridge, cave, and water. He looked over the top of the book, staring downriver, where the water flowed into a wall of darkness.

"There's something here." It was Winn's voice, issuing from a triangular beam of light up the riverbank.

Jack finished his drawing, clapped the book closed, and strode over the rocks to where Winn's light was shining. She was in a half-crouch, examining something large sitting just off the riverbank, partially submerged in the shallow, surging water.

"It's a boat," Jame said, lifting his head. A black, grease-streaked hull came into the view of his headlamp.

"Not a boat—a mining cart." Neave flicked the side of it with a painted finger. "It's got wheels."

"Maybe it's both," Nalissa offered.

Jack opened his flashlight, swinging the beam over the strange machine. His first impression was of Captain Knots' ferry, if the ferry had been smaller and wider—but the comparison wasn't quite right. This machine was sturdy and sleek. It resembled a boat with an open, rectangular deck and two glistening metal wheels on each side.

"It's a cart." Winn donned her thick gloves, then unclipped a tool from her belt and wedged it between two metal plates. "But it's been adapted for traveling on the river." She gave the metal a shove, and a hatch swung open, revealing steps up to the deck. "Someone built this to transport people."

"Three guesses who," Jame said.

Jack peered around the cart's front end. Jame was right; its construction was imposing, sharp corners fused from slabs of steel and brass. He was reminded of King Faraday's red-sailed warship, sitting outside the palace in Ar. The puzzle box might have been something Winn could make, but there was no mistaking this cart. It was Faraday's design.

A glint of red paint caught his eye around the cart's far side.

"It's empty," Neave said, sweeping her light through the hatch. She stuck the flashlight under her arm and plucked at the tops of her laced boots. "I'll go first."

As she pulled herself up the steps to investigate, Jack wandered away to try catch a glimpse of the paint on the outside of the cart. It was some kind of design, but only its edge would appear in the beam of his flashlight.

"There's something written on here," he said to the others. "I'm going to look."

There was a round of acknowledgement. Jack clipped his flashlight to his belt and waded into the river.

Lukewarm water slopped up to his waist. The current was strong, forcing him to drag his feet across the riverbed. He needed to be careful. One wrong step and he could be swept down the river.

When he reached the far edge of the cart, he grasped it with two hands and pulled himself around the corner of the machine. The painted design slid into the light of his headlamp, gleaming blood-red.

Jack's body went rigid. He rubbed a spray of water from his eyes. There it was: three concentric squares, with points at the corners and in the middle of each line.

Nine Men's Morris.

For a moment, he just stared. The feeling of *sameness* returned, making his vision cloud at the borders. How could a Nine Men's Morris board be here? The Shute was miles away, on the surface to the southwest. A coincidence? He began to reach into his jacket to retrieve Gravel and Lode, but he stopped himself. The pages would get soaked.

"Cameron." Water splashed around his hips. "Cameron, there's—"

But his sentence died. At his feet, something long and white detached itself from the riverbed and slid out of sight.

A chill ran down Jack's spine. He whipped around, his headlamp swinging across the river's shimmering surface.

Empty. Rocks rolled past his legs, heading downriver like sea-bottom tumbleweeds.

Jack wiped a hand over his wet face. Had he imagined it? Was the dark playing tricks on him?

A slimy length of skin darted through the water and grazed his ankle.

Gasping, Jack raised his arms and backed away, moving with the current, until he glimpsed the others standing on the riverbank. Their headlamps swiveled, blinding him with Adrudian light. He shaded his eyes with his forearm.

Cameron said, "What's going on?"

"There's something here," Jack responded, and at the same moment, words were spoken into his head. A whisper, as if the speaker were curled inside his ear canal.

The voice sounded like the rattle of dead leaves. Inhuman. Familiar.

"*I found you*," the man-snake said, and a pair of twitching, pale hands closed around Jack's ankles.

4

RICHARD GRAY

ISALINE

One second Jack was standing in the river, and then he was gone. Isaline blinked and the water roiled, closing over Jack's falling figure like an envelope. His headlamp winked out.

Cameron bolted to the edge of the river, swinging his flashlight across the water. "Jack! Where are you? Can you hear me?"

Jame and Winn rushed to the riverbank, splashing into ankle-deep water, calling Jack's name. Isaline tried to join them, but her legs had turned to stone. *I found you.* The voice had spoken into her mind, dry like a shaking wind. It was the creature that had attacked her and Jame in the forest. The creature that had tried to steal the pendant.

The creature that had killed Nalissa.

Her vision shuddered, overcome by the memory of her final night at Casret Academy. Nalissa's drooping head, her body slipping down the wall of their shared dorm room. The creature's black blindfold tumbling across its long, slimy back. The memory was visceral. She was *there* again, cowering in the corner of Nalissa's bed, flinching at the crunch of broken glass. That night, Isaline had been a terrified Watchling, pushed into a fight she didn't understand.

Neave came flying down the steps of the cart, boots thumping on the metal. "He's gone. That snake thing is back." She dropped her pack to the ground and shed her jacket, pulling her Flash Camera from her belt. "I'm going to find Jack."

"I'm coming with you," Cameron said, already stepping out of his boots.

Isaline tried to speak, but the creature's voice echoed in her mind a second time, making her throat seize.

"Tell the others to stay. Come alone. Give me the lock, and your friend will live."

"Wait," Isaline said, catching Neave's arm. She touched the pendant, pressing the heavy, round stone into the space between her collarbones. "Let me think."

The creature was bargaining with her. It had taken Jack as a hostage. Why? Nalissa had never been a hostage. The creature had killed her outright; an innocent girl subjected to a cruel, horrifying death.

Isaline's instincts thumped. That was it—killing Nalissa had been a fear tactic. The creature had been trying to frighten Isaline into handing over the pendant, but now it wasn't trying to scare her. It knew she was protected by her friends.

I'm meant to be here. I won't let another friend die for me.

Determination came to her, flooding her body with energy. She met Neave's eyes and released her arm.

"It wants me to go alone," she said. "It's trying to get to me. The pendant."

Neave stared at her, lashes fluttering. "It'll drown you both."

"I won't let it." Isaline's stomach was a beehive. She glanced at the others. Winn was frowning, stock-still, water rushing below her boots. Cameron looked sick and strained, one hand covering his mouth. They couldn't have known the spark that had been buried in Isaline's heart. The blaze inside her now.

I'm going to kill it.

She threw off her backpack and thrust it into Jame's arms. He took it, doing a double take.

"But—"

"I have to fight it. It murdered ..." She swallowed Nalissa's name before it could burst from her lips. "It murdered my best friend."

A pause, then a flicker of understanding crossed his face. He wordlessly held out his hand for her blazer. She freed the trident from its sling and pulled the stiff fabric from her arms. The trident's metal was cool in her fingers.

"I don't like it," Neave said, pulling on her jacket

again, "but fine. Take this." She dropped the Flash Camera into Isaline's hand, a brass rectangle with a domed bulb on the front. "It helped last time, and it'll still work if it gets wet."

Isaline rotated the Flash Camera, examining the glass bulb and the iron slats beneath. The button that controlled the flash mechanism rested comfortably against her index finger. She recalled Neave's instructions in the Harper and Cup: aim, fire, and hope the flare of light disorients the enemy enough to finish the job.

She clipped the Flash Camera to her belt, mimicking Neave's weapons configuration. "Thank you."

"If anything happens, we're coming to get you." Winn planted herself on a large rock, digging her heels into the riverbank. "We'll be watching."

Isaline nodded. She inhaled deeply. Then, sparing a last look at Jame hugging her backpack to his chest, she took a shuffling step into the river.

THE WATER WAS BATH-WARM, soaking her legs up to the waist. Isaline clutched the trident in one hand and propelled herself across the current, past the King's mining cart and deep into the river. Her companions' lights shrank into the distance, leaving her with the cone of her headlamp and the press of the solid dark.

She stopped in what she guessed was the river's

center. There was no sign of Jack or the creature—no sign of life at all. Rushing water tore at her legs and feet. She wiped moisture from her brow and spun in a slow circle, scanning the empty riverbed.

"I have it," Isaline said, raising her voice over the roar of the water. She dug the pendant out of her collar and held the sparkling stone between two fingers. "The lock. Let him go."

There was a moment of quiet, only the sound of water coursing around her hips. A prickle worked up her spine. She was being watched, but from what direction she couldn't tell. The river seemed giant and tiny at once, as if her cone of light were a little world inside an abyss.

A flapping noise met her ears, followed by the twittering she had heard at the three passages.

The bird.

Was it helping her? Was it even real?

"I *said*," she called, swallowing a rising fear, "I have what you came for. Let my friend go."

A squawk erupted from the darkness at her right. Without a second thought, Isaline lunged toward the noise, orange light skimming the river's surface. She pressed the button on the middle grip of the trident, readying an attack, but hesitated. The figure that appeared under the water was clad in black, not wormy and pale. A body slipping across the riverbed. A tangle of black hair. Blue-lined skin.

"Jack!" She plunged her hand into the water, trying to

seize his flailing wrist, but the current carried him out of her reach. He surfaced, gasped, and was dunked under the water again. The river was only waist-high—why couldn't he stand?

It didn't matter. If she couldn't catch up to him, he would be swept downriver and lost. Heart pounding, Isaline dashed over the smooth rocks, letting the water's torrent push her. She was vaguely aware of her friends' lights receding; there was now a length of river between them, and if Isaline needed their help, they wouldn't be able to get to her in time. She was truly on her own.

But she had to save Jack. As he surfaced again, she made another grab for his waterlogged sleeve, but the fabric passed between her fingers. She stumbled, one knee falling hard on the riverbed.

"No—" she tried to say, but water rushed into her mouth. She pushed to her feet, coughing, and wiped her eyes. Jack was gone. Washed away.

"Jack," she called, water trickling from the corners of her mouth. "Jack!"

"No more running."

The creature's voice was a deadpan scratch coming from behind her. Isaline whirled, one hand slapping over the pendant at her chest. Her headlamp illuminated nothing but glistening water.

"Show yourself," she said, as bold as she could manage. "Bring back my friend."

At the sound of her voice, the crown of a bald, fishy

head emerged from the darkness, parting the river at the outer edge of her light. "*Give me the lock.*"

"I ..." The sight of the creature sent a shockwave through her body. Nalissa's face rose in her mind and the fire inside her chest hissed. "You need to bring back my friend."

"*He will live.*"

A lie. Wasn't it? He had been drowning—but she couldn't think about that now. She needed to focus.

Isaline forced herself to take a step closer to the creature. The reach of her light lengthened, and its tail appeared, rippling beneath the water. A huge, white snake. "You killed Nalissa," she said. She was stalling, toeing around in the riverbed, looking for divots.

The creature rolled its neck, lifting its head from the river. The black strip of its blindfold glistened, lumps wriggling beneath the soaked fabric. "*Give me the pendant, girl.*"

Isaline renewed her grip on the trident. In the forest, she and Jame had been fighting with an advantage: they were on land. This creature's domain was the water. She needed to steady her legs and keep her feet. Brushing her hair out of her eyes, she wedged her left foot between two rocks, leaving her right foot free to pivot. It wasn't ideal. She could trip and hurt her ankle, but even that would keep her from being swept away.

Like Jack.

The thought made her jaw pinch. She was fed up being scared.

"Enough talk, now," Isaline said, raising the trident. It was no tree branch. Three points glimmered, sharp enough to slice through the wood of a clockwork's belly. "I won't give you the pendant. So ... come and take it."

It simply stared at her, head bobbing in the rushing water.

Isaline wouldn't be taunted. Clutching to a memory of Nalissa—arms flailing, feet scrambling across her desk and sending letters flying like snow—Isaline yelled, "*Come on!*"

The creature streaked toward her, its body slicing the raging river. Isaline anchored her left foot, bent her knees, and plunged the trident into the water. River stones stirred. The creature dodged the blow and circled out of her light. She wrenched the trident up and rotated the staff in her hands.

Her light swiveled as the creature's arms materialized to the left, moving slickly across the riverbed, overlong fingers reaching for her ankles. Beneath the water, they were twisted and claw-like. The fingers of a corpse. She scraped the points of the trident across the rocks, warding off its quivering arms.

As the creature slid backward through the river, preparing for another lunge, Isaline readied another jab. She wouldn't be able to spear its torso if she couldn't get past its arms. She needed dry ground.

But before she had finished the thought, the creature

came at her again. It pushed itself to the surface of the river and made a grab for her shoulders. Isaline thrust the staff of the trident across her body, barely keeping the creature from smacking into her. One slithery hand closed around the trident and pulled. She forced her center of gravity back and into the current.

"You," the creature groaned. *"You ... you ... you ..."*

Isaline's headlamp lit its face—the cavern of its mouth, the decaying, fleshy nose, the lumps of its eyes squirming beneath its blindfold. Her skin shrank in horror. What had Nalissa seen beneath that blindfold? What hideous glare had she witnessed during her life's last moments?

The creature's sour breath gusted into Isaline's nose. She redoubled her grip on the trident, praying she was strong enough to keep the creature from pulling it away. Desperate, she kicked at its tail, but the current and the creature's weight threatened to drag her down.

"Let go," she said, breathing hard. They were locked in a precarious balance, neither giving way. "I won't give you the lock."

"Dead girl," the creature said, and there was glee in its voice. River water leaked from its immense mouth, sloshing onto her fingers. *"You already have."*

The words had scarcely registered before there was an odd sensation at the nape of her neck. Isaline's breath stuttered. She'd been so focused on gripping the trident that she hadn't noticed the creature's other hand, creeping around her side, up her back, fingers hovering at the top of her spine.

A long finger hooked beneath the bronze chain of her necklace and jerked upward.

The chain drew taut around Isaline's throat, ripping into her skin. Searing pain bit through her neck. On instinct, she released a hand from the trident and clawed at her throat, trying to free the chain's clasp—but it had buried itself into her throat. Her lips parted. Was it water moistening her collar? Or blood?

She groped at the pendant. The chain was strangling her. A gurgling sound escaped her mouth, and the creature sighed, a grating whistle of rank air that turned Isaline's insides to ice.

"I saw you born, girl," it said. The words didn't enter Isaline's mind. Spots swam in her vision, her headlamp light dimming. *"I didn't want to see you die."*

Saliva pooled at the base of Isaline's throat. *Don't pass out,* she pleaded with herself. If she lost consciousness, she was going to die. She would never see the light again.

Light. Her fingers fell from her neck and grazed a brass, rectangular box clipped to her belt.

Isaline's arm was heavy, but somehow, she unclipped the Flash Camera. It fit into her hand, trigger resting beneath her index finger. Her mind was screaming—*don't look at the eyes, don't pass out, don't look at the eyes, don't pass out*—but she knew what she had to do. No time to wait.

Choking, her chest heaving, Isaline squeezed her eyes shut. The creature's face vanished.

"*Surrender the pendant,*" the creature said. "*Surrender to—*"

Isaline released the trident, struck out, and tore its blindfold from its head. The creature screeched, eye-slime grazing the side of her finger, and she fired the Flash Camera. A blinding strike of light cast the world in white-orange. Adrudian lightning. She felt the creature's body go rigid as darkness swept in and the Flash Camera fizzed, preparing another shot.

The chain digging into her neck loosened. A modicum of air entered her lungs. This was her chance.

Blind, she groped for the trident pressed between them with her free hand. She seized the slick metal in her palm and pulled the staff back and across her side. With a gasp, she thrust the three points into the creature's chest.

The trident lodged, making a horrible crunching sound, and then there was stillness. Isaline wheezed, sucking lungfuls of air into her burning chest. Before her, the creature whined, tail waving weakly. Its arm left the back of her neck and the bronze chain peeled from her skin, the pendant settling into her collar. A thick, chalky ooze dripped down the trident and onto her hands.

"*Open your eyes,*" the creature said. Its voice had gone quiet, inaudible if it hadn't been speaking in her head. "*Look.*"

Unable to think, Isaline cracked one eye open, careful

to keep her gaze down. The amber light of her headlamp slid over the three points of the trident, wedged in the creature's torn, pale skin. She winced, a wave of nausea turning her stomach. Orange slime was seeping from the wound, covering her hands.

"*Look,*" the creature repeated. One hand was tapping at its impaled chest, drawing her eyes to the slashed skin. "*Here.*"

Grimacing, Isaline used her upper arm to rub water from her eyelashes. She had thought she was imagining it —or hallucinating—but something was moving beneath the creature's skin. The glint of rotating metal. A clanking sound.

Gears. She took her hands from the trident, staring at the orange slime stretching between her fingers. A memory emerged: her pointed branch, wielded like a sword, scraping across the creature's back in the forest at Casret Academy. Orange slime had burst from the gash and coated her legs. She hadn't recognized it.

Adrudian Milk.

The creature was a clockwork.

"*My name was Richard Gray.*" Its breaths were short, clattering within collapsed lungs. From the periphery of her vision, Isaline saw that it had pressed a hand to its eyes, shielding her from its gaze. "*I pretended to be the King's servant. I planned to destroy the lock. He changed me. He ...*" The creature coughed, a line of Adrudian Milk dripping from the corner of its mouth. "*Don't let Johannes have the pendant. Pass it on. Then you will remember.*"

Isaline tried to speak, but her voice was a rasp. She whispered, "Okay."

"*If Adrises is freed, tell my—*" It coughed a second time, curling its palm over its eyes. Despite her best efforts, Isaline caught a glimpse of a closed eyelid between two long fingers. With a start, she realized the eyelid was human. Just human. "*—tell my family I tried to stop it. Don't tell them what I became.*"

Words failed her. Something was rising in her chest. A wail, or a scream. She couldn't let it go. Instead, she whispered, "Okay."

The creature exhaled, its limbs beginning to droop. Isaline's mind was a whirling blank. All she could think was that she didn't want it to die hiding its face.

Absurdly, ridiculously, she clamped her eyes shut and plucked at the creature's thin wrist, lifting its hand from its eyes. She stared at the backside of her eyelids, sensing the creature looking up, around, and then at her.

A strange sound escaped it. "*Ah,*" it murmured, as if understanding something for the first time. "*Not you ... not you ... not you ...*"

His voice faded, a sighing winter wind. Then his head sank back, dipping into the water, and Richard was dead.

ISALINE STOOD in the river's current, trembling, until an engine boomed in the distance and a searchlight came up behind her, casting her eyelids in a greasy orange glow. Richard's dead weight had sunk to the bottom of the river, held in place by her trident.

"To her side," Winn said, and something huge and rumbling slid through the water beside Isaline. She wanted to lift her hand from her eyes, but found it impossible to move her palm, as if her hand had been glued to her face.

Neave's voice. "Don't look at that thing's eyes. I've got her."

Someone splashed into the water and grasped the staff of the trident, wrenching Richard's body from the sharp points. Isaline's limbs slackened as another pair of hands grabbed beneath her arms and hauled her out of the river, onto the deck of the King's mining cart. She was placed upright in a hard metal seat, and her shoulders were covered with two dry jackets. The vibration of an engine made her brain shake in her skull.

Gentle fingers pried her hand from her eyes. Jame's features resolved in front of her.

"Are you okay?" he said, searching her face. Someone had closed Isaline's headlamp. His freckles shone in the light from a lantern across the deck. "You did it. You killed it."

Isaline opened her mouth, but no sound came out. She touched her neck, exhaling in relief when she felt the pendant tucked into her collar. And no blood—the chain hadn't cut her.

"She's in shock." Neave sat on the seat across from them. She patted the jackets draping Isaline's shoulders, pulling them tighter around her arms. "Do you know where you are?"

"Yes," Isaline croaked, throat like sandpaper. She looked around the giant mining cart. Winn was at the helm, her goggles strapped over her eyes, feeding glowing rocks of Adrudian to a hot engine. Cameron was at Winn's side, staring at the expanse of water. They had opened lanterns around the cart, illuminating a rectangular deck with three rows of rough metal benches.

"What happened to Jack?" Neave asked. At the same moment, Cameron shouted Jack's name from the front of the cart, calling for him in the coursing river.

Isaline swallowed painfully. "He's gone. S-swept down the river. I almost caught him but ..." The words died on her tongue. The creature—*Richard*—had said Jack would live, but Jack had been struggling to keep his head above the surface.

Neave nodded gravely, as if reading Isaline's thoughts. "We're headed downriver. The cart rolled onto a pair of rails near the edge of the cavern. Tracks. He could be alive."

Isaline couldn't bring herself to respond. She handed Neave the soaking Flash Camera, and Neave clipped it to her weapons belt.

Jame gestured to the Milk-splattered trident lying at Isaline's feet. "And that monster?" He still hadn't let go of her hand. She was thankful for his proximity, but her chest was solid ice. The sound of the trident impaling Richard's metal insides played over and over in her mind.

"It said ..." Isaline let go of a shaky breath. "It said it had been working against the King. Only pretending to be his servant. It wanted to destroy the pendant, not steal it for the King. It said its name was Richard Gray."

"Richard Gray," Neave repeated. She ran a painted fingernail across her scalp. "Where have I heard that name before?"

"He was in the photo." Isaline shuddered, remembering the lean man with the muted gray hair. He had kind eyes. "Faraday did something to him. There were metal parts inside his body. Like—like a clockwork."

Jame let go of her hand. He fiddled with the rings on his index finger. "If Richard wasn't working for the King," he said, staring at the dark water flowing outside the cart, "that's why he didn't kill us right away. In the forest."

Isaline chewed her bottom lip. Of course. Richard had stolen the pendant and tried to escape, but Jame had spotted him and followed him to the river. Later, when Isaline took back the pendant, Richard had trailed her into Casret Academy to retrieve it. He had killed Nalissa when they attacked him.

"There's more." Isaline turned to Neave, who had

started restlessly re-lacing her knee-high boots. "Richard said a name. *Adrises.* Do you know who that is?"

Neave tilted her head to the side. "*Ah-dry-sees,*" she said, lengthening the word. "Sounds Ancient Benemournian. I've never heard it before, though." She got to her feet, brushing the legs of her pants. "Was there anything else?"

Don't let Johannes have the pendant. Pass it on. Then you will remember.

"No," Isaline said quickly.

Neave gave her an attempt at a smile and strode over the shaking cart to join Cameron and Winn. The engine spewed out a ball of smoke, oily haze drifting upward. Isaline lifted her gaze. There was a rock ceiling passing over them, spiked with stalactites. When had they entered another tunnel?

Jame took the seat Neave had vacated. He ducked his head to catch Isaline's eye. "You sure you're okay?"

Isaline pressed her palms together, examining her fingers. The river had washed the Adrudian Milk from her skin, but still she felt dirty. Contaminated. She had gone after Richard for Nalissa. But was revenge a good enough reason to kill someone, monster or not? Richard had been trying to thwart the King's plans. Would his effort be wasted now that he was dead?

She sniffed, fighting sudden tears. Jame covered her hands with his own, softly releasing her grip into his.

"I don't know why I'm crying," Isaline said. A tear

leaked from the corner of her eye. "I thought I knew what I was doing."

None of this would have happened if Nalissa were on the expedition. Nalissa wouldn't have gotten herself buried in an Adrudian vat. She wouldn't have let Jack slip through her fingers. She wouldn't have killed Richard—Nalissa hadn't even been able to kill the rat that had sneaked into their dorm room.

"I think I ..." Isaline said to Jame, who was rubbing her palm with the pad of his thumb, "I think I've ruined everything."

Jame let out a short breath. He smiled, his eyes turning into half-moons, and entwined her fingers in his own. "Not everything."

The quality of his voice opened a hollow in her stomach. She looked at him, and he was staring back with a sincere expression, gaze roaming her face. Their noses were inches apart, his breath nudging the wet curls of her hair. The urge to kiss him was overwhelming.

But Isaline leaned back, swallowing a fresh wave of tears. She couldn't kiss him knowing he thought she was Nalissa. There was nothing right about how much she wanted him to like her. Not when she had lied to him about her name, and who she was, and everything else.

The pendant rolled on its chain. She closed her eyes, breathing in and out. Even if she could tell Jame who she was, what would she say about herself? Days ago, she had been a Watchling. Now she was ... nothing. A question.

She couldn't offer Jame the truth until she found the answer.

Pass it on. Then you will remember.

Isaline tugged her hands from Jame's and lifted the bronze chain from around her neck. Jame blinked as she placed it over his head, arranging the pendant behind the collar of his white shirt. Her nerves thrilled at the warmth of his skin.

His smile faded. "Why give it to me?"

She dropped her palms in her lap. "I can't bring myself to wear it right now. Richard tried to use it to kill me." She was also following Richard's instructions: if she passed the pendant on, just for now, maybe she could remember what she had forgotten.

Jame gave her a nod, leaning back in his seat. There was a hint of pink on his cheeks. "I'll keep it safe," he said, "and you should get some rest."

Isaline didn't remember falling asleep, but she woke sometime later from a familiar dream. Nalissa had been sitting beside her, smiling, patting Isaline's closed hands. Something cold pressed between her palms. There were lush leaves all around them, green and blue in moonlight, and a stone wall at her back.

But when Isaline opened her eyes, she saw nothing but orange and black, the ceiling of the tunnel passing above the King's mining cart, and her own tired body, stretched on the hard metal bench.

A ball of shadow was nestled beneath her breastbone. She shifted, startled. It was an image carved from dreaming, a bird's silhouette filled with the points of faraway stars. As soon as she moved, the image disappeared, dissolving into air.

The bird. *Are you real? Or my imagination?*

Isaline turned her head, rubbing the sleep from her eyes. In the Harper and Cup, Neave had warned her that the dark could disorient and corrode the line between real and not real. Hallucinations. Waking dreams.

She pushed herself to sit and rolled her stiff shoulders. Jame was asleep on the opposite bench, his mouth parted slightly, breaths even. The pendant spilled from his collar. Isaline spent a moment gazing at his hair sticking up in all directions, warmth rising in her chest.

Beyond Jame, Cameron was lying on the third bench, curled as best he could on the thin seat. One hand was tucked beneath his head, the rest of him covered by a thin blanket. At first, he appeared to be asleep, but his breaths were rapid. Isaline suspected he was wide awake.

The reverberation of the cart's engine shook the deck beneath Isaline's boots. She peered toward the helm of the cart, where Neave was bent over the engine, feeding it rocks of Adrudian one by one. The goggles strapped over her eyes were smeared with soot. Next to her, Winn was taking a break, leaning over the cart's edge and examining the rushing river below.

Isaline watched them until she couldn't sit still anymore. She got to her feet and picked her way to the front of the cart.

As she approached, Neave dropped a rock of ore into the red-hot engine, bracing as a blast of light and energy pushed the cart forward along the river. She dug a finger under the strap of the goggles, making a frustrated noise.

"You're going to break the strap," Winn said. Her profile was silhouetted against the bright searchlight.

"They're too small," Neave replied. "How do you wear these things?"

"They're not too small for me."

Neave dug into a bucket of Adrudian and selected a large, lumpy rock. "It's not my fault you have a tiny head, Princess."

Winn let out an abrupt laugh, a hand flying to her mouth. Neave chuckled and dropped the rock of Adrudian into the engine. A blast of light illuminated their faces, and Isaline joined them, giving a half-hearted wave.

Neave acknowledged her through soot-dusted goggles. "You're awake," she said, brushing her gloves—also Winn's—over the side of the cart. Her braid was tied in a bun at the back of her head to keep it from falling into the engine.

Isaline hesitated, then leaned on the cart's edge on Winn's other side. "How long did I sleep for?"

"Better part of an hour." Neave pointed in the direction of Cameron and Jame. "Them, too. Once I convinced Cameron to lie down, that is."

Their figures were bathed in shadows cast from the Adrudian lanterns around the deck. Isaline scratched a hand over her sore neck, confused.

"But it's ..." She pushed back her sleeve to check the watch Neave had given her at the Harper and Cup. "Shouldn't it be lunchtime?"

"Should be," Winn said. "The dark makes you want to sleep."

Isaline shifted uncomfortably. Days had passed since they had been above ground. If she thought about it too hard, her mind threatened to bend, so she forced the thought away.

The searchlight stretched before them, illuminating an expanse of torrenting river. Rock walls slid by on either side of the cart, rough and craggy. Isaline imagined skimming her fingertips across the glittering streaks of mica darkened with splashes of river water.

"Any sign of him?" she asked.

Neave shook her head, her face somber. "But the current is moving faster than we are, and the river keeps getting shallower, branching off into side streams. He could still be ahead."

The implication hung in the air between them: Jack's *body* could still be ahead. The memory of his figure beneath the water made Isaline's stomach roll.

"Don't lose hope," Winn said. "Not until we know."

Isaline nodded, clenching her jaw. She reached up to fiddle with the pendant. A ripple of dread went through her when her fingers grazed bare skin, but then she remembered she'd given the necklace to Jame. Her reflexes would take some time to catch up.

Winn watched her rub her empty collarbone. "You've decided, then," she said, looking at Isaline from the corner of her eye.

"Decided what?"

"To take off the pendant."

Isaline's hand fell to her side. She had hoped no one would notice. Taking off the pendant felt personal, as if trying to remember her past were the same as admitting she was empty. Featureless, like the bare rock of the tunnel.

"*The wearer forgets,*" Winn said. "Seems logical enough. Maybe something will come to you."

Something already has, Isaline thought, imagining the bird and its faraway stars. But she couldn't find the words to describe what it looked like, how it had helped her, or how her senses seemed to be buckling. She squinted, waving her hand as a burst of smoke from the engine floated into the air.

"You think it's a good idea? Trying to remember?" she asked Winn.

"Maybe. Maybe not. We'll find what we need to know at Faraday's workshop either way."

"If we're lucky," Neave added, attempting to loosen the strap of Winn's goggles.

Another blast of smoke, and their faces were obscured in oily gray. Isaline coughed. "What do you think we'll find?"

"At the workshop?" Winn asked. The smoke thinned and her face appeared, framed in twists of hair and engine grease. "Information. If I can't find a way to destroy Faraday's clockwork army, the Seven Thrones will never be rebuilt, and Benemourne will crumble. Clockwork soldiers raiding homes. Adrudian disappearing. I can't let that happen."

The solemn tone of her voice, coupled with the distant look in her eyes, made Isaline stand up a little straighter. Neave rolled a bright chunk of Adrudian around in her palm.

"You'll get Benemourne back," she said to Winn. She opened her hand and the Adrudian fell into the engine. "No one else can do it—before you showed up, there hadn't been a new Throne admitted in decades. No wonder they call you the Princess."

The ensuing blast of light hit Winn's face in tones of orange. Isaline shaded her eyes, but Winn didn't flinch.

"*Princess* is a name they gave me," Winn said, "but I'm not sure. The Thrones told me it was because I'm young, and a leader, and I'm not afraid of responsibility." She didn't look at either of them, just stared down the murky passage. "It seemed like they were talking about a different person."

"Well, that's the person *we* know," Neave said, looking at Isaline for confirmation. Isaline nodded.

Winn smiled her soft, angled smile at both of them. "I'll be honest. There's something else I hope to find in Faraday's workshop." She lifted her chin, a nervous set to her jaw. "I hope I'll find that those things are true, and that I know them. Without someone having to tell me."

A pause followed her words. Isaline took a deep breath. Winn made it sound as if she were on this expedition not just to save Benemourne, but to prove something to herself. To answer her own questions. Wasn't that why Isaline was here, too?

She reached for the pendant again but found her collar empty. Winn's gaze flicked to hers, then returned to the river, her expression inscrutable. She pulled a box of matches from her belt and selected one slender stick of wood.

Neave's face had gone thoughtful. "My mom used to tell me: *The brightest treasures are the truths you find inside.*" She shrugged, giving them a devilish grin. "But then I became a Treasurehunter."

Winn let out a breathy laugh. She struck the match, and it flared and fizzled like a tiny star. "Funny," she said. "My dad's version is: *Wear your truths. Everything else is just clothes.*"

Neave made an amused noise. "Same concept."

A minute passed in silence, each of them listening to the rush of the river beneath their feet. Then Isaline's eyes focused on something in the distance, in the dark beyond the searchlight. Her hands held tight to the side of the cart.

"Do you see that?" she asked.

Neave let out a rousing whoop. She took the rock of Adrudian in her hand and banged it against the engine, clanging it like a bell's toll. "Wake up, people!" she called. "There's a light!"

The light was a pinprick far down the passage, a tiny, hovering beam. Neave hunkered into a crouch behind the engine, filling her arms with bright Adrudian rocks.

"If it's Jack, he could be hurt," Winn said, pushing her sleeves up to her elbows. "We should hurry."

"Took the thought right out of my head, Princess." Neave grinned, wicked in the orange shine of the Adrudian. "Permission to see how fast this thing can go?"

5

THE EIGHTH GOD

JACK

Water, darkness, and he couldn't breathe. The river carried him tumbling down its channel, his arms and legs flailing in the current. The water was shallow, but he couldn't get his feet beneath him. The man-snake had broken both of his ankles.

He'd felt his bones snap—*pop, pop*—beneath the creature's twitchy fingers. Pain radiated from the breaks, his ankles heavy and swollen as the river roared. Water gushed into his nose and white spots burst and re-burst in front of his eyes, like bubbles.

Jack couldn't die. He had come so close. The House of Matchsticks had called to him. He'd Drunk Adrudian. He'd shaken Cameron's hand.

At some point, the man-snake had left him, and he was

alone, struggling against the torrenting water. How long would he last? His teammates could be miles away. His headlamp had been ripped from his head and lost. He was in the pitch dark.

Don't drown. Not yet.

The river deepened, and suddenly his throbbing feet couldn't find the smooth rocks on the riverbed. Jack pawed at the deep water, but still he sank like a stone. The space surrounding him lost shape and meaning; he was in a void, suspended as gravity towed him down. The same sensation as his Adrudian vision on the train to Ar, when the woman in the mines had spoken to him.

I'm someone like you, the woman had said. *Someone who looks through doors. Someone who wants to be free.*

Jack's chest convulsed, his lungs starved for air. Was the current carrying him? He didn't know. The world had hushed. He imagined the woman from his visions, her dripping-wax skin, her black, round eyes. She had asked Jack to bring Nalissa. She had assured him he would remember the lost expedition. But he was going to die before he could.

"You say that as if I won't keep my promise," a voice said.

A burble of precious air leaked from Jack's mouth. His eyes snapped open. There was nothing around him: no lights, no figures. Just the stillness of drowning.

"At least call me by my name." The woman's voice was

inside Jack's head. She sounded reproachful, as if speaking to a child. "*Adrises.*"

Jack was too busy dying to be surprised. He'd heard the name before, but where? His research? A book?

"*You will live, Jack.*" Adrises' voice lowered to a gut-vibrating pitch. "*We'll meet soon. For now, sleep. Dream.*"

Her last words followed Jack into the blackness. He didn't understand what they meant, but he had no choice. Water encased him. Gravity stretched him, and he drifted down

down

down.

THE BOTTOM of the pit came into view only after they left the surface behind. Jack and Cameron stood firm on the middle of the Nine Men's Morris board as it descended from the plateau. Above them, the trap closed with a deafening grind, the mechanism spiraling back into the stone platform. A board awaiting more players.

Dead players, *Jack thought grimly. If he and Cameron had almost fallen into the pit, others would surely plunge to their deaths.*

They descended into a round, open cave, lit by slants of light from cracks in the ground above. The hill they had climbed to get to the plateau was hollow, and Jack traced a path on the wall with his eyes, imagining himself and

Cameron hiking up the other side. Cameron with his walking stick, talking about Mivnia's ring. He almost missed the one-sided conversation; the cave was quiet, nothing but the click-click-click *of their lift lowering into a bed of spongy moss.*

As they came to a stop, Jack spotted a scatter of white littering the ground. His skin puckered into goosebumps. Human skeletons. From years ago, based on the level of decay. He scrunched his nose at the stench of death and dampness.

"That's a lot of bones," Cameron said, finally breaking the silence. They were standing back-to-back, Cameron with his elbow pressed to Jack's arm to keep them stable. "You think anyone got past the trap?"

Jack didn't respond. His insides were churning. He had been sure no one else knew about the House of Matchsticks, yet there were people here.

They're not Treasurehunters, *he told himself.* They played the game and fell into the pit by accident.

But his confidence wavered.

Holding his breath, Jack stepped off the stone and kneeled by the nearest skeleton, examining the crumbling bones spread with an insidious black mold. A leather belt was strung around the collapsing hips. Jack's heart sank. The fashion was old, but the belt was unmistakable. A weapons belt. They were all wearing weapons belts. Jack was far from the first Treasurehunter here.

He stood, weaving his fingers through his hair. The

hum of discovery inside him shrank until it was nothing but a tiny pinch.

Cameron had opened his flashlight and was shining it over an aging metal crank at the edge of the stone square. He tested it, turning the handle. With a groan, the mechanism reversed, carrying the square back up to the Nine Men's Morris board.

"So, that's how we get back up," Cameron said. He stood and pointed across the cave. "And that's *the direction we should be going."*

Jack followed his gaze to a stone archway carved into the wall, rough-hewn, leading off and into darkness. "How do you know?" he asked. He was the one with the map.

"Process of elimination." Cameron winked. "It's the only exit."

Jack dug the toe of his boot into the squishy moss, casting around the cave. The space was large, the walls shaggy with roots and soil, but there were no other archways. Cameron was correct. Again.

They passed beneath the arch and into a narrow tunnel, the smell of earth filling Jack's nose. He was eager to leave the cave and its skeletons behind. The next landmark was close—a bridge; his research said to proceed beneath it, instead of across it—but all he could picture were the eyes that had seen this passageway before his. The Treasure-hunters who might have made it here might have made it even to the House of Matchsticks.

For the first time, Jack wondered what he would do if he

got to the House of Matchsticks and the cave was empty. The thought made his face heat. No keystone, nothing to learn, the site scraped clean by explorers with well-connected families, bigger libraries, better relationships. Explorers like Cameron.

The tunnel was slim, forcing them to walk in single file. Jack stared at the back of Cameron's neck, gaze running over his strong shoulders, his head of golden hair flawlessly mussed. It was as if the skeletons in the cave had woken Jack from a days-long trance. How had he grown so comfortable? Worse than comfortable. Jack had been enjoying *himself. He'd enjoyed rolling his eyes at the stupid Mivnia story. He'd enjoyed playing Nine Men's Morris. He'd enjoyed ...*

Jack closed his eyes. He'd been entertained, that was all. But he had no business being on this expedition with another Treasurehunter. Had the times Cameron had stolen victories from him been erased from his memory? The Golden Chalice? Even Mivnia's ring, which Jack had been researching when Cameron had found it. Jack had been only halfway through his map when Cameron had emerged from the Shute, ring held aloft, eyes flashing gold in the daytime sun.

Not real. *Jack shook his head. He hadn't been there when Cameron had returned with Mivnia's ring. He'd just imagined it that way. And Cameron's eyes were brown.*

His thoughts were interrupted by the sound of running

water, bringing with it the scent of fresh air and trees. Cameron hurried his pace, forcing Jack to jog to keep up, and the passage opened onto a massive space carved into the base of one of the Shute's low mountains. A grotto.

Jack squinted, eyes adjusting to the flood of daytime light. A great ceiling of rock hung overhead, sheltering the gently curving end of a creek. Sparkling water wound through the grotto and out into the crisp, green trees of the Shute, which stood tall outside a large, natural opening to their left. Jack stepped into the grotto behind Cameron, both of them craning to watch a family of brown-winged birds soar beneath the ceiling.

"It's beautiful," Cameron said. The breathless tone of his voice surprised Jack. He kneeled and dipped a hand into the creek, shaking water between his fingers. "Have you ever seen anything like this?"

"No," Jack replied truthfully. He turned away and retrieved his map, trying to keep thoughts steady. It was *beautiful, a natural wonder, but he couldn't afford to be distracted.*

Jack fixed his gaze on the map. If they walked parallel to the creek, they should find the bridge at the other side of the grotto. He ran his finger along the route—grotto, creek, bridge—but soon his attention slid over the top of the map and landed on Cameron. He was standing now, running a moistened hand over the back of his neck. The light dancing through his hair was blinding.

Jack squeezed his eyes shut. Not blinding. Normal sunlight.

"We should ..." He cleared his throat and tried again. "We should follow the creek."

Cameron nodded, running a thumb along his brow. "I think I hear a waterfall."

They strode across the green, lush ground, picking their way between clusters of shiny plants. As they rounded a corner, the head of the creek came into view, fed by a babbling waterfall issuing from a crack in the grotto's wall. The thin sheet of tumbling water glimmered, so practiced in its falling that it reminded Jack of rippled glass. At the base of the waterfall, leading over the creek and off into the forest, was a wooden footbridge.

Jack stowed the map in his jacket, the knot in his spine loosening a degree. He might not be the first Treasurehunter here, but at least he was on the right track.

A moment passed before he noticed Cameron was being uncharacteristically quiet. He turned to see him standing a few steps away, one hand drumming the side of his face, regarding Jack with interest.

Jack's stomach jumped. "What?"

"Just watching."

"Watching me?"

"Watching you watch that waterfall. You look like a hawk tracking a mouse. You see everything, don't you?"

The comment brought Jack up short. Was it a compli-

ment? It sounded like one, but he couldn't find a reason Cameron would be praising him.

"It's just a waterfall," Jack said. That was its own kind of false. His research had revealed as much: proceed beneath the bridge, not across it. He would have bet a hundred gold pieces there was a hidden door behind that sheet of water.

Cameron gave him a cheery smile. He was standing between Jack and the rest of the grotto, leaning on a wedge of rock. "I mean, I like it," he said, shrugging one shoulder. "The way you look at things."

There was no mistaking it. That was a compliment. Jack opened his mouth, trying to find a suitable response—but something about the rock behind Cameron caught his attention. Black lines swirled and dipped like brush strokes on its surface. His heart thumped. There was a painting on the rock, half-covered by creeping vines.

"I've always been ..." Cameron trailed off, smile waning. "You're not listening."

He was right. Jack moved toward the rock, one hand outstretched to brush away clumps of tangled vines. The leaves and stems shifted easily, parting like a green curtain. Behind them, a rudimentary mural materialized, no taller than Jack, but five or six paces across. Lines of glyphs arched across the top in a language Jack didn't recognize. The mural itself was drawn in the style of Ancient Benemournian art: thick, black lines, rounded figures, and bulging eyes. Ancient depictions of people made Jack think of fish with arms and legs, as if the artist had seen the first humans crawl from the sea.

But these weren't humans. They were gods.

Cameron made a noise of amazement. He turned to survey the mural, and a light pressure appeared at Jack's side. Their arms were brushing together. He glanced at Cameron out of the corner of his eye, but Cameron didn't move—didn't even seem to notice—so neither did Jack.

The mural depicted eight figures standing behind an empty table. The figure at the center of the table was broad-shouldered and heavy-browed: Arias, the sovereign of the Ancient Benemournian pantheon. Arias had their hands spread in a gesture of welcome to the lesser gods on either side, gods of precious stones, elements, and states of nature. Jack recognized Dodia, the god of floods and famine, and Tuphin, god of quartzes, as well as most of the others.

Ancient Benemournians had worshiped gods and performed rituals to them, but their beliefs had been nothing more than superstition. Jack guessed that, aside from Treasurehunters, the average person wouldn't know Arias' name, let alone any of the lesser gods.

Cameron pointed to each figure in the mural from left to right, naming them. "Dodia, Gomos, Wudtar ..." He stopped at the end of the line, pointing to the last figure on the right. "Who's that?"

Jack hadn't recognized that one, either. The figure was wild-haired, vaguely feminine, with circular eyes and no pupils. Her hands were resting on her chest, as if pulling apart the folds of a coat, and there was a small marking between them.

"Eight gods," Cameron said. "There's usually seven. She's an extra."

"An uninvited guest." Jack wasn't sure what he meant by that. He was having trouble thinking. Had he ever seen an eighth god? No—but he couldn't be sure. He was distracted by the alarming sensation of Cameron leaning into his arm more readily. Not a mistake. Not unconscious.

"There's a symbol here," Cameron said. He stepped toward the mural, breaking their contact. "Nine Men's Morris."

There was a tiny Nine Men's Morris board etched into the eighth god's chest, between her spreading hands. Jack rubbed his arm, confused. Not about Nine Men's Morris—that was simple enough. About Cameron. And him. What was Cameron trying to do? Throw him off?

Cameron cast a glance over his shoulder. "You thinking what I'm thinking?"

"No," Jack said with confidence.

"Well, it's obvious to me." Cameron gave him a sly look, tapping the mural with the flat of his hand. "The ritual held at the House of Matchsticks. They were praying to this eighth god. That's why we keep seeing her symbol."

It made sense. None of Jack's research had told him what kind of ritual had been performed at the House of Matchsticks, or to what god the ritual-makers had prayed.

Cameron ran his fingers down the mural as if memo-

rizing it with his hands. "We'll have to write to Ar's library," he said softly. "Tell them what we found."

We. The word made Jack's skin prickle. Unpleasant and ... pleasant. He took a step backward, sitting on a nearby rock. Of all the things that could have gone wrong on this expedition, he had been stuck here with Cameron, who seemed to be playing some kind of game with him. Talking as if they hadn't been enemies for years, as if they were friendly. Complimenting him and touching his arm as if they were ...

Jack's mind had trouble forming the idea. Something more than friendly.

He rubbed his palms into his eyes. Jack had experienced his share of casual attention, but it had always come from stoical, wayward men: a childhood friend who later left on a mission with the Thieves' Quandary; a mysterious stranger across the tavern when he turned eighteen; an ill-tempered archivist who would write him stacks of letters.

Not a rival, not a celebrity, and certainly not Cameron Agustin.

When he surfaced from his hands, Cameron had taken off his weapons belt. He laid the belt on a patch of grass, shedding his leather jacket.

"What are you doing?" Jack asked, his voice a rasp.

"Getting comfortable." Cameron lay down on the grass with his jacket bunched under his head like a bulky pillow. He crossed his legs and rested his ankle on the opposite knee, thighs making a perfect triangle. "We've been up for

..." Yawning, he checked his watch. "A long time. Seems like a good enough place to sleep."

"Here?" Jack looked around the massive grotto. "We'll be exposed."

"We don't all have your limitless energy, Jack Fael." Cameron stretched, sighing in a way that sent a shiver straight up Jack's spine. He turned and flashed Jack a grin. "Besides, who's going to come strolling through this part of the Shute? We're all by ourselves."

Jack coughed. "We're—um—" A day ago, he would have brushed off the comment. Now he wasn't sure Cameron wasn't flirting with him. "I—I don't have limitless energy."

"Of course you don't. You use it all up being delightful company."

Jack found himself unable to form words for a response. Cameron smiled at him a moment more, as if enjoying Jack's speechlessness, then turned to the ceiling and closed his eyes.

The morning went on, and soon the noonday sun cast the grotto in shades of white. Cameron relaxed on the ground, picking at the grass and reading from a book he'd pulled from his jacket. The thought of lying down anywhere near him sent Jack's head into a tailspin, so he settled for sliding off the rock he was sitting on and using it as a backrest. When afternoon came, they ate a meager dinner, talking sparsely and listening to the trickle of the creek, and when the light tilted through the trees, Jack's exhaustion outpaced his nerves and he fell into a dreamless sleep.

He woke as the air was turning blue. Twilight crept along the ground, drawing lines on the mural and draping the wooden footbridge in shadows. Cameron was asleep on the grass, turned on his side with his forearm over his eyes. He had built a fire while Jack was asleep—burned down to embers, now—and left a cup of fresh water beside him.

Jack stared at the cup, then at the mural. The gods seemed to be scrutinizing him through the growing darkness, willing him to make a decision.

He took a deep breath, pine-scented air filling his lungs. Months of research had gone into finding the House of Matchsticks. Endless hours spent in his shabby boarding house room, bent over scrolls, books, or carvings. He'd thought about Cameron during those nights. Wondered what he was working on, if his team had gone into the Shute, if he would show up on Jack's expedition with that gleaming smile. That was how it had been for years. Normal, for Jack. A semblance of balance.

Now the scales had tipped. Traveling with Cameron had upset Jack's stability, and there was a dark feeling in his chest that told him it was intentional. With Jack's guard down, Cameron could take the prize for himself. Why else would he be here? Cameron had romanced half of Ar, if the gossip was true. It wouldn't be the first time he had employed his charm and looks to get what he wanted. Just the first time he'd gotten brash enough to try it on Jack.

The fading evening cast the grotto in cool light. To anyone else, it was day's end. To Jack, it was the opportunity to sneak into a new beginning.

He stood, quietly gathering his things. He left the cup of water untouched. It crossed his mind that he could be wrong—that Cameron could simply want to share the expedition with him—but there was no sharing in their line of work, and Jack was never wrong. Only insensitive to particular shades of truth.

He tore a page from his notebook and scribbled on it with black ink.

Nice try. Don't bother following me.

Tiptoeing across the grotto, he pinned the note under dry rock where Cameron would see it. Then, with a last look at Cameron's sleeping form, he climbed to the head of the creek and edged through the waterfall. The water cooled his flushed skin, and Jack continued on as he was meant to: alone.

In the mines, he woke up with a wrenching gasp and opened his eyes to dim light.

Water ran across his back, warm and foamy, but shallow enough to coat only the crown of his head. For a moment, Jack had the absurd thought that he was lying in the creek, the grotto ceiling high above him with its sunlight and brown-winged birds. But the rock overhead was pegged with stalactites, and the light coating them in greasy orange was Adrudian.

Jack lay still and focused on filling his body with air. He was alive. How was he alive? Turning his head, he watched river water funnel through a slot in the rock wall of the passage. He was at the river's end, or at least at the point where the tunnel pinched it off.

To his left, a round passageway spilled hazy amber light over the narrow riverbank. How did he get here? He racked his brain for the last thing he remembered before the vision. The world had been blackness, his weight sinking into a basin, unable to swim because of his broken ankles.

His ankles.

He gingerly bent at the waist, lifting his back from the water with a splash. Grasping at his legs, he pulled back the wet cuffs of his pants and examined his ankles. They were pale and soaked, but unmarked. He prodded one with a finger, poking around his ankle bone and across his heel. No pain, not even any swelling.

Jack's mind whirled. His ankles had been broken. Just the memory of the creature's slimy fingers snaking around his skin, contracting and crushing, made him shudder. There was no way he could have imagined it.

Muscles quivering, Jack pushed himself to his feet, windmilling his arms for balance. His ankles held. He was weak, but not injured. That was good—but it was also impossible. How could his ankles have healed so fast? And how could he have survived sinking into a deep part of the river?

You will live, Jack.

The woman in the mines. Adrises. She had saved him, and if he wasn't hallucinating, she had healed his injuries. Even his broken nose didn't hurt anymore.

Jack hugged his arms around himself, fighting the chill working up his body. What kind of woman could do this? Adrises hadn't been with him in the river. She was trapped; she had said so herself in Little Space, when they had looked through the lock: *I'm in a cage. Underground. Help.*

In Jack's vision, she had been in a dark, cave-like space, peering through a keyhole to the world beyond. Yet she had saved him from dying, healed his body, spoke into his mind, and controlled his visions. No woman could do that. No human.

His own words came back to him, the words he'd spoken before Adrises had placed her waxen hands on his temples and flooded him with memories.

I don't mean to be rude, but you don't seem *to be someone like me.*

The realization hit Jack like a brick. The mysterious figure from the mural blazed into his mind: wild-haired, vaguely female, eyes round like buttons. He'd seen those eyes. The eighth god.

Adrises was the eighth god.

A shot of adrenaline forced him into movement. Jack

lurched out of the river and kneeled on wobbly knees, squinting in the light from the tunnel. He opened his jacket with shaking hands and retrieved his two stolen books: *Gravel and Lode: Rocks and Gemstones of the Shute* and *Ancient Benemournian Rituals and Their Uses*. He let the covers of *Gravel and Lode* fall open. The pages were mostly mulch, but the map he'd been drawing of their progress through the mines was legible.

Ancient Benemournian Rituals was in better shape—wet, but salvageable. He didn't know how it was possible, but it could be Adrises' doing. She was drawing him to the right information. She wanted him to know.

Jack cracked the back cover and thumbed through the moist pages to the index. When he had stolen the book from a hidden room in Fort Upper's library, he'd known there must be secret information within the pages, but he hadn't been able to find any new information in the text. Then again, he had never made it to *Chapter Five: Types of Rituals*.

He skimmed his finger down the *I* section of the index, looking for *imprisonment*. Nothing.

He tried the *T* section, looking for *trap*. Nothing.

He flipped to the S section and scanned the list. His lips parted, releasing a shallow breath. *Something*.

Sealing Rituals, page 408.

Heart pounding, Jack flipped to the fifth chapter of the book. The text was soaked through, making the words impossible to read, but that didn't matter. What Jack was looking for was emblazoned squarely in the center of the page. Three concentric squares, connected with points at each intersection, gazing out of the book like an odd, angular eye. Nine Men's Morris.

Cameron had been wrong, in the grotto. He'd thought Nine Men's Morris was Adrises' symbol. It wasn't—it was the symbol of the ritual used to imprison her.

A deep, quaking rumble shook through the ground, rippling up the walls of the tunnel and vibrating the stalactites overhead. Jack froze, watching as a cloud of dust fell from the ceiling. He didn't dare breathe until the trembling had stilled, the mines settling again into silence.

Adrises was a god, sealed deep under the earth during a ritual held at the House of Matchsticks. The idea spread Jack's mind uncomfortably thin. He had never believed the Ancient Benemournian gods were real. Yet a god had spoken to him, healed his injuries.

Despite his shock, Jack felt a smile blooming on his face. No Treasurehunter had come back from an expedition with the news of a trapped god.

Jack would be the first.

He stood, resting a hand on the side of his dripping face, and let go of an incredulous laugh. The hum of discovery inside him expanded, harmonizing with the rhythm of his new memories. Strange and familiar. The memories were his, undoubtedly his, but the more he remembered, the more Jack was aware of how much had changed since the lost expedition. He had been wrong about so many things, that evening he'd sneaked from the grotto. But he'd been given a second chance.

As he turned to face the glowing tunnel—the way forward—there were no thoughts of the Treasurehunters that had come before him, the skeletons in the cave. Instead, Jack had grown sensitive to a particular shade of truth. He wished Cameron were here.

6

TWO RITUALS

ISALINE

Isaline braced her feet against the deck of the cart as Neave dropped Adrudian rocks into the engine with renewed fervor. There was a staccato blast of light and heat, and the cart barreled through the tunnel, picking up speed. Behind them, there was a thumping sound and a muffled curse. Jame, falling off the metal bench and bumping his head.

"What's the rush?" he said, appearing at Isaline's side. He rubbed his head with his forearm. "Did we find Jack?"

"Maybe. Look." Isaline had to shout to be audible over the engine. She pointed to the light in the distance. It had grown into a tiny, orange circle shining from the side of the passage. At first, she'd thought it was the beam of a headlamp, but now it appeared to be a passageway leading from the main tunnel.

The river beneath them thinned, branching off into

smaller tributaries on either side, and the wheels of the cart burst from the water with a thundering splash. Neave whooped. Her braid had come loose from its knot, whipping around her head in the wind. She tipped more Adrudian into the mouth of the engine and the cart roared, hurtling through the tunnel.

Cameron clawed his way from the benches and joined them at the helm of the cart. "Is it him?" The edges of his eyes were pink, his sleeves buffeting in the thrashing air. "Do you see him?"

Isaline started to reply, but her voice was lost in another blast from the engine. The cart's searchlight bled into the light from ahead, and their destination came into view: a brightly lit passageway overlooking a shallow riverbank. What was left of the river funneled past the passageway, straight into a slot in the rock. Stalactites hung from the ceiling, casting stripes over the tunnel's end.

The tunnel's end.

Isaline's blood ran cold. They were headed for a solid wall.

"Slow down," she yelled, waving her arms at Neave. "We can't follow the river. It's a dead end."

Neave let two rocks of Adrudian fall into the engine, skin shining with grease and sweat. "It's a what?"

"A dead end!"

"A *what?*"

A rush of smoke enveloped them as the Adrudian combusted and sent the cart tearing down the tunnel.

Isaline clutched Jame's arm, trying to keep her balance. The river had slowed to a trickle, its glimmering surface disappearing into the rock ahead.

Winn was bent at the waist, one hand holding herself up and the other flailing at Neave, miming pulling a brake.

"There's no brake," Neave shouted in the tumult. She was frantically looking for a lever or switch, but there was none.

Isaline's heart jumped into her mouth. Ahead, their searchlight and the glow from the passageway had merged, the end of the tunnel coming at them like a shot from a pistol.

"Jump," Cameron cried above another engine blast. He was braced against the corner of the cart, his hair lifting from his forehead in one mass. "We need to jump!"

Neave and Winn nodded, but Isaline shrieked, "*Jump?*" The cart was big. They would pitch to the stony riverbed.

"Thank me later." Cameron wound his hand in the back of Isaline's blazer. He grabbed Jame with his other arm and sprinted across the deck, hurling all three of them over the side of the cart.

The world blurred, heat rushing through Isaline's hair, her stomach somersaulting into her ribs. She screamed, but an earth-shaking explosion stole her breath, rending the air behind her. A ripple of force shook the mines, her body, and the world flickered into momentary darkness.

A stone wall was at her back, lush leaves enveloping

her and Nalissa. They were two children huddled at the base of Casret Academy's dormitory, sharing secrets on the first night they'd met. Something heavy was pressed between Isaline's palms. Nalissa patted the outside of her hands, a smile playing over her face.

"You'll always remember," Nalissa said.

Then the ground *whumped* against Isaline's back, and she tumbled, rocks scoring her blazer into ribbons. She slid to a stop, lying sideways in the riverbank, and stared at the bare wall of the tunnel, powerless to do anything but breathe as the ground shook. Rock clattered against rock and dust whooshed from the explosion, turning the tunnel white.

Finally, the noise subsided. The last falling pebbles skittered to a stop, and the air cleared. Isaline wiggled her toes and twitched her fingers. Was she hurt? No—no agonizing pain. She squeezed her eyes shut. If she concentrated, she could still see the moonlight and smell the greenery at the base of Casret Academy's dormitory.

The memory scraped at her. It was the same memory she'd had during her dream only hours before. Why?

You'll always remember.

Before she could reflect further, a sound emerged from the quiet, breaking her from her thoughts. A familiar voice. Deep. *Laughing.*

Isaline hinged at the waist, sitting up in the warm light. The round opening to the passage was to her right, and there, knees bent with his back pushed into the wall, was Jack. Soaked like a drowned rabbit and laughing so hard, he doubled over.

"You all …" He gasped, wiping at his streaming eyes. "You all know how to make an entrance."

Isaline's throat thickened. She looked over her shoulder. The remains of the cart were in a crumpled heap, buried beneath an avalanche of rocks. The end of the tunnel had caved in, folding around the cart and splintering into chunks.

Groaning came from the river, followed by movement: Neave, ripping off her goggles and rolling onto her side; Winn, raising herself from a pile of little rocks; Cameron, flopping onto his back, clothes smeared in dust. Next to Isaline, Jame lifted onto his hands and knees, his hair wild and muddied with powdered rock. The point of his nose was eggshell white.

"Are you all right?" Isaline asked him, and he coughed in reply, a cloud of dust puffing from his lips. Surprised, he tried to speak, but more dust puffed out. The absurdity of it pinched Isaline's chest. She giggled, tears welling behind her eyelids.

Jack peeled himself from the wall, holding his sides. "Why were—oh *stars*—why were you going so fast? I thought it was an earthquake."

The sound of his laughter was infectious. Isaline dissolved into giggles. Jame chuckled, too, and the third puff of dust from his mouth killed Isaline's voice. She wheezed, laughing so hard her stomach hurt. Behind them, Neave let out a wicked cackle and plopped onto her back in the shallow river. Winn's shoulders were shaking.

For a minute, there was nothing but giddy laughter from each of them, the silence of the tunnel suffused with their relief at being together and breathing.

You're losing it, Nalissa said in Isaline's head, but she didn't care. She was alive. Her friends were alive.

Winn wiped a hand over her face, then pointed an unsteady finger at Neave. "You're not allowed to drive anymore."

This set them off again, clutching their stomachs and curling into balls in the shallow river. The only one not laughing was Cameron, who was lying limply on his back, taking deep breaths. Jack strode toward him and stretched out a hand to help him up.

"Am I dead?" Cameron asked. He didn't move, just looked from Jack's hand to his face, and back again. He blinked hard.

"Would I be here if you were?"

Cameron considered this. "Possibly."

"Good thing I'm not dead, then." Jack grasped Cameron's hand and hauled him out of the river. "And neither are you."

Isaline stood on weak knees, her lungs burning. The tunnel was domed, rock walls knitting together above their heads. The small passage entrance lay to her side. Adrudian light spilling from the opening was bright enough to illuminate the tunnel for a long stretch.

She turned to Jack, who was reluctantly wrapped in a bone-crushing hug from Cameron, patting Cameron's side and looking a little dazed. He wasn't wearing his head-lamp. Where was the light coming from?

The others wobbled to their feet. Cameron released Jack, and Neave clapped him on the back with a power reminiscent of Captain Knots. Winn shook his hand, holding her other arm close to her body.

"Looks like you remembered how to swim," the Princess said.

"Lucky me," Jack replied. He stood with a relaxed posture, his hands resting in his pockets. How could this be the same man caught in the river's current, unable to lift his head from the water? Isaline's relief mingled with uncertainty. He was unscathed, but how?

Cameron's face split into a shining grin. "I knew you were alive," he said in a shaky voice, dragging a finger beneath one eye, "but how did you get here? What happened?"

Jack's blue gaze didn't leave Cameron's. "I was drowning. Then I wasn't." He shrugged one shoulder. "I woke up here. It was a—"

"A miracle." Jame stepped up beside Isaline, rubbing rock dust from his nose.

"Magic," Neave suggested.

"No such thing," Winn said. "Only luck." She studied Jack with a keen eye. Isaline caught a hint of suspicion in the curve of her mouth. "Luck and context."

Jack shifted from one foot to the other. The veins on his face purpled in the light from the passageway. "Fortune is ours, then. Any idea what's through there?"

They turned as one to look through the side passage. The others shook their heads, but Winn's gaze landed on Isaline, waiting for any sign of a memory. Isaline reached for her intuition, searching for familiarity in this place—the dimensions of the passageway, the trickle of the river—but there was nothing.

Winn's attention slid away, silent acceptance. A knot wrapped beneath Isaline's ribs.

Jack gestured to the open passageway. The hoops in his ears glittered, hints of gold tangled in twists of his black hair.

"Come with me," he said. "There's something you all should see."

THEY FISHED the belongings they could salvage from the rubble, then Jack led them down the passage, Isaline with her trident slung over her shoulder. The corridor was short, only about fifteen feet, then turned at a sharp angle. Jack ushered Winn and Neave ahead of him, and as Neave rounded the corner, her fingers froze mid-pull on her long braid. Winn's expression didn't change, but a slight twitch in her left hand revealed her surprise.

"What is this?" Neave murmured as the rest of them crowded around.

"His workshop," Winn replied. Her voice had gone tight as a bow drawn with an arrow. "Faraday's workshop."

The passage led into a broad, round cave lit by Adrudian lamps fastened to sconces. Hundreds of aging papers had been stuck to the walls, the lamps dripping orange light onto countless shelves crammed with books and odd, spindly instruments. Faraday had arranged three giant worktables in a triangle, leaving the center of the room bare.

The hair on the back of Isaline's neck spiked. She didn't know what she had expected, but this room felt *dislocated*, like an arm out of its socket. This was the kind of place no one should find this deep in a mine.

As the others spread into the room, Isaline stepped up to one of the walls, where a long shelf held rows of lanterns, headlamps, and basic cooking equipment, all covered with a layer of grime. Her toe brushed a pile of bedrolls shoved beneath one of the worktables. The fabric was ratty, similar to the blankets they had found in the cave with the glowing mushrooms.

People had been sleeping here.

"Look at this," Jame said. He was standing at the other end of the shelf, rubbing his thumb over the dirty glass of a picture frame.

Isaline joined him and they stared down at the faces of Mining Team 5. Richard and the woman with the short, curly hair—Mio—were at the edge of the frame, their shoulders slumped, eyes glassy. The athletic-looking man, Haris, had a soot-streaked hand resting on the shoulder of the brown-haired woman. The ends of her long hair were matted and oily. She was facing the camera, but someone had ripped off the edge of the photograph, taking her head with it. Johannes Faraday was nowhere to be seen.

Isaline took the frame from Jame, bringing it close to her face. What had happened to Mining Team 5 between this photo and the last? They looked exhausted and starving, gaunt bags beneath their eyes, hair unbrushed, clothes unwashed.

Jame pointed to the woman with the brown hair. Theresa. "She's pregnant."

Isaline pulled her brows together. Yes, there it was: a bump beneath Theresa's dirty mining clothes. She opened her mouth to reply, but Jack's voice came from behind them, cutting through the silent workshop.

"I didn't get much chance to look around before you arrived ... but I found this." He walked to the center of the room, to what appeared to be a large, carved circle of iron set flat into the ground. The three tables had been arranged to make space for it. "Listen," he said. He tapped the circle with his boot. An empty *clang* sounded out. "It's hollow."

"A well cover?" Cameron asked, tapping it with his own foot. He crouched, running his fingers over the carving in the iron. His voice grew quiet. "And a Nine Men's Morris board."

"A symbol." Jack's eyes shone glacier-bright. He bent and hooked his fingers around an iron bar protruding from the cover's side. "Help me move it."

Cameron hesitated. "You sure?"

"Of course I'm sure."

Isaline tucked the picture frame under her arm, watching as Jack and Cameron heaved the cover from the floor and slid it to the side. A perfect well of darkness emerged, letting forth a groan and a gust of hot air. Gagging, Isaline clapped a hand over her mouth. The smell was rancid. Rotting flesh and putrefying wood.

"Charming," Jame said from behind his hand.

"There's more." Jack traced the ground around the hole with his toe, digging out layers of dust. A long divot in the floor appeared, curving outward from the edge of the hole. Isaline hadn't noticed the pattern before, but as she spun in a slow circle, her mouth opened in a soundless gasp. The divot was sculpted into the workshop's entire floorspace, spreading from wall to wall.

Neave scratched a hand over her chin. "Art?"

"A spiral," Jack breathed. His features were alight. He took Cameron's arm and led him to one of the worktables, where he had laid open the book he'd been scribbling in since they'd left the mine shaft. Isaline caught a glimpse of the map he'd been making, a freshly drawn spiral shining from the page. "The spiral carving is old. Older than everything else in here, including that iron cover."

Cameron pressed his hand to the map. Isaline had the sense he was looking at it, but not really seeing it. "So, someone found this hole, and the spiral, and decided to cover it?"

An idea clicked into place in Isaline's mind. "The King," she said. She slipped the picture frame from beneath her arm and held it out to Winn, who took it with her left hand. "The King found it. Maybe his whole mining team did. They were staying here—look."

Winn studied the picture, her eyes narrowing. Neave peeked over her shoulder.

"They've looked better," Neave said. Her painted lips stretched into a grimace. "That would explain why they stopped signing that mining ledger. Mining Team 5 stopped coming to work. But why would they hide out here?" Her nose scrunched. "It doesn't exactly smell like a vacation."

They passed the picture frame around, and Jack said, "I think I know the answer."

He grabbed a roll of white paper from beside his open book. Sweeping aside a collection of rusty tools, he unrolled the paper over the thick tabletop. Isaline didn't like the look of the reddish-brown stains sunk deep into the wood. She resisted the urge to prop her elbows on the table.

"Winn," Jack said, smoothing the paper's edges, "what can you tell us about this?"

Looking at the paper, a shiver walked across Isaline's shoulders. It was a blueprint. The diagram looked vaguely like a man, but his legs were fused together at the ankles and feet, his fingers elongated. With a pencil, Faraday had sketched a complex network of machinery inside the man's outline.

"The man-snake," Jame said.

"Richard," Isaline corrected. She reached out to touch the blueprint, but shrank back before she grazed Richard's likeness. Faraday had left human parts on the diagram. A brain, two eyes, a heart. There had been organs inside his body. Human and machine.

Revulsion rocked Isaline's stomach. To see Richard in the photo, and then like this in the blueprint—she thought she might be sick.

Winn hunched over the paper. "It's like Faraday's body," she said after a moment. "The engineering doesn't make any sense. This creature ran on an Adrudian engine, but the Adrudian should have only supplied his internal machine with power. He shouldn't have been *alive*. Able to think. He certainly shouldn't have been able to speak inside someone's head."

"Or kill with his eyes," Isaline added. She could barely look at the eyes on the diagram.

Jack smacked the table with an open hand, making

them all jump. "Exactly." He covered the diagram with a stack of papers from beneath the table. "And these?"

Isaline was grateful not to have to look at Richard anymore, but the other blueprints Winn was sifting through one-handed weren't much better. There were diagrams of clockwork soldiers, pickaxers, and puzzle boxes. Isaline's heart quivered, all her senses trained on Winn. These were the blueprints the Princess had been searching for. The coveted information on how Faraday's mysterious clockworks functioned.

But Winn's expression was anything but joyful. Her face grew stormy as she studied each picture. She tossed paper after paper to the ground, her shoulders trembling.

"It's all the same," she whispered. Her eyes were glossy, the whites flashing against her skin. "There's nothing special here ... just clockwork machinery that runs on Adrudian."

Jame tugged at his hair. "Then how do they have senses—"

"I don't know."

"—or activate with a voice?"

"*I don't know.*"

Winn pushed away from the table, a palm plastered to her forehead. She started pacing back and forth, the heels of her boots coming perilously close to the open hole. Isaline could only look on, anxiety weighing her body into the floor.

If I can't find a way to destroy Faraday's clockwork

army, the Seven Thrones will never be rebuilt, and Benemourne will crumble.

"There has to be something," Winn muttered, turning to a nearby bookcase. She dashed to the wall and began wrenching books from their shelves, glancing at their titles and throwing them to the ground at her feet. "There *has* to be something else."

"Winn ..." Jack said, but the Princess was too frenzied to notice. She ran to the other side of the room, pulling rolls of blueprints out of boxes and shoving one arm into trunks of tools and instruments. The rest of them watched, paralyzed, as she began to tear the workshop apart, searching for the scrap of information that meant Benemourne could be saved.

"Winn, stop," Cameron said gently. He placed a hand on her arm, but she shook it off. He kneaded his fingers through his damp hair. "Destroying this place won't help us."

"Won't help *you*, maybe." Her words were scratchy with panic. She whirled on him. "Do you have any idea how many people are counting on this? How are we —*ahh!*" Cameron had rested his hand on her wrist. Winn jerked her arm away, holding it to her middle, face twisted in pain.

A beat passed, then Neave said, "You're hurt."

Winn opened her mouth to retort, then closed it again. Isaline's gaze fell from Winn's dismayed face to her wrist, pressed protectively above her toolbelt. Her skin was puffy and swollen, purple bruises spreading like blots of ink. An injury from the cart crash.

Cameron took a half-step backward. "Why didn't you tell us?"

"Because—" Winn's gaze darted to each of them, like an insect unsure where to land. With a pang, Isaline realized her eyes were filling with tears. "Because I—I can't stop, not now. We're here. We made it, and if I can just find—but what if there's *nothing*—"

Her tears spilled over, glistening tracks streaking her face. She sank onto a wooden crate filled with books, bowing over her injured wrist, sniffing.

Isaline glanced at the others. Had they come all this way for nothing? Jame had averted his eyes, studying his boots. Cameron was rubbing his fingers into his temples, his features pained. There was nothing to say.

A moment passed, then Neave dug into her backpack, retrieving a roll of gauze. She dragged the end of a wooden bench beside Winn's box. "Let me see, Princess," she said, and Winn held out her arm. Neave rested Winn's injured wrist in her lap, examining the bulging skin with gentle hands. "I don't think it's broken, but it's a bad sprain."

Heavy silence descended as she unrolled the gauze and started wrapping Winn's wrist. Isaline wrung her fingers. Where would they go from here? Back to the surface? Winn's questions would go unanswered. Isaline's, too, if they had to leave in defeat, never having found the

House of Matchsticks, never knowing if the pendant was a keystone, or how Isaline came to have it.

Moonlight, lush leaves. Nalissa's fingers over her closed hands.

You'll always remember.

She shook her head, pushing away the persistent memory.

Behind her, Jack was bent over the tabletop, studying the clockwork diagrams, fiddling with the collar of his jacket. He pursed his lips, then turned in Winn's direction, finding the words none of them had been able to conjure.

"I have a hunch," he said.

Winn shot him a brief frown and returned to hanging her head. "A hunch is nothing. You said so yourself."

"It's something." Jack strode to the circular iron cover. He nudged it with his boot. "Faraday's technology. I think it has something to do with this. Do you recognize the symbol?"

Isaline tipped her head to the side, examining the carving in the iron. Three concentric squares, connected with intersecting lines like a kind of geometric constellation. Winn leaned off her box to study the design, nearly pulling her wrist from Neave, who tutted and drew her back.

"I've never seen it before," Winn said, wiping tears from her cheeks with her good hand. "What did you call it?"

Cameron snorted. He arranged a piece of hair over his forehead, leaning backward against one of the tables. "You'd think I was the only one having any fun around here."

"It's called Nine Men's Morris," Jack said. "It's a kind of game. Since we left the mill, I've seen it everywhere. In my visions, on the side of that cart, on this iron cover." He slipped a book from inside his jacket, a slim volume with wrinkled corners. Flipping to a dog-eared page, he held the book out for them to see. "And it's here, in this book."

Isaline squinted at the page around Jame's side. The symbol printed in the book was a perfect match for the design on the iron cover. Three concentric squares with intersecting lines. Cameron reached forward and lifted the front cover of the book with a long hand, revealing the title: *Ancient Benemournian Rituals and Their Uses.*

They weren't touching, but Isaline felt Cameron's body go suddenly rigid. He asked in a hushed voice, "Where did you get this book?"

But Jack didn't hear him. He clapped the book closed and placed it on the table next to his hand-drawn map. "At first, I thought Nine Men's Morris was a symbol for an Ancient Benemournian god. A god that you and I discovered on a mural in the Shute." He pointed to Cameron, who had gone completely still at Isaline's side. "But it's not. It's the symbol of a ritual."

Jame hopped up on a table, perching with his elbows on his knees. "What kind?"

"A sealing ritual." A hint of a smile appeared on Jack's face, his veins curving around the corners of his mouth. "A ritual for trapping someone behind a locked door. Imprisonment."

His last word seemed to echo, imbuing the air with a crackling energy. *Imprisonment.* Isaline reached up to grab the pendant, but found her neck bare. She cast a glance at Jame, who had the pendant out and was rolling it between his fingers. Glittering, crimson purpesia in the shape of a lock.

If Adrises is freed, tell my family I tried to stop it.

Neave ripped off the end of Winn's bandage with her teeth. "What do you mean? That eye that showed up in the lock ... you're saying it has something to do with an Ancient Benemournian god?"

Jack shook his head. "Better than that." He paused, scanning the room, gauging their reactions before he spoke. "I'm saying it *was* an Ancient Benemournian god."

A quiet second passed, then another. Winn glowered, tugging her arm from Neave, who had her mouth hanging open. Isaline couldn't process Jack's words. The idea of a trapped god made no sense—it was impossible. Ancient Benemournian gods were fictional. Her professors hadn't even bothered to teach about the gods in school. She didn't know their stories or their names.

Except one. She knew one name.

"Adrises," Isaline said.

Jack lifted his head, but it was Cameron who whipped

around to look at her, his eyes curiously sharp. "What did you say? Where did you hear that?"

"Richard mentioned the name." She raised her palms, surprised at Cameron's tone. His nostrils were flaring as if she'd just spilled his darkest secret. "I didn't know what it meant. Richard talked about—about Adrises being freed."

Jack's eyes flicked to Cameron, his brows arching the tiniest fraction, but then his gaze settled back on Isaline. "I've heard the name, too. In my visions." He rubbed a hand through his wiry beard. "My hunch is that Winn was right. Your pendant—it *is* the keystone. The keystone for the ancient ritual that imprisoned Adrises here, in the mines." His voice lowered. "In the House of Matchsticks."

A sudden tremor shook the ground, clinking the spindly instruments on their shelves and clattering tools in their boxes. Ice shot through Isaline's veins, but Jack merely raised his head to watch rock dust rain from the ceiling, a strange smile bending his lips.

"It's her," he whispered as the tremor ceased and the noise settled. Isaline's flesh rose into goosebumps. The glint in his eye unnerved her.

Cameron was clinging to the table, his breaths ragged. "I ... I think we should leave. We should go."

Neave raised her hand. "I second that."

Jame nodded. "Me, too."

"*Waiting,*" another voice said. "*In the mines.*"

They all startled, Neave leaping from her bench with a little shriek. Isaline's hand flew to her trident, but then she noticed the Listening Spider sitting on Winn's palm. Its eight wooden legs were bent at the middle, copper knobs gleaming in the orange light.

The King's voice came from it next. *"In my workshop? And now you're here. Then it must be ... she's awake. I—I should have known. My clockworks have been mining less Adrudian. She's using it, isn't she?"*

"Yes," Richard replied, his words like dry autumn leaves. *"And she's given you time enough to enjoy the gift of her power. Now you must find what you lost, and try again to open the door."*

Winn pressed the top of the box with her thumb and the legs retracted, disappearing into the wooden cylinder. When she looked up, her eyes were large. "That's it. That's the secret to his technology, why it doesn't make any sense. He and his mining team found the House of Matchsticks and he used her power to invent ... and that's where the Adrudian is ..." She clenched her jaw, pressing her head between her forearms. "What am I saying?"

"No, Princess, you're right." Jack seized the photograph of Mining Team 5 and rubbed the elbow of his leather jacket over the glass. "See the bedrolls? The portable stoves? They were staying here, using this room to camp. They tried to free her. *Try again to open the door.*" He cocked his head, a realization spanning his face. "They must have tried another ritual."

Handing the photograph to Winn, he rushed across the room and grabbed *Ancient Benemournian Rituals and*

Their Uses. Isaline's knees wobbled. This was too much for her unraveling mind. The King, using the power of a trapped god to manufacture an army of clockworks?

She imagined the clockwork she'd fought during her Weapons Portion and the clockwork guards in the mill. They had *sensed* her, hadn't they? Come to life with a word, predicted her movements, like no machine ever should. Was it so hard to believe they could be supernatural? Magic?

Jack flipped to the index of his book, running his finger down a list of words. Cameron stood nearby, hunched over a table, staring at Jack's drawing of the mines and the map of their forgotten expedition. Stress lines had appeared at the corners of his mouth. He kept flinching, as if barely restraining himself from tearing the maps into pieces.

"Forget the book," he said. "I really, *really* think we should go."

Jack wasn't paying attention. He had opened *Ancient Benemournian Rituals* to a new page, jabbing a run of text with his index finger.

"Here it is," he said. "Sealing rituals can be altered. The seal can be broken, too, but that would require too much power for a group of pickaxers. To *alter* the sealing ritual, Faraday would have needed the original keystone —" He pointed at Isaline, who looked at Jame, who closed a hand over the pendant. "*—and* a new keystone. Something living."

"Living?" Winn said. "Like an animal? But I thought you said keystones were always objects."

"The book says it right here: *A living keystone.*"

Jame hooked his ankles around the legs of the table. His cheeks had gone pallid beneath his freckles. "If a keystone can be an animal, there's not like ... a sacrifice, is there?"

Isaline's stomach flipped, but Jack shook his head, thumbing through the soggy pages of his book. "I don't know. A keystone just needs to be present for the ritual. It doesn't say why."

"Well, that's a relief," Neave said.

Jack's reply was interrupted by another rumble in the ground. In unison, they turned to stare at the hole in the floor, as if waiting for it to groan or emit a blast of hot, stinking air. But it remained silent, a yawning chute of darkness.

"We can still leave," Cameron said when the shaking faded. He kneeled in front of Winn, attempting to catch her eye. "We can still go, Princess. Regroup. Try to ... to figure something out where it's safe. I don't like these—these tremors."

Winn was holding the photograph of Mining Team 5 in her lap, her bandaged wrist weighing down the bottom of the frame. Her little finger traced their features. Richard, Mio, Haris, Theresa.

"Winn?" Cameron prompted.

"I'm just ..." Tears had dried to salty tracks on her face.

When she looked up, her focus bypassed Cameron and drifted over his shoulder, landing on Jack. "Can a person be a keystone?"

Cameron moaned quietly and buried his head in his hands.

Jack said, "I don't see why not." He seemed taken aback by the question. "I've never thought about it before."

"This woman in the photo." Winn pointed to Theresa with her oily brown hair. "She's pregnant. Could it be that ..." She glanced at Jack through twists of her hair, black coils bouncing loose and floating over her forehead.

Isaline's mouth went dry.

The baby was used in the ritual.

"No." Neave stood from her chair, pacing anxiously in front of the thick worktables. "*No.* I refuse to believe anyone could be born down here. And for a keystone? It's evil, even for Faraday."

"It is," Winn said. "It's just evil enough."

Jame ran a finger beneath his headlamp. Isaline had the urge to grab his hand, to anchor him to her, but she hugged her arms around herself instead.

"If they tried to free Adrises," Jame said, "with the pendant and a—a baby, what happened to the rest of Mining Team 5? What happened to the baby? Their ritual failed, but then what?"

Jack waved toward the shelves lining the walls. "This equipment is old. Maybe they died in the mill fire. That was sixteen years ago. It could have ..."

He trailed off, and the room fell silent. Isaline had the sense of a collective understanding hitting each of them at once, a ripple moving through the room with the force of a tidal wave. She held her breath while the moment grew taut.

Then every single one of them—Jame, Jack, Cameron, Winn, Neave—turned to stare at her.

"What?" she asked, squirming under the intensity of their gazes.

Jack stepped forward. He pointed a finger in her direction. "The pendant. You said it was yours. It didn't belong to your roommate."

"Yes, it's mine. I've had it for as long as I can ..." Isaline's mouth tightened, trapping her voice. She shuffled backward. "What are you saying?"

"How old are you?" Jack's eyes were blue fire.

"S-sixteen." She marked their faces: Neave's slightly parted lips, Jame's arched brows, Winn's jutting chin, Cameron's bloodless, shocked expression. They looked as if she had grown a third arm, or turned green, or spouted some magical power.

All at once, it dawned on her.

"I'm—you think *I'm—*" She couldn't get the words out. Her ears had begun to ring, memories clamoring inside her skull like angry bees.

Cameron's voice in her room at the Harper and Cup: *It's not a coincidence ... You're meant to be here.*

Jack, speaking to her on the dock: *With you and that*

pendant, we have our best shot.

Richard, rotten breath blowing from his mouth, eyes wiggling beneath his blindfold: *I saw you born, girl. I didn't want to see you die.*

I saw you born.

Isaline had dreamed about having an important past. Something special. But *this*? Her head swam. If her friends were right, she was a living keystone. Born underground. Used to try to release an imprisoned god.

She took the photograph from Winn with a trembling hand. Theresa's dirty clothes, haggard frame, and long tresses had taken on a bright quality, glaring from the frame like noonday light. *Was this my mother?*

The world muffled. There was a fluttering noise, and a shadow dropped onto the glass of the picture frame. Bird claws obscured Theresa's baby bump. Two bright, black eyes stared from within a starling's sparkling silhouette.

The bird.

Isaline swallowed a lump in her throat. "Is this real?" She didn't know whether she was asking about the bird, about being born in the mines, or about the actuality of living, ancient gods.

The bird twittered at her, singing a song Isaline couldn't begin to understand. Then it sprang into the air, zoomed around her head, and was gone. As if reality had folded down upon its wings. As if it had always *existed*—lived, breathed, remembered—and she had simply never opened her eyes.

7

SLEEPWALKING

JACK

Beyond the waterfall, Jack's path sloped downward at a sharp angle.

He edged through the wall of the grotto, finding himself at the head of a narrow tunnel. Breathing hard, he unclipped his flashlight and thumbed the slats open, releasing a beam of bouncing orange light. Cameron had been asleep when he'd sneaked away, but he could wake up anytime. Jack needed to hurry.

He half-ran, half-slid down the slope, one hand pinned to his chest as if his map—his lifeline—could jump from his jacket and be lost in the dark. The tunnel beyond the incline was a tight squeeze. Jack sidestepped, worming between slabs of rock. He envisioned his path: grotto, creek, bridge. What was next? Tunnel, tunnel, tunnel. No discernible landmarks on the map until the House of Matchsticks. A straight shot.

Jack shuffled sideways for a long time. He imagined Cameron waking in the grotto, finding his note. Don't bother following me. *Would he try to follow Jack anyway? Or would he return to Ar in defeat? Jack told himself he didn't care what Cameron did, as long as he wouldn't be distracted. As long as his head wouldn't turn.*

Moments later, the ground ended. Jack was still sandwiched between the walls of the tunnel, but suddenly there was no support for his leading foot. Just a sheer drop into a crevice. With a gasp, he tipped, grabbing at the stone on either side. He couldn't find purchase.

The rock released him, and Jack plunged, his guts zigzagging into his ribs. He fumbled his flashlight midair. It rolled out of his hands.

"Open your eyes, Jack," a female voice said from another part of his mind. "You're close, now. Come. Leave the girl. She'll bring herself, now that she knows the truth."

He opened his mouth to shout, but instead he

WOKE UP.

Faraday's workshop was dim, lit by a single lamp. Jack sat up, knocking the wooden bench beneath him with his ankles.

Images of the crevice remained behind his eyelids. The memory had been clear, as clear as one of his Adrudian visions, but he hadn't Drunk before going to sleep.

Had he? No—the flask of Milk in his pocket was the same weight, undisturbed.

Jack's body thrummed. It was *her.* Like in the river, Adrises had gifted him a vision. She wanted him to remember.

A rumble shook the workshop as Jack stretched his neck and rolled his shoulders, joints popping beneath clouds of dust drifting from above. Small quakes had become periodic vibrations through the rock that put his companions on edge. For Jack, the tremors plucked a well-played string: the *pull*, calling him down into the hole. Into the House of Matchsticks beyond.

If it had been up to him, they would have left for the cave hours ago. But with Nalissa's revelation and Winn's sprained wrist, the others had decided to rest before making a decision. Jack had been frantic, his nerves on fire with the end so close, but he wasn't the man he had been in the Shute. He chose to wait.

Jack pulled back his sleeve as the ground's rumbling faded, squinting at his wristwatch through the thin light. It hadn't been long since he had gone to sleep. His dream-memory had been short.

You're close, now. Come. Leave the girl. She'll bring herself, now that she knows the truth.

He leaned to the side, peering beneath the closest table. Nalissa was stretched on the ground, a pile of curly hair peeking from beneath her neck. Her fingernails were digging into her palms, even in sleep. Did she feel the *pull* now, too? That perpetual longing to find the House of Matchsticks?

Jame was asleep beside her, with Neave and Winn close to the wall. Jack suspected none of them needed sleep, but being underground was playing with their senses again, making them drowsy.

There was only one person who seemed immune to the effects of the dark.

Jack glanced over his shoulder, at a series of huffing breaths coming from the center of the room. Cameron was on his hands and knees, trying to shove the heavy iron cover back over the hole in the ground. He gave the iron a hard push, but the cover was massive, far too much weight for one man to move. He might as well have been trying to shift a rock wall.

Trying to protect us, Jack thought, a warmth rising in him. He suppressed a smile as Cameron circled to the cover's other side and fruitlessly lugged at its handle. He had never met anyone so determined to help his friends in secret.

Resisting the temptation to keep watching, Jack swiveled on the bench and whispered, "Do you ever sleep?"

Cameron jumped like a Thief caught inside a bank vault. He blinked at Jack a moment, then recovered himself. "I tried. I couldn't."

Easing off the bench, Jack tiptoed toward him round the edges of bedrolls. Cameron paused, then got to his feet, brushing his hands over the forearms of his coat.

"Why cover it?" Jack asked him. "That's our way forward, whether we like it or not." He peered into the pure, circular blackness of the hole. Earlier, he had pointed his flashlight down the opening, but the darkness was impenetrable. At least the smell had dulled.

Cameron was silent for a long moment, then said, "You're right. I don't like it."

He sunk his hands into his pockets. Jack looked at him from the corner of his eye, keenly aware of how close they were standing, the subtle graze of Cameron's arm. When had it become Jack's habit to be alert to him? His stances, the tone of his voice, even his distinctive smell, as if he'd been reading by the light of a candle. The smell of libraries at night.

"Liking is beside the point," Jack said, choosing his words carefully.

Cameron sighed and turned away, sitting on a nearby bench. He wouldn't meet Jack's eyes. "Doesn't matter anyway. Winn can't continue, not with her wrist. It's too dangerous."

"I know." Jack looked at her sleeping silhouette, tucked between Neave and a box of blueprints. It was just as well. The Princess had found her information on the clockworks, and though Jack had decided to wait to continue on, it wasn't Winn he had been waiting for. Winn or any of the others.

Jack rubbed the back of his neck. "There's something else we could do."

Cameron let out a hard laugh, tracing the side of his boot with his index finger. "We could leave."

"No. We could stay." Jack was surprised to find that his feelings were nestled in his chest, ready to be spoken. His stomach gave a nervous twist. "We could stay and finish the expedition."

"Well ..." A sick look crossed Cameron's face. "About that. There's—there's something that I should—"

But Jack had already kneeled, bringing them eye-to-eye. Cameron lifted his head, sentence fading into a surprised breath. Jack slid a hand into his pocket and pulled out the map. The same aging parchment he'd used on the lost expedition.

"Send the others back," he said. "We'll go forward. Together." Cameron's hand was resting palm-up on his thigh. Jack gently uncurled his fingers and placed the map inside, hand lingering on his knee. "We'll find the House of Matchsticks. You and me."

Another rumble shook the workshop, vibration shuddering beneath Jack's legs. Cameron's eyes grew round. He closed his fingers over the map, unfolding it with a careful hand. His gaze roamed over the contents, and his features softened, falling into an intensity that made Jack's heartbeat quicken.

"Jack." Cameron's hand tightened on the map, crinkling the parchment. "We already did."

Around them, metal instruments jingled on their shelves, tools rattling in their boxes. When the ground's shaking dwindled, it left the workshop in crisp silence.

Jack shook his head. "What?"

"You weren't ..." Cameron let out a soft sigh. He swallowed, the cords in his neck tensing and releasing. "You weren't supposed to find that book."

Jack stared at him. *Ancient Benemournian Rituals and Their Uses* grew heavy, hanging within his jacket like a brick. He envisioned the book as he'd found it: hidden behind a puzzle door at the end of a secret hallway in Fort Upper's library. The puzzle had been gold. Glittering gold.

The truth sparked.

"It was you," he said in a bare whisper. "You hid the book."

In answer, Cameron slipped his hand into his pocket. It emerged holding his ring of keys. An ornate, golden key clanked against the rest. The key to the puzzle door.

"After we got back from the Shute," Cameron said, "I scoured every library. *Ancient Benemournian Rituals* was the only book I could find that had Adrises' symbol. The Nine Men's Morris."

Jack's arms deadened, hand slipping from its perch on Cameron's knee. "You hid it from me."

"I wanted ..." Cameron's shoulders sagged. "I wanted

to tell you. I started a hundred letters. I took a hundred useless trips to Lower Village." The keyring dropped from his fingers and clattered to the ground, forgotten. "But if you knew about Adrises, you would have found your way back."

His eyes were fathoms deep, liquid enough for Jack to drown in. Jack could only repeat himself. "You hid it from me."

"Jack."

"You lied to me."

"*Jack*. Listen." Cameron took him by the arm, giving him a delicate shake. His face grew frightened. "You can't go back."

The words barely entered Jack's mind. His neck heated in an involuntary flush. Cameron's strange behavior when they had entered the workshop hadn't been lost on Jack, but how had Cameron known about Adrises after the lost expedition?

Looking at Cameron's expression, a feeling returned to Jack. *Sameness*. Time rolling onto itself like a scroll. An overwhelming sense of déjà vu.

"Beginner's luck," Jack murmured.

Cameron's breath was rapid. "Hm?"

"In the cave. You said that me winning Nine Men's Morris was beginner's luck." Why hadn't he recognized it before? The *sameness* hadn't been déjà vu. It had been a warning. "How did you know? If you forgot the expedition, how did you know I'd never played that game?"

Cameron stiffened, his cheeks draining of color. He opened his mouth to reply, but Jack cut him off.

"You never forgot, did you?"

To this, Cameron said nothing. He looked down at his boots.

There was silence, a long moment drawing tight. Jack squeezed his eyes shut, and when he opened them, he was

FALLING *through the darkness of a crevice in the Shute. He landed on a bed of something soft and sticky, his fall broken, but his forearm caught beneath his side. A searing pain sliced through his wrist.*

He lay there, stunned, until he gathered the courage to bring his arm in front of his face. His flashlight had rolled some ways off, and in the faint light his forearm glistened wet with blood. Something had cut him—he felt around on his side until he found it. The lump of purpesia, a jagged edge forced through the leather of his jacket.

Where was he? Jack pushed himself up with one hand. The squishy ground let go of his back with a soft smuck. *He had landed on a patch of odd, gluey black moss. Roots hung around him, woven into the soil edges of the tunnel. Hadn't the walls been rock moments ago? Slimy, waving black vines hung from the sides of the crevice in bunches.*

"Jack," a voice said as he stood himself up and stumbled forward, sticking his flashlight into one armpit, a palm pressed to his bleeding wrist. The passage had become low

and round and moist. An endless burrow. A rabbit hole. "Jack."

A HAND SHOOK him back to the present. Cameron's face swam into focus, a concerned wrinkle between his brows. "That's it?" he said. He released Jack's arm. "I tell you I remember, and you have nothing to say?"

Jack's eyelids fluttered, awareness returning. His heart contracted, the *pull* vibrating in his chest like a moth trapped in a box. That root-lined tunnel had led to the House of Matchsticks, hadn't it? It was the *straight shot*, wasn't it?

Cameron had lied to him. He had looked Jack straight in the face and said *we didn't find the House of Matchsticks in the Shute.*

But they had.

Jack's body flooded with heat. He wrenched away from Cameron and pushed him two-handed on the chest. Cameron lurched. He fell off the bench but caught his balance before he hit the floor. The map skated through the air and unfurled on the ground by Jack's feet.

"How?" The memory of the root-lined tunnel shimmered in Jack's mind. He stood and white-knuckled his own hands, fighting to keep from pushing Cameron a second time. "How did I forget, and you remember?"

Across the room, there was the shuffle of bedrolls, sleepy heads lifting from the ground.

"What's happening?" Winn's voice, drifting from the corner.

Cameron's eyes didn't move from Jack's. "The purpesia. I dropped it after we left the stream. I lost an hour, maybe two, but not the whole expedition. I didn't realize why until you mentioned the purpesia before. The curse must ... I don't know how it works. Nalissa's memories weren't taken the same way."

Jack let off a strangled laugh. Maybe the pendant being a keystone changed its properties. His own lump of raw purpesia had been missing when he woke outside the Shute. He must have lost it, too, but when? Did that mark the line between remembering and forgetting?

It didn't matter. He had lost the expedition. The *pull* had come for him, draining every moment. And all the while, Cameron had been sitting on the most significant Treasurehunting discovery in modern history, waiting to unveil Adrises and take the credit. Letting Jack suffer.

How could he have been so foolish?

"I was right about you," Jack said, and despite his best effort, there was pain in his voice. "You're a selfish, two-faced fraud."

Cameron flinched, bringing his arms around his middle. "You can hate me if—if that's what you want. You never have to see me again." He pointed a trembling hand at the hole in the ground. "But you can't go down there. If you go back to the House of Matchsticks, Jack, you'll be killed."

Venom coursed through Jack's body. He ran his fingers down the sides of his cheeks, stretching the blue veins, and said, "Too late."

The ground shook, a rhythmic tremor that snaked through the walls, through the floor, through Jack's bones. A flash of pain crossed Cameron's face, a look of hurt so acute that for a moment Jack felt it himself.

"Th-that's not my fault," Cameron said as the shaking stopped. "I didn't know you were going to Drink. You can't put that on me."

"I can put it wherever I like," Jack replied. An ice chip had sneaked into his heart the first time he'd Drunk Adrudian. It mingled with the words he had read in Fort Upper's library, the words that confirmed what he had been trying to forget for months.

By consuming Adrudian Milk, the Drinker foretells they will one day die by Adrudian poisoning.

Jack had destroyed himself looking for the lost expedition, and for all Cameron's talk of truth between them —*friends, allies, something*—Cameron had only ever wanted to make sure he wouldn't discover the House of Matchsticks.

"Hold on a second." This was Neave, huddled with the others on the floor. "You went looking for the House of Matchsticks in the Shute. That's two days' travel from here. It can't be in two places at once."

Jack dragged his gaze from Cameron to stare at the

open map at his feet. Grotto, creek, bridge. Neave was right. If there were paths to the House of Matchsticks in the Shute *and* the mines, it was a geographic anomaly—but how was that less extraordinary than a trapped god?

"I didn't think we'd find the House of Matchsticks here," Cameron said, pressing his fingers over his eyes. "You think I would have asked Jack to come if I did? I just didn't want him to keep Drinking. I thought if we went looking for it, and couldn't find it, he would give up the ..." He shook his head. "I didn't think finding it here was possible. But this hole, and the spiral, and even the smell ... it's the same."

It's the same.

Jack stooped and picked the map off the ground. He unclipped his flashlight, opening the slats and brightening the room with a triangular beam. Holding the map as he had grabbed it, upside down, Jack ran his eyes over the landmarks he'd drawn in another body, in another life.

The Dead Tree, the giant, withered tree that marked the entrance of the Shute, was inverted in the bottom right corner. At the top left of the map was the straight shot: the crevice with the black roots and vines that should have led him into the cave, into the House of Matchsticks.

The straight shot. His vision pulsed. Something about the parallel lines he'd drawn seemed familiar.

Heart pounding, Jack pulled *Rocks and Gemstones of the Shute* from his jacket and opened it to his map of the mines. He stuck the flashlight between his teeth and rucked the map of the lost expedition against the spine of the book. In water-blotted ink, he had drawn the mine shaft, then the branching tunnels, followed by the cavern with the bridge, and the river, and finally the spiral carved into the floor of Faraday's workshop.

The mine shaft. It was two parallel lines. The same as the straight shot.

It's the same map.

Every landmark on one map had a counterpart on the other: the straight shot and the mine shaft; the creek and the river; the grotto and the cavern; the spiral pit trap and the spiral he was standing on now; the iron footbridge across the gorge and the wooden bridge in the Shute. *Go beneath, not across.* They had done that, hadn't they? They had traveled beneath the iron footbridge and down the river.

The Shute and the mines—they were mirror images. Two sides of a symmetrical figure. A fractal, spiraling impossibly down and down to the center. To the House of Matchsticks.

He had been right all along. He had been *right.*

A tremor shook the workshop, so strong it nearly knocked Jack off his feet. Cameron staggered, catching himself on a worktable, while Winn, Neave, Jame, and Nalissa hunkered together.

Jack let *Rocks and Gemstones of the Shute* drop to the floor. He didn't need it anymore. He had the map.

As the noise began to thin, Jack strode to the edge of the room and stuffed his hand inside the nearest backpack. Neave had given them all the same supplies. Waterskins, pistol-shaped fireworks, and basic rappelling equipment. Rope and carabiners.

Jack clipped a carabiner to his weapons belt, looped the rope, pinched it off, and tied them together. The belt wasn't meant to be a harness, but if he passed the rope beneath his legs, it would work well enough. It had to work.

Cameron's eyes were heavy on Jack's back. "You're not going to stop, are you?"

Taking a headlamp from the worktable, Jack strapped the band around his head. "For you?" he said. He looped the rope around the handle on the heavy iron cover and pulled it taut. "Next time, don't waste your wager on me."

Jack stuck one foot into the hole, testing his makeshift harness. The belt hitched around his waist, the rope digging into his thighs, but the friction was strong enough to control his descent.

He could think of nothing but getting away. Leaving Cameron behind. Never looking at him again.

"Jack, please—"

"Don't bother trying to stop me, Head Inspector." Jack retrieved his flask of Adrudian Milk and sent it skidding along the floor. The metal bumped the toe of Cameron's boot. "You can have that back. I don't need it anymore."

Cameron picked up the flask, staring at it. "What is this?"

Jack descended another foot. The inside of the hole was smooth, a duct into an unknown sewer. "The Adrudian you burned out of my lantern at the Harper and Cup. For someone trying to keep me from my memories, you're not very good at it."

"Adrudian Milk?" Cameron turned the flask over in his hands. "This wasn't me."

"Then who was it?"

Silence fell between them, but a voice emerged from the huddle of bodies across the workshop.

"I did it."

Both Jack and Cameron turned to see Jame sitting up in his bedroll. Jack frowned. The Thief boy? It explained why Jack hadn't woken up that night—Thieves' feet were quiet as a whisper—but what stake did Jame have in the lost expedition?

"You burned the Adrudian in Jack's lantern?" Nalissa asked him. "Why?"

"I was told to," Jame said innocently. "By her."

He pointed to Winn. The room's collective gaze slid to the Princess. She had her bandaged arm curled around her middle, her eyes wide and dark as coals.

Jack cocked his head. He had noticed Winn whispering to Jame after their meeting in Little Space, but he couldn't imagine what motivation she would have to give Jack a flask of Adrudian Milk.

Cameron was just as perplexed. "You?"

Winn shrugged one shoulder. "Jack had a vision when that eye showed up in the lock. I saw it. I thought if he kept having visions, it could help us. I didn't tell you, Cameron, because I knew you didn't want him to Drink, and I didn't tell *him* because—" She jabbed her thumb in Jack's direction. "—he'll do the opposite of whatever he's told."

"But ..." Cameron wound his fingers into his sleeves. "You lied to me?"

That was the problem with liking. It made you blind.

Jack couldn't help it; he threw back his head and laughed. Without another thought, he loosened his hold on the rope and took a step, then another, letting the ground enfold him. He laughed all the way into the hole.

In the Shute, Jack stumbled through the root-lined tunnel toward the House of Matchsticks, trying to run and simultaneously bandage his wrist with a torn strip of his jacket.

The space between the black, twisted roots protruding from either side of the tunnel was unsettlingly thin. Reaching tendrils swiped mire onto his face and hair. A vine poked into his mouth, and he spat, retching. The slime tasted like the tunnel had begun to smell: rotting and rank, like wood moldering in stagnant water.

His knees were rubbery, dread sprouting from the pit of

his stomach. What was this place? What vegetation did these roots belong to, and why did they seem to wriggle at the corner of his vision, as if alive? The hairs on the back of his neck bristled. Why did he feel there was something curled in the dark ahead, watching him?

Jack sucked in a breath and held it. Keep moving, *he coached himself, afraid to stop for even a second.* You'll find it.

Minutes later, the tunnel widened, opening onto an enormous cave. The House of Matchsticks. Jack skidded to a stop at the cave's mouth and lifted his flashlight. Up and up it went, and his mind bent, failing to understand what he saw. At the center of the room was a gigantic knot of dark, gnarled branches hovering in the air, as if a tree had been strung upside down in space.

Without warning, the Adrudian in his flashlight dulled, dimmed, and winked out.

"Closer and closer," Adrises said in his head. "Come, come, come."

In the mines, Jack forced himself awake, pinching his arm.

The memory dissolved, leaving him alone in the present. He collapsed against a rough stone wall. The hole in the workshop had led into a featureless rock passage leading off into darkness.

He was finally away from Cameron. He could stop and think—but as he unhitched his belt from the rope, another memory began to surface, eating hollows in his vision.

"Wait," he said aloud. Adrises was listening—she *had* to be listening. "Just wait. Give me a minute."

The memory receded. Jack's legs wouldn't hold him anymore. He slid to the ground and clutched his knees to his chest, lungs tight as iron, breaths coming in hoarse wheezes.

Cameron had betrayed him. Cameron had deceived him. Beyond finding the House of Matchsticks, Cameron had never spared him another thought.

Only now, out of the sight of his companions, could Jack let himself feel how much that hurt.

The expedition, Cameron had said, brandy on his lips in Jack's room at the Harper and Cup. *What happened to us was just* gone, *but it wasn't meant to be gone.*

Everything he had said was an omission or lie. Manufactured words to get close to Jack and to keep him close. Their exchanges in the grotto, in the Harper and Cup, in the mill—they had been fake. Cameron had woven a thread to make it seem like they had something in common, a thread built to snap at the smallest tug, lightning-quick.

But the link had *felt* real. Jack's chest ached. Something inside him had been ripped away.

Stop. Stop it. Jack thumped his forehead with a closed

fist. He retrieved *Ancient Benemournian Rituals and Their Uses* and picked through the warped paper. The book opened to the page he had written on as they had traveled to the mill aboard Captain Knots' ferry. There it was, scribbled in his own hand, blotted ink in the margin:

Bring the girl into the mines. Find the House of Matchsticks. Uncover the memory.

Don't let him distract you.

Jack lifted his head and gazed into the blackness of the tunnel. His next step was obvious. The House of Matchsticks was somewhere inside that darkness, his goal closer than he dared dream. Why was he sitting here paralyzed? Was it his memories, returning at a pace he could no longer control? Or was it the look in Cameron's eyes?

Don't let him distract you.

The memory he had pushed away began to surface again. Jack stood on shaky legs, blinking spots from his vision, and widened the slats in his headlamp. The light illuminated nothing but a tunnel, nothing but a lone walk into the deep.

"*Nothing is nothing, Jack,*" Adrises said. Her voice echoed in his mind, setting his skin alight. It was deep as splitting rock, vibrant as a hornet buzz. "*There are no choices when my handprint is on your heart.*"

Jack pressed a hand to his chest, where the *pull* shook, turning his blood to tar and his heart to stone. He took three heavy steps down the tunnel. Four steps. Five.

"*No use in fighting. Surrender. I will carry you.*"

This time, Jack could feel it when Adrises reached into his mind and picked at a thread. Darkness spread across his vision. He urged himself to resist, to decide for himself, but by then he was merely sleepwalking, one foot in front of the other, down the tunnel and away from the light.

8

ENGINE AND PISTOL

ISALINE

Isaline stood from the workshop floor and folded her bedroll. She didn't know how long she had slept before Jack and Cameron had begun to fight, but it didn't feel like long enough. Her bones were frail, her body numb and stunned. She fiddled with her sleeves, listening absently to Winn and Cameron arguing.

"What did you expect me to do?" Winn said. "It's not like you're a beacon of common sense with Jack around."

The anger in their voices rang painfully in Isaline's ears. Were the bonds between their group so fragile? Based on thin deception?

Jame planted himself beside her. He had detached from Neave, who stayed near the center of the room, watching Winn and Cameron fight.

"You all right?" Jame asked. He folded his hands in his lap, rings glimmering red-blue-green. "This isn't great."

"I'm fine," Isaline replied, but she wasn't. Her mind was caught in a whirlpool. In the last hours, she had finally found answers—but the answers had only begot more questions. How had she escaped the mines when she was little enough to be put into an orphanage? What had happened to her mother and the other members of Mining Team 5? How had she come to have the lock?

The story seemed wrong. What was she missing?

Surrounded by green, Nalissa said, "You'll always remember," and patted the outside of Isaline's hands.

"Have some." Jame held out a water bottle. "It's like an oven in here."

He was right. Even as Isaline's hair dried from the river, her neck had begun to moisten with sweat. Isaline tilted the bottle to her lips and water cooled her feverish mouth. She eased her eyes to the hole in the floor. If they kept on after Jack, it would get hotter. Suffocating.

She dropped onto the bench beside Jame and passed him the water. He took a swig and stowed the bottle in his backpack, gaze trained on the argument before them. Winn had propped one hand on her hip, staring as Cameron sputtered something about broken trust.

Jame heaved a sigh. "We should go back," he said quietly to Isaline. "Jack's gone. This isn't helping anything."

Isaline could only bring herself to nod. She wanted to leave this place, to see the sky again, but her mind had become tormented. She was obsessed with knowing more about her past. Finding proof. Solving her lingering doubt.

She balled her hands. Richard had said *I saw you born.* What other proof did she need?

After a minute, Jame looked at her sideways and dug into his collar, resting the pendant on his palm. "Want this back?" His knee bumped hers in an attempt at playfulness. "Sounds like you earned it, being a keystone and all."

Isaline exhaled. Richard had said her past would return if she passed the pendant on, but her memories hadn't appeared. She needed to know the truth. She needed to figure out why she could only produce one memory: Nalissa at the base of Casret Academy's dormitory.

You'll always remember.

"Keep it, for now." Isaline watched him drop the pendant into his shirt. The fabric's pull around his shoulders exposed the lines of his arms. She laughed despite herself. "Remember when I thought you were trying to steal the pendant? Turns out you were going to take it anyway."

Jame chuckled, eyes sparkling. She could look at them all day and night.

He said, "Funny you should mention that. This has all been part of a very long, very elaborate scheme."

Isaline's answering laugh was cut short by another quake rippling through the ground. She pressed her knees together as a fresh sprinkling of dust fell from the ceiling.

"Tell me something," Jame said as the trembling began to fade. "When this is all over, will you go back to Casret Academy? Back to being a spy?"

When this is all over. Isaline pressed her hands to her knees. She didn't know what would happen after the expedition. Casret had expelled her, but her future no longer hinged on passing a Weeklong Review. Ar's Head Inspector was standing only feet away, listening crossly to Winn as she said, "You could have told the truth. If you didn't carry such a torch for him, we might not be in this mess."

Winn and Cameron were some of Benemourne's most powerful people. With their favor, Isaline could have a chance to take the City Watch oath, Weeklong Review or not.

But is that what she wanted? Is that what she *should* want?

The ground was still rumbling, and she hadn't answered Jame's question.

"I think ..." She scrambled for words. *I think I have to find out why I'm here. I think my past has to tell me what to do. I think destiny will decide.* "I think I'll have to think about it."

He nodded, slowly, his eyes wandering the workshop. Isaline watched his palms pat against his thighs. She sensed he wanted to say something, but, like her, he was having trouble finding the words.

"What about you?" she prompted. Her stomach gave an anxious jump. "What will you do?"

"I was going to go back to Sunrest." Jame inclined his head, rotating a large, emerald ring around his index finger. "But I might stay in Ar for a while instead. Something about—" He released his hand and waved it in a deliberately nonchalant way. "—a girl I met in a forest."

She stared at him. Too late, she remembered she had said there was a boy at Casret Academy waiting for her, and by showing hesitance to return she had changed her story. Or changed her mind.

Ahead of them, Cameron was gesturing to the hole, saying, "You have no idea what it was like. We almost died."

Isaline had little right to feel betrayed by Cameron. Her whole identity was a lie. If Jame knew the truth, he would be angry, undoubtedly, and heartbroken about Nalissa's death. He might decide he never wanted to speak to Isaline again.

But her heart had leaped at his words: *A girl I met in the forest.* He hadn't said *a girl who wrote me letters.*

When they had met in the forest, she had been Isaline, not Nalissa.

Jame gave her a placid smile, unaware of the chaos his statement had sparked inside her. His expression was so genuine it made her breath tighten.

Tell him.

But how? How could she say it?

She opened her mouth to speak, but her attention was dragged away by the ground's ongoing rumble. The noise hadn't stopped.

Jame had noticed, too. His smile vanished. "Why is it still going?"

"It's ... different." The quality had changed, less a sensation and more a sound. Isaline looked to the center of the room, where Cameron and Winn's argument had come to a halt, each of them with their heads cocked, listening.

"It's close," Neave said. Her braid was draped around her shoulders like a black scarf. "The noise was far away before, wasn't it?"

Winn wrapped her hand around something in her toolbelt—a knife. "That's a different noise. That's an engine."

They were silent, listening with growing dread to what was now obviously an approaching engine. Isaline flew to her feet and seized the staff of her trident. Could it be another mining cart thundering down the river toward them? Possibly. They hadn't seen extra carts hidden along the riverside, but they hadn't had time to look. Her ribs shrank.

Cameron's fingers were stretched and rigid. "Who would be this deep in the mines? Another clockwork?"

"We haven't seen a single clockwork since leaving that cavern with the bridge," Winn said. She stuffed a collection of Faraday's blueprints into her backpack. "And this is a secret part of the mines, remember? Faraday hid the entrance with that puzzle box."

Neave's back straightened. "So whoever it is, they either know we're here, or are going to find us."

A tense beat passed. They all looked at each other, blinking.

Then, like a bubble popping, the workshop burst into activity. Isaline swung her backpack over her shoulders and dropped the trident into its sling. Jame scooped up the remaining bedrolls and distributed them. Winn and Neave slid books onto their shelves and replaced fallen tools. Cameron stood, dazed, and started rummaging through his backpack.

The rumbling grew louder and shook Isaline's blood in her veins.

"If someone is coming down the river," she said to the others, "how are we going to get back without being caught? This is a dead end, unless we go down that hole."

"Maybe we can sneak by them," Neave replied. "Stay quiet—I'll be right back." She leaped fox-like over a table and skidded out into the passage, drawing a gleaming dagger from her weapons belt. "I'll see if I can get a look at what's coming."

"Wait." Winn froze in the middle of donning her backpack. "It's not safe. There's no time."

But Neave was already gone.

"She does that," Cameron said flatly, pulling a coiled rope out of his backpack. "You get used to it."

Winn eyed the workshop's entrance. She turned to Cameron and said, "Would you ..." but she trailed off at the sight of him passing the rope around the handle on the circular iron cover. "What are *you* doing?"

"Going after Jack." Cameron looped the rope through a carabiner and attached it to his belt. He strapped a headlamp over his forehead. "Get yourselves out. We'll ... I'll meet you outside the mill."

"You shouldn't—"

"No, I shouldn't. But you can't stay, and I'm not leaving him here alone."

A tense look passed between them. Isaline stilled. If Winn and Cameron started fighting again, there was no telling how long their argument would last, and the roar of the engine was swelling. They didn't have time to disagree.

Winn closed her eyes, then gave Cameron a terse nod. To Isaline's surprise, she held out her hand to him, offering a truce.

A wave of relief passed over Cameron's face. He clasped her hand in both of his own, squeezing. Their eyes met, and it was decided. Their group was separating.

"Be careful," Winn told him.

Cameron flashed her a white-toothed grin that didn't reach his eyes. "Not one of my natural traits." Nodding at Isaline and Jame, he tested his rope with a hard tug and lowered himself inside the hole. His shining headlamp faded from sight.

Isaline, Jame, and Winn stared after him, then Jame said, "What about us? Are we supposed to just waltz back down that tunnel? Wade through the river?"

"Not much choice," Isaline replied. She squinted at the workshop's entrance, willing Neave to come back and tell them it was a mistake, that no one was coming down the tunnel after all. They needed time to regroup.

But long seconds passed, the rumbling grew close, and Neave didn't return.

"Princess?" Jame said, raising his voice above the noise. All three of them were watching the passage opening now, waiting for any sign of Neave. "What should we do?"

Winn had sucked her bottom lip between her teeth, her eyes swinging as if reading an invisible book. "It's not safe to go out there. Neave could have been ..." Setting her jaw, she unclipped a small, rectangular box with a tiny wind-up crank from her toolbelt. "I'm going to send out a decoy."

She popped the box between her teeth and wound the crank with her good arm. The roar of the engine sounded just outside, and if Isaline strained her ears, she thought she could hear splashing. Someone was in the river.

Adrenaline flooded her body as she cast around the workshop. There were sharp tools and tripping obstacles strewn everywhere—if someone picked a fight here, this room could quickly become a tomb for all of them.

"Stand back," Winn said, freeing the box from her

mouth and holding the crank between index finger and thumb.

Isaline and Jame shuffled back as Winn set the box on the ground. It shuddered and rose on four spindly legs, reminding Isaline of the Listening Spider. The crank unwound with a rapid *click-click-click-click* and the little box scuttled over the floor, wooden legs tip-tapping out and into the empty passage.

Isaline had time only to inhale before a sharp *pop* sounded, a discharge from a pistol, and the box exploded.

Wood and metal debris went flying, ricocheting off the rock walls of the passage. Isaline recoiled, banging her head on the wall. Winn made a choked noise and stumbled backward. Her face had gone slack, eyes sinking into her head.

"It's him," she murmured. "How did he find us?"

"You can come out now, Winn," came Neave's voice floating into the workshop. There was something wrong with her tone; it was high-pitched and whistling, air hissing from a teapot. "I'm out here by the ... by the cart."

Isaline clamped a hand on Jame's arm. Firearms were rare in Benemourne. Adrudian was volatile when stuffed into the barrel of a pistol, likely to blow up or backfire. She'd never heard a gunshot before, even in school. The only person she could think of who would own a gun would be ...

Her focus locked on Winn, who visibly swallowed and took a step toward the workshop's entrance.

"I'm here," she said above the beating engine. "Don't hurt her, Johannes."

Johannes.

"She stays alive if you come out." This voice Isaline had heard on Winn's Listening Spider. A booming bass that had a wet, gurgling quality, as if the speaker had swallowed oil. "And if you don't come out, I'll come *in.*"

Winn delayed for the count of two breaths, and another gunshot exploded into the empty passage, cleaving a chunk out of the rock. Isaline's knees liquified. What good would their knives or her trident do against such a weapon?

"Don't shoot. I'm coming," Winn said. To Isaline and Jame, she mouthed, "*Hide.*"

They stared as Winn edged into the passageway, her palms held up in surrender. When she passed from sight, Isaline led Jame to the nearest table. They wedged themselves underneath.

"Should we ..." She gestured in the direction of the hole in the ground. "We could find Jack and Cameron, tell them."

He whispered into her hair. "If the King comes in, we'll all get caught."

"We need to help Winn and Neave."

"I know. But he has a gun."

Isaline shook her head. There was no way they could just hide and let Neave and Winn get killed. But how could they get past the King? Anger warred with terror inside her. This didn't feel real. She could hardly believe only hours ago their team had been together, safe, discussing keystones and the House of Matchsticks.

Richard's voice from the Listening Spider returned to her.

Now you must find what you lost, and try again to open the door.

Ideas clicked into place. At the Harper and Cup, Cameron had spoken of destiny. *Her* destiny. Sixteen years ago, the King had meant to use Isaline in a ritual to free an ancient god. The ritual had failed, but he wanted to try again. She had been born for this purpose; for the ritual.

Didn't destiny mean there were no other options? No decisions to be made?

She drew a shaky breath. The King wouldn't kill her. He couldn't—not if he wanted to complete what he had started. She had leverage, no matter how small, no matter her doubt. It couldn't be a coincidence to find herself with a chance to help now. She had to act.

That's dangerous, even for you, Nalissa's voice said in her head.

Isaline ignored her.

"Jame," Isaline said. "I'm going out there." Internally, she repeated the prayer Cameron had given her, the words that had dug themselves under her skin and planted hope where there had long been none.

I don't need to be scared. I'm meant to be here. I'm the keystone. Me. Isaline.

Isaline.

Isaline.

"Nalissa," Jame whispered. His hand settled on the small of her back, fingers spread. His touch sent a prickle through her, even entangled as they were.

"I'm not Nalissa," she breathed. Fear and worry and grief had filled her since Nalissa's death. They had buoyed her until this moment, but now the feelings were too much. There was no space left. The truth leaked.

She could sense Jame's confusion. "What do you mean?"

"I mean—" Isaline captured his chin in her hands and tilted his face to hers. His breath grew clipped, the tip of his nose grazing her cheek. "—I'm so glad I met you."

Before she could talk herself out of it, she kissed him. He tensed, then pressed his hand into her back, pulling her against his chest. The kiss was daylight, the brush of clouds over a clear sky, but still it ended before it began. Isaline extracted herself from Jame's arms and slid from under the table.

"Wait—no, wait—" Jame said, struggling to get his taller body out from their hiding spot, but Isaline couldn't stop to reply. She shed her backpack, leaving it on the floor. Then she unslung her trident, pressed the button on the middle grip, and watched the three razor-sharp prongs click into place.

She walked from the workshop and into the passage, her heart pounding in her ears.

IN THE TUNNEL, amid shards of rock and the ruin of their cart, were Winn, Neave, a man, and a monster.

A second cart had been parked in the river, similar in design to the one they had crashed. Winn had been backed against its hull, a knife hovering at her chest. The man holding the blade wore a City Watch uniform and snow-white gloves. His sickly-sweet cologne stung her nose.

Donborough. Isaline's steps stalled. Why was he here? Could he—

But the thought vanished when she caught sight of the King. Giant, stooping, his brass body glinting in the harsh Adrudian light, he had one metal-jointed hand clutched severely in Neave's braid and the other holding a pistol to her neck. His expression was gruesome, his face half-man and half-clockwork. A black suit stretched across his bulging limbs, and his massive feet parted the trickling river like boulders.

Inside, his engine looks new, Winn had said during their meeting at the Harper and Cup. *But the human parts —the parts that should have been there in the first place— they're gone.*

Faraday wasn't half-man, half-clockwork. He was *all*

clockwork. The human inside him had decayed, his heart-engine powered by Adrudian and the influence of a trapped god.

King Faraday turned his immense head to look at her, and his teeth flashed iron, and Isaline wondered too late if she had made a mistake.

"You don't look much like her, do you?" was the first thing Faraday said. His eyes were beady and bloodshot over his brass cheeks.

Isaline gripped the trident. "Theresa?"

"Don't you dare speak her name." Faraday's hand tightened in Neave's hair, and she gasped, knees wobbling. "You're the reason she's dead."

"Where are the others, then?" Donborough said. Next to Faraday, he was vibrating with barely controlled energy. He glanced at Isaline, then back at Winn, who stared defiantly at him despite being held at knifepoint. "That little Thief is here somewhere. I know he is." He prodded Winn with the tip of the knife. "They were all together at the inn, like I told you, Highness. Should I go looking?"

The inn. Isaline's mind sailed back to the Harper and Cup. In Little Space, after Adrises' eye had disappeared from the lock, Jack had climbed off the table and wrenched at the latches on the row of windows.

The windows blew open, he'd said to Cameron. *Do you want all of Ar to hear you?*

Isaline swallowed. Donborough must have been in the alley. He had seen and heard everything.

Faraday ignored Donborough's question with an irritated look. He flattened his pitch-black gaze on Isaline.

"You made it farther than I thought you would, girl. Adrises calls to you, doesn't she, even without your memories?" His lips split into a grin, black teeth glistening, and Isaline was compelled to nod—despite the fact she had never heard such a call. "It's been pleasant, imagining what would happen to your little group down here."

"Why did you wait?" Winn asked. Her voice dripped vitriol, her hands curled into fists. "If you knew we were coming, why not just stop us at the surface? At the mill?"

The King chuckled, the sound crawling beneath the beat of his engine. "Oh, I tipped off the mill warden. But Rhody Charlotte proved useless, and even my dear friend Richard Gray couldn't stop you. No matter. They were only distractions. You've done the work for me, haven't you, Winn? You've brought the girl and the pendant into the mines." Neave struggled in his grip, and he hauled her against his chest as if holding a wriggling child. "I knew I could count on you doing the right thing, Winn, no matter how foolish."

"S-stop talking to her," Neave said. Her face contorted in pain and rage, her hands tight on the King's fingers wrapped in her braid.

Faraday looked down at her. He was so tall he could have lifted her off the ground by her hair. "I'll speak to whomever I please."

"Not her," Neave said, her eyes watery. "She's a

member of the Seven Thrones. You treat her with respect."

There was a pregnant pause. Isaline's stomach dropped like a stone. Neave would be killed for treason—all Faraday had to do was pull the trigger—but the King only clicked his silver, fish-like tongue, another smile crossing his face.

"I see," he said. "Winn, you have a protector."

Neither Winn nor Neave responded, but Isaline caught the twitch of Winn's uninjured hand, betraying some hidden feeling. Faraday chuckled again. He pushed the barrel of the gun harder into Neave's neck and looked back at Isaline.

"And you, girl? Who's your protector?"

Isaline prayed Jame wouldn't seize this moment to come running out of the workshop. She drew herself up, attempting a City Watch impression Nalissa would be proud of, and said, "I need none."

The King regarded her in a way that made her insides squirm. "You sound like her, though, don't you?" he said, as if speaking to himself. Louder, he added, "Surely you must desire to return to the one who has called you. To go into the House of Matchsticks and complete the ritual."

Isaline's throat dried. She looked shakily inward, searching for a memory or an intuition that would guide her. But there was nothing. Except for a strange, starry bird, probably a hallucination dredged from her subconscious, her past had never made itself obvious.

Fate wouldn't come to her. Maybe it was waiting for her to come to it.

To the King, Isaline said, "Yes, I want to go to the House of Matchsticks."

He studied her. "And the pendant?"

She opened her left hand and the pendant fell, swinging at the end of its bronze chain. Another move Nalissa, a Thief, would have been proud of. Isaline had slipped the chain from Jame's neck as she'd kissed him.

"Good, good." Faraday released Neave, who dropped into the river on her hands and knees, her breathing ragged.

"You don't have to go with him," Jame said.

To Isaline's dismay, he came walking out of the workshop behind her. Donborough's head whipped in their direction, his wide, worm-long mouth opening in an expression of glee.

"I knew it. I knew it, didn't I?" Donborough's arms trembled, the blade in his hand slipping an inch from Winn's chest. To Jame, he said, "I told you I would wipe that smirk off your face. Where are the others? The Head Inspector? That Blueveins? I owe *him* a visit, too. I owe—"

In a flash, Winn grabbed Donborough's arm and stole the knife from him, one-handed. She spun the blade in her fingers and pointed it at the base of Donborough's throat.

"Don't move," she said, and Donborough held up his hands.

Faraday's engine made a turnover growl. He hadn't

moved, hadn't even blinked. Just kept the pistol pointed at Neave in the river.

"Kill him if you must." He stretched his brass neck. "Watchmen tire me."

"Why bring him, then?" Jame appeared at Isaline's side, his hand seeking hers. She had to fight to keep from sagging into him. Her knees were weak.

Donborough's face distorted into a snarl. But before he could speak, Faraday said, "Adrises might be hungry."

"Might be *what?*" Donborough said. Isaline felt a splinter of pity for him. Faraday had told him nothing. Maybe the King had offered him something in exchange for coming into the mines—something, judging by Faraday's annoyed expression, Donborough would never get.

Winn turned her head without shifting her gaze from Donborough's gawking face. "Nalissa. Stay behind. We can get out of this."

"*Can* you?" Faraday brought his free hand up to his face, tapping his brass jawline with a glinting finger. *Tap-tap-tap.*

Isaline bit back a moan. The implication was obvious. They couldn't kill Faraday—not until they knew how his clockwork body worked—but Faraday would murder them where they stood. Winn had betrayed him. Neave and Jame were of no consequence to him. And Isaline ...

She pushed the button on her trident with the pad of her thumb. The three points retracted into the staff with a metallic *sheen*, and she slung the weapon over her shoulder. Her course was plain ahead of her. She would see this through if it meant they could be safe.

Her stomach roiled. A destiny was what she had wanted, wasn't it? It was why she had kept pretending even when it put her and others in danger. It was why she had clung to fate; why she had closed her eyes, held her pendant, and wished and wished. She had wanted nothing more than a clear-carved path, for someone to take her hand and say, *This way. This way is for you.*

Winn's chest rose and fell. "Nalissa?"

Isaline took a step to the side, letting go of Jame's hand. If she was going to follow her destiny, she was going to do it as herself.

"My name is Isaline," she said. Her voice was strong. "Nalissa was my best friend, my roommate. She's dead. The pendant was mine and has always been mine. I'm not a Quandary Thief. I pretended to be Nalissa so that I could find out where I came from. I'm ..." Her heart throbbed as Jame backed away from her and sank against the wall. "I lied to you."

A heavy quiet followed her admission, punctuated by Faraday's thundering chest. Winn stared at her, mouth open. Jame was silent as a grave. Isaline couldn't look at him, or her courage would lock up and die.

I'm sorry, she wanted to say. *I never wanted to hurt you.*

But she couldn't speak. If Faraday saw her feelings, he would use them. Wield them like a weapon. Better Jame hate Isaline and get a chance to survive than like her and be killed.

Neave fell into a cross-legged sit, her laced boots splashing in the thin river. "The dead girl in the dorm room," she said, cradling her face in her hands. "Cameron's going to kill me."

Faraday was grinning again. "So ... *Isaline*. You speak like a true follower of Adrises." He gestured with the gun at the others. "What shall we do with them?"

"Let them go. Free them, and I'll go with you."

"So be it. Their lives won't matter, soon." Faraday deposited the pistol in a holster behind his back. When he brought his arms forward again, he was holding a puzzle box. He spun it, twisting dials and pressing buttons on its exterior. "Go to the surface," he said, glancing at Winn. "Tell Benemourne the Seven Thrones are never coming back. Tell them that before the night is through, they will have a new Queen."

Winn said nothing, only looked from Isaline to the King, and back again. Donborough's knife wobbled in her hand.

Faraday's puzzle box divided in two and a portion of the tunnel wall began to shake, a slab of stone shuddering to Isaline's left. Jame leaned to the side as the wall retracted, revealing an archway similar to the secret passage in the cliffside cave. A blast of heat and the smell of rotting flesh and wood assailed the air. Sloping rock led beneath the workshop.

Jame's eyes were trained on Isaline. His gaze brought a burning heat to her face. If she looked at him, what would she see written in his expression? Disbelief? Hatred?

Faraday gestured with his chin to Donborough. Scowling, Donborough slid his knife from Winn's limp fingers. He came toward the newly revealed doorway, wagging the blade at Jame, who shuffled out of his way.

"In here?" Donborough said, peering into the blackness beyond the archway. "It stinks. I thought we had to go through your workshop, Highness."

Faraday pocketed the puzzle box and clanked across the river. He moved like a clockwork guard, thudding steps and a mechanical smoothness that made the hair on the back of Isaline's neck spike. He had to hunch to keep his oiled, black hair from scraping the top of the passage.

"The House of Matchsticks has many entrances." The odor of burning Adrudian surrounded Faraday like a cloud, mingling with the smell of rot. He waved Donborough into the secret tunnel. "This happens to be my own pathway. Go."

Donborough hesitated, squinting into the dark as if trying to make out a trap beyond.

"Adrises is waiting." Faraday pointed into the passage. "*Go.*"

Still, Donborough didn't move. With a rolling exhale, Faraday placed one giant brass hand on Donborough's back and shoved. Donborough whimpered and clopped into the dark, struggling to keep upright.

When he was gone, Faraday swung his head to peer at Isaline, taking the same hand he had used to push Donborough and holding it open in front of her.

Isaline stared at his skinless palm, breaking out in goosebumps.

You're really going to do this, Nalissa said in her head.

Yes, Isaline thought back. *If no one stops me.*

She glanced at Winn, slouched against the mining cart, at Neave in the river, and finally to Jame, who was sitting against a new patch of wall. Each had their eyes on the ground, mouths drawn tight. They wouldn't acknowledge her, let alone try to stop her from following the King.

Their anger was justified, Isaline knew, but still their silence felt like a rejection. A dismissal from the friends who had kept her safe—the friends who would have kept Nalissa safe—and the boy who might have loved her. Would have loved Nalissa.

Tears stung her eyes, but she blinked until the emotions withdrew. Faraday couldn't see her weakness.

She dropped her pendant into the King's waiting hand. He gave her a broad, unsettling smile, crunching his fingers closed around the keystone. Then, turning, he followed Donborough into the passage, his great bulk disappearing into the dark.

In the quiet moment that followed, Isaline inhaled for a count of four and exhaled for five. Her arms flexed and relaxed. She took a step into the passage, shadows reaching for her with their encircling squeeze, and something pressed into her hand. Something with a trigger.

Looking down, Isaline caught the flash of Jame's fingers as they passed her the object and retreated, fearing the King's discerning gaze. She rolled the object in her palm.

A firework, shaped like a pistol and about the size of the flare she had used during her Survival Portion.

If you are in life-threatening distress, activate your emergency flare, and the examiners will arrive at your location shortly.

She almost smiled. This was no Weeklong Review. If she faltered, or froze, there was no coming back. Isaline cast a look at Jame, but he had retreated into the workshop, leaving the passage empty. A shell closed around her heart.

Don't think. Go.

She slid the firework into her pocket, a secret just for her, and walked after the King.

9

THE GAME'S END

JACK

Beneath the Shute, Jack stood at the threshold of the House of Matchsticks, prodding at the slats of his dark flashlight. His stomach sank when its orange glow didn't return. Something had killed his Adrudian.

Jack thrust a hand into his pocket and forced the drawstring top of his extra Adrudian pouch open. No light. The Adrudian rolled out and clattered to the ground, as worthless as plain rocks.

A rattling breath escaped him. Without light, he wouldn't be able to find his way through the giant cave before him. He wouldn't be able to find his way back to the grotto.

As a last resort, Jack groped for a box on his weapons belt.

Fingers shivering, he struck a match.

The tiny point of light flared, barely piercing the heavy

darkness. Jack ran his knuckles over his mouth. The match's glow was minuscule, but he could see by it. He could continue.

Steeling himself, Jack took a step into the cave—into the House of Matchsticks—holding the fizzling match out with one hand. The air was still and quiet as a corpse. He followed the wall, afraid to venture into the huge space in case he should lose his way. Clouds of steam blew from his mouth. The temperature had plummeted, leaving his sweat icy on his skin.

His path curved around the thick, leafless branches of the inverted tree at the center of the cave, the tip of its massive canopy suspended ten feet above the floor. Jack craned to look at the thick trunk he imagined sprouting from the ceiling, but his light wouldn't reach that far.

How could a tree grow upside down in a cave? Did its roots extend from the Shute's surface, drinking the sunlight in reverse?

Hot pain burst on his fingertips. The match extinguished.

Jack reached into his weapons belt and lit a second. On the wall, he skimmed his fingers over the charcoal-black marks of ancient paintbrushes. Murals in the same style as the painting on the rock in the grotto.

He stared into the bulging, painted eyes of Arias, sovereign of the Ancient Benemournian gods. Arias' broad shoulders were arched, arms protectively circling the lesser gods, who crowded beside them. A dense black rectangle surrounded the group. The seven figures Jack recognized had yawning, open mouths, every jaw slack. Masks of elation or fear.

He shuddered. Were the gods singing? Or screaming?

The eighth god, the one with the Nine Men's Morris on her chest, was the only figure with a different expression. She grinned.

Jack's match went out.

HE RETURNED to consciousness in the mines, wracked with the bizarre feeling of involuntary movement. His boots were thudding on the level ground of the tunnel, one after the other.

Adrises was moving his body. She was walking *for* him.

With a conscious effort, he stopped mid-stride and planted his feet. The *pull* in his chest complained, but his legs remained under his control. He shone his headlamp around the tunnel. Directly ahead was a cavern, its ground fractured into a deep ravine with a long, gravel-strewn slope climbing the opposite side. The trickle of a stream upset the silence.

Some part of Jack wanted to laugh. He didn't have to check his map to know Adrises had brought him to the right place. Of course, there would be a ravine this close to the House of Matchsticks. When he had entered the

Shute a year earlier, the ravine had been at the beginning of his map instead.

He hadn't known the ravine's significance when he had almost fallen over the edge, Cameron saving him by grabbing the back of his jacket.

Graceful, that, Cameron had said, accompanied by one of his sly smiles.

Jack entered the cavern with quiet feet. He unfolded his map of the lost expedition and flipped it over. Upside down, the only landmark after the ravine was the Dead Tree, inverted at the bottom of his parchment. No doubt this was the tree he had seen in his memory, springing from the ceiling of the House of Matchsticks.

There was a narrow, winding footpath swerving above the ravine to the other side. Jack walked carefully across it, releasing the *pull's* tension fluttering in his ribcage. He ignored the glimmer of a shallow stream below him, and ignored even harder the scattered, red-purple glint of a purpesia deposit. His attention was glued on the smooth wall at the other side of the ravine.

No distractions. No reminders of his feet swishing through frigid, ankle-deep water in a distant streambed, Cameron's splashes trailing him through the night.

I assume you're looking for that ritual site.

The House of Matchsticks.

Right. I'm looking for it, too.

As Jack walked, the cavern wall emerged under his headlamp, running parallel to the ravine. A strip of flat rock extended along the wall's base, spare feet of even earth before the ground sloped into the ravine.

But the slope wasn't what caught Jack's attention; it was the design that appeared on the wall before him, the immense Nine Men's Morris board carved into the rock, that made his breath pause.

He stepped off the narrow footpath and up to the board, his fingertips tingling. The carving was elaborate, far more detailed than the board he and Cameron had played in the Shute. Florid, spiraling lines stretched from the three concentric squares, disappearing into bunches of fungi that had grown on either side of the board. Long-dead roots and vines framed the Nine Men's Morris in black, woody tendrils. Sculpted on the center square, at Jack's chest-height, was a giant, ornate lock.

The last board was a trap, he thought, eyes wandering to the ground, where two stacks of tiles were partially obscured by a curl of roots. *This one is a door.*

He placed his palm on the center square of the board and the Nine Men's Morris burst into light.

Jack lurched backward, nearly losing his footing and rolling into the ravine. Mouth agape, he watched as the center of the Nine Men's Morris illuminated orange. Light spread from the place his hand had touched the rock, flowing across the lines of the board. Even the fungi lit up, blue glow mingling with Adrudian amber.

The board released a low hum, emitting energy as if it had been struck by lightning. Jack swiped his headlamp from his head and let the bulb clank to the ground at his feet. He didn't need it. The glowing Nine Men's Morris lit the cavern wall-to-wall.

Jack approached the board and felt at the corner of one of the squares with cautious fingers. Yes—there were slots in the wall to accommodate tiles, openings about the length of his palm.

The toe of his boot came up against a boulder at the board's edge. Had rocks been hauled here and used as steps so players could reach the highest points of the Nine Men's Morris? If so, who had done the hauling—the ancient engineers that built this place? Or Mining Team 5 and Johannes Faraday?

It didn't matter. The board was meant to be played. Jack crouched, picking through overgrown roots until he uncovered the two stacks of tiles. Nine red, nine blue. He slid a blue tile into his hands. They were just like the game pieces he and Cameron had discovered in the Shute.

"Jack."

The word came slipping down the tunnel behind him, making his muscles seize. He dropped the tile and whirled around, but the sound was faint, the speaker not yet arrived.

"Jack, where are you?"

It was Cameron. Of course it was. Jack's heart jumped into his throat. Somehow the argument in the workshop hadn't deterred Cameron from following Jack into this place.

Panicked, Jack wrung his hands and cast around the empty cavern. He had precious few options. He could retrace his steps and try to head Cameron off inside the tunnel, or he could wait and deal with Cameron here. Neither was ideal. How would Jack go about stopping him? Jack didn't know if he could fight Cameron off. Even if they were matched in strength, Jack feared the brew of rage, loathing, and longing inside him. He wasn't able to predict what would happen.

No. Jack's only option was to try to get through the door and inside the House of Matchsticks before Cameron could catch him.

But when he turned to the Nine Men's Morris board, he was

THRUST INTO THE PAST, *his fingers striking a third match.*

Jack edged past the mural of the wide-mouthed, boxed gods and continued following the outer rim of the House of Matchsticks. Upturned branches floated behind him, unmoving yet present. *He couldn't shake the feeling the tree was staring at him, anticipating his movement, recording him in its ancient consciousness.*

His own mind was beginning to turn, courting the idea of finding the keystone and getting out of this place. But he wouldn't be able to find the keystone without Adrudian light.

You'll find it, *Jack encouraged himself.* You'll bring the keystone back.

He suppressed a wave of goosebumps as a new mural came into view. Unlike the others, this painting depicted only the mysterious eighth god, her circular eyes leering, features framed by strings of black hair. She was boxed, as in the previous mural, but she had moved into the center of the rectangle, where Arias had stood. As if the other gods and their sovereign had disappeared between this mural and the last.

Despite the sheen of fear on his skin, Jack's insides were abuzz with curiosity. What had happened here? The murals were unlike anything he had seen at other ritual sites. Ancient Benemournians had prayed for simple desires: prosperity, fortune, guidance. The House of Matchsticks was something else.

As he was stepping past the mural, a twig snapped.

Jack's body jolted. The sudden movement extinguished his match, darkness cocooning him in a cold embrace. He pressed against the wall and clutched at his matchbox with shaking hands.

"Who's there?" His voice returned to him in an echo. "Cameron?"

He dragged a match across the rough surface of the box. The head ignited with a fizz and the smell of phosphorus. Its light revealed a vacant space in front of him. Not even the tree was visible.

"Alone," someone whispered, a soft hiss cutting through the quiet. "So alone."

Jack shrank against the wall, waving his match side-to-side. He couldn't tell where the voice was coming from. It seemed to be all around him and inside his head at the same time.

The whisper came again. "Are you here to help me?"

He straightened, one hand resting on the hilt of his dagger. He couldn't envision the person such a voice might belong to; the intonation was vaguely female, but multiple, as if many people were speaking at once.

"Depends who you are," he said, lifting his match, searching the shadows. "Show yourself."

"Why? You already know what I look like."

He blinked. "I do?"

"Oh, yes. You've seen me in those paintings." The voice drew out its words, vibrating in his ears. "But I'm still a stranger to you."

A stranger. *Jack shakily drummed his fingers on his weapons belt. The murals surfaced in his mind: Arias, Tuphin, Dodia, Gomos, Wudtar ... all the way down until the last. The one other—the unfamiliar god.*

"You mean the ... eighth god?" he asked, baffled.

"You can call me Adrises." A beat passed in which Jack imagined Adrises stirring, preparing to come closer. "Tell me. What do you know about gods, Jack Fael?"

A shiver skittered across Jack's shoulders. "How do you know my name?"

"You're going to ignore my question?"

"No, I—" Jack swallowed. This woman must be playing a joke on him, but there was something in her inflection that told him he shouldn't argue. The answer to her question spilled from his mouth. "Ancient Benemournians believed in gods, but then Adrudian came, and there wasn't … there wasn't a need for gods anymore. They were forgotten."

"Not by you."

"I'm a Treasurehunter. It's my job."

Adrises laughed, a bitter, grating sound. "Treasurehunters—you're all so proud. But you have one thing wrong, don't you? I'm not a god." She was quiet for a moment, and when she spoke again her voice was low, dangerous. "I was trapped here in the walls with the rest of them, but I'm not *a god."*

Jack blurted the question without thinking. "What are you?"

Nothing but an ominous silence followed, so charged it pressed on Jack's chest. His match died with a curl of smoke. In the bare seconds it took to strike another, he could feel Adrises looking at him through the dark, waiting for him to ask a different question. He flattened his free hand on the wall behind him.

"You said trapped. *The gods were trapped? Is this a myth I've never read?"*

Adrises sighed. "Not a myth, Jack. When the Benemournians discovered Adrudian, Arias and the other gods tried to stop them from using it. The gods thought Adrudian would bring humans too close to gods themselves." Jack envisioned her waving a dismissive hand. *"Or something like that."*

"So … someone trapped them in the walls of this cave? The House of Matchsticks?"

"Yes. Seven ritual-makers. Your kind's first Adrudian engineers."

Jack's mind was spinning. Benemourne's founders—the first Seven Thrones—had been engineers. They had been the ones to introduce Adrudian technology to the world. The same technology that had replaced the need for rituals and gods.

As much as Jack couldn't fathom it, the idea made sense; based on the spiral pit trap, Cameron had guessed that the people who had hidden the House of Matchsticks were engineers.

Adrises continued. *"Thanks to Adrudian and a powerful keystone, they managed a ritual strong enough to seal Arias and their little friends here. Unfortunately for me, your power-bloated ancestors thought I was a god and caged me in here, too. Even though I'm the one who* made *your beloved glowing rock."*

"You …" Jack's words failed him. He gulped and tried again. *"You made Adrudian?"*

"I made it, I use it. I am *it. Where do you think your light went, Treasurehunter? Who could control Adrudian in such a way but me?"*

Jack's whole body was prickling. He needed to leave, to get into the open air. Either he was speaking to an ancient presence that had been imprisoned in this place for thousands of years, or he had lost his mind. He wasn't sure which was worse. But where was the keystone?

"If—if Arias and the lesser gods were trapped here," Jack said, taking a tiny step back the way he had come, "where are they now?"

A pause, then Adrises said, "I consumed them."

Ice trickled down Jack's spine. She'd consumed *them? What could eat gods?*

He took another step, ankles trembling, and struck a new match before the last one extinguished. He weighed the odds of finding the keystone if he went running through the cave. Would he be able to grab it before Adrises stopped him? Would *she stop him?*

The only thing he could think to do was keep her talking.

"You asked if I was here to help you."

Adrises made a breathy, amused noise. "You're not the only one, Jack, who can ask meaningless questions. I know you're here to help me."

"How?"

"Because you all are—the Treasurehunters who come to visit me." Jack had the sense Adrises was creeping toward him, but he couldn't tell from what direction. "You're all curious. Determined. Reckless enough to come and find me. Besides the worthless group of pickaxers that tried to free

me by placing a living keystone in my prison years ago, six Treasurehunters have already been here. And I've been using them in a little ritual of my own. Arcane magic to break the seal, something humans could only dream of." She laughed again. Jack's flesh crawled over his bones. "The last Treasurehunter to find me was a member of the Seven Thrones. Can you believe that? One of the Justs. Unlike the gods, I have a sense of irony."

Jack squeezed his back against the wall of the cave. How many steps had he taken inside? How many would it take him to escape? He gripped the hilt of his dagger.

"And that was a hundred years ago," Adrises went on. "I've waited a long time for you, Jack Fael. You will be the seventh. The last. Then I will be free."

Holding his breath, Jack slid along the rock. "The seventh what? The last what?"

But Adrises wasn't answering questions anymore. Her voice grew loud. "Sit where they sat. Be what they were. A mirror of souls breaks the seal. Seven is seven. Seven is ..."

Her fingers landed in the center of Jack's back, protruding through the wall, and he yelped. The terror that had been inching to the surface broke inside him. He ran. His match blew out. The world was lost in blackness, but panic had overtaken his legs. He stumbled blindly from the wall, straight into the open space of the cave.

"A mirror of souls breaks the seal," Adrises roared.

Jack's hands found an object in the dark. His desperate fingers felt around it. Could it be the keystone? Or the slimy roots bordering the exit? No—it was dry, ridged, and crumbling. And the smell ...

He gasped and wrenched away. They were bones. Human bones. A skeleton slumped on the seat of a thick stone chair.

Adrises' laughter echoed in his ears. "Sit where they sat."

Jack staggered backward, white spots sparkling in his eyesight. Something hit him behind the knees, and he sat, his back coming up against an empty block of stone. His shoulders slammed into a rock backrest.

"Seven is seven is seven is seven is seven is ..."

"Jack."

He cracked open his eyes.

Light seeped beneath his eyelids, orange and turquoise. Jack blinked once, hard. There was blackness at the outer edges of his vision, but in the center, a face.

Cameron shook him a second time, his hands gripping Jack's arms. "Come on, you're scaring me, here," he said. His face emerged into Jack's focus. Brown eyes bright with alarm. The flash of white teeth worrying a bottom lip. "I'm two seconds away from slapping you."

Jack pushed him back with an open palm. "Slap me and you're dead, Inspector."

His limbs were groggy from memory. Jack sank against the glowing Nine Men's Morris board as

Cameron laughed with relief, twining a hand into his hair.

"Stars," he said. "I thought I lost you for a moment. Again."

The comment made Jack's stomach twist. He clenched his fingers around the tile in his hands, the same tile he had dropped before losing consciousness. When had he picked it back up? If he had stayed awake, he could have played the game and entered the House of Matchsticks before Cameron found him. Now it was too late, and Cameron was here, and the moment was growing long and tense, and Jack didn't know what to say.

"I ..." Jack started, at the same time as Cameron said, "Do you—"

They both stopped, staring at each other. Cameron broke their eye contact first, waving a hand toward him.

"You go first."

But Jack had forgotten what he'd meant to say. There were too many words to speak and, at the same time, far too few. His brain was bursting. Adrises wasn't a god. She was something *else*, something that had destroyed Arias and the lesser gods.

I've been using them in a little ritual of my own.

You will be the seventh. The last.

What did it mean?

Meanwhile, Cameron had discarded his headlamp and his hair was mussed on one side. His jacket was askew, and his soot-streaked collar hung open, revealing the bare hollow of his throat. Blue crescents lined his lower lids. He had never looked so disheveled.

Trying to order his thoughts, Jack felt he might shatter. The *pull* tugged painfully at his chest, Adrises wasn't a god, he had been to the House of Matchsticks, he hated Cameron, and he didn't.

Whatever passed over Jack's face in the silence, Cameron was watching it carefully. He gestured to the tile Jack was clutching. "Were you planning to play the game?"

Jack nodded. "I was going to, before I ..."

Before he *what?* Drifted away? Was granted a memory he had lost and couldn't recover because Cameron had decided to keep their expedition to himself?

Cameron's gaze traveled from Jack's face to the stack of tiles below the board. Without a word, he crossed to the wall and gathered nine tiles, red to Jack's blue. He examined the Nine Men's Morris and slid a tile into a slot on the board's left side. Then he inclined his head at Jack.

"Your turn," he said.

Jack's mouth fell open. "You've lost your mind. Do you know what this board is? It's a door."

Cameron gave him a weary look. "Play. If you win, you can go. I won't stop you."

"And if I lose?"

There was no reply, just a long stare. Jack understood. If Jack won, Cameron would forget the House of Matchsticks, turn around, and climb to the surface.

If Jack lost, they would fight.

Jack swept the rest of the blue tiles from the ground. He recalled Cameron's explanation of the rules: *You need to get three in a row. That's called a mill. We take turns, and if you get a mill, you get to take one of my pieces. And vice versa.*

Simple enough. Jack slid a tile into place on the opposite side of the board. He had won the game in the Shute. If he focused, he could win this one, too.

But Jack couldn't focus. He lost his first tile to Cameron, then his second. He felt the tension between them as sharply as if it were a physical ache. An ache that married with the *pull* in his chest—which, in spite of the fact he was trying to get into the House of Matchsticks, remained intent on squeezing his ribs until they hurt.

He spoke when he couldn't stand it anymore, and Cameron had taken another of his tiles.

"You should have told me."

Cameron sighed quietly. "I know."

"It was selfish."

"I ..." Cameron bit the inside of his cheek, as if he had almost agreed with Jack's statement, then stopped himself. "Maybe if you had mentioned you were going to—"

He broke off, fiddling with the stolen tiles stacked on his palm.

"Going to what?" Jack plucked one of Cameron's tiles from the board, watching as Cameron hesitated and avoided his eyes. "Go on. Say it. I poisoned myself looking for the memory. The memory you kept from me."

"I wouldn't have lied if you had come to talk to me."

Jack scoffed. "Yes, you would have. You kept lying even after I Drank. Even when you asked me to come here. Even *hours* ago." He made way as Cameron shifted one of his red tiles to another slot. They had both played their hand—now there was only rearranging the board until one of them won. "But I guess you got what you wanted either way, didn't you?"

Cameron's spine stiffened. He turned, aiming his gaze fully at Jack for the first time since they had started playing. "What are you talking about?"

"In the Shute." Recalling their hike through the forest, their close call with the pit trap, and their time in the grotto melted Jack's insides like hot wax. "You were trying to distract me. You wanted to steal the keystone, to take all the acclaim."

A dark look slid over Cameron's features, his eyes flashing. "Acclaim? You think *I* wanted to steal the keystone?"

"I'm right, aren't I?"

"No. You left me. You left me and I had to wake up and come after you and—and—"

Jack crossed his arms while Cameron labored to speak. He hadn't remembered this part yet. Maybe if Cameron came out with it, he wouldn't need to, and the lost expedition would finally be leveled between them.

Cameron struggled with himself for a moment. When he spoke again, his voice was razor-sharp. "I'm not selfish. *You* are." He took a step toward Jack, pointing an accusatory finger. "You let me come with you, and then you just *left*."

"I left, but you lied," Jack said. "You lied when you knew the lost expedition was ..." His voice broke, more emotion flooding through than he was prepared to show. He swallowed. "It ruined my life."

Cameron's expression was stony. "I didn't want it—"

"But you decided to go back yourself. Without me."

"No, I didn't want to go back. I—"

"You wanted to get me out of the way."

"I wanted to *protect you*." Two pink spots formed high in Cameron's cheeks. "If you weren't so ... so obsessive, so reckless, I could have told you the truth. But you couldn't get your nose out of that stupid map. You were going to get yourself killed! Do you think I have anything to prove? Look at me." He swept an arm down his body. "I lost everything after that expedition. My career, my—my sanity. Every time I think about the Shute, I feel like I can't breathe. I have nightmares. I can't sleep ... all because of what happened to you."

Cameron's eyes were ablaze, his shoulders heaving. An honest admission at last—yet poison still flowed through Jack's veins. Nightmares were nothing. What did Cameron know about the *pull*?

Jack wrenched a tile from one slat in the wall to the

next. "Sorry your life is so hard, *Head Inspector.* I feel sorry for you, with your mansion, and your inn, and your badge." He punctuated each word with a jab of his finger. Cameron pressed his lips into a line, scowling. "You're right. I can't see an inch past that map. But you were happy to follow the map when you crashed my expedition."

"I didn't *crash your expedition.*"

"You did. And the expedition before that, and the one before that. Don't stand there and pretend like you're better than me. If you didn't care about discovering the House of Matchsticks, why follow me? Why come to the forest in the first place?"

"Because I ..." Cameron clenched and unclenched his fists. His cheeks were pinched, pupils dilated, the bow of his mouth stretched into a grimace.

Breathing hard, Jack let his hand fall. It was satisfying, in a cold way, to see Cameron Agustin tongue-tied.

He turned, trudging back to the board, and Cameron found his voice.

"Because I'm in love with you."

For a moment, Jack could feel nothing but his own heartbeat. He spun around. Cameron had both palms covering his eyes, his head thrown back. The tiles he'd stolen from Jack were set aside on a rock, gleaming sapphire in the orange light.

"What?" was all Jack could say.

Cameron exhaled, long and slow. He kept his hands

over his eyes, pushing into his temples with his thumbs. "I'm tired, Jack," he said. "Why else? I've been in love with you for years."

There it was again. Jack lifted his eyebrows. None of his stoical, wayward men had said *that* to him before.

Leaning against the Nine Men's Morris, Jack set his tiles on the ground by his feet. He didn't know why. He just needed to move to keep his brain from falling out of his head.

"But ..." He sifted through the last week with clumsy recollection: Cameron at the mill, asking him to come on the expedition; the letter stuck to Jack's door in Lower Village with a booking for an inn; the hug Cameron and Winn had shared in Little Space, and the twinge that had gone through Jack every time they had put their heads together since. "I thought you and Winn ..."

Cameron laughed grimly, running a hand through his hair. "*Friends*. I'm allowed to have friends, aren't I?"

The bitterness in his tone surprised Jack. "Never said you weren't."

"People speculate about me, you know. In rumors, in newspapers. Tell one person you're bisexual and suddenly you've dated half of Ar." Cameron shot him a steely look. "Not that dating half of Ar would be a problem."

"No," Jack said, truthful. He had believed those rumors himself. He wished he hadn't, now, along with a wealth of other things that weren't true. Cameron hadn't been trying to manipulate him during the lost expedition.

Jack had been the one misled by ambition; he had been blind to Cameron's kindness, his charming enthusiasm for a contest—too often hidden behind taunts and his famous smile.

Cameron loved him.

It seemed impossible, but the rage inside Jack dampened, nonetheless. In its place, a warm feeling stirred.

Impossible and possible.

Plainly aware of Jack's eyes on him, Cameron heaved another sigh and said, "I can't take back the lie. I *am* sorry I did it, for what it's worth." Reaching for the Nine Men's Morris, he shifted one of his tiles to the left. He patted it in place with his palm. "Three-in-a-row. I win."

Jack's stomach flipped. In the confusion of the last minutes, he had completely forgotten about their game. He stood back—more than conscious of how close the movement brought them—and surveyed the board.

Cameron *had* won. There were two blue tiles left. To finish the game, all they needed was to remove one of Jack's remaining tiles from the board. The last steal.

"I don't know if—" Cameron started, but Jack's hands moved of their own accord. He reached across Cameron and pulled the nearest blue tile from the wall.

Deep, bone-shaking resonance emerged from the Nine Men's Morris. Jack's insides hummed as the roots framing the board shook. Then, with a deafening rumble, the center square of the Nine Men's Morris began to lift. The ornate, carved lock rose on a thick slab of stone, releasing a whoosh of frigid air.

When the mechanism stopped, a perfect square of darkness faced them at waist-height. An entrance.

The House of Matchsticks lay beyond.

Cameron sucked in a breath. "We have to get out of here."

Jack looked at him askance. He had blanched, the fine curves of his profile tense. Moments ago, Jack would have climbed through the door without hesitation. Now everything had changed. Cameron loved him, and had lied to protect him from whatever was waiting in that cave.

But the *pull* clawed at his ribs, insistent. Jack squeezed his eyes shut. Finding the House of Matchsticks was more than a simple discovery. It meant being free, ridding himself of the inexplicable longing that had plagued him since the lost expedition.

Jack had never told Cameron about the *pull*, only assumed he felt it, too. Now Jack knew he had been wrong; Cameron still believed going into the House of Matchsticks was a choice.

Nothing is nothing, Jack. There are no choices with my handprint on your heart.

Jack's mind shivered. A memory began to form, borne on Adrises' breath, her hand creeping into his mind and pulling at threads. Dizziness weakened his legs. He didn't want to leave Cameron. He didn't want Adrises to control him. He brought his hands over his ears, attempting to force the memory back.

"Not now," he mumbled. "Wait. Let me think."

"What's wrong?" Cameron said, sounding alarmed, but Jack couldn't respond. Adrises didn't care to listen to him.

The memory washed over his consciousness, bringing him

INTO THE PITCH-DARK *of the House of Matchsticks, where he was slumped over on a cold, stone seat.*

A minute earlier, Adrises' voice had been roaring, echoing off the cave walls and filling Jack with clean panic. She had hushed, now, as if retreating and leaving him alone. The silence was thick. Jack's terror had ebbed, but his thoughts were spreading thin. He couldn't move from his chair. Phantom weights had grown in his muscles, his head too heavy to raise on his neck.

Something was happening to him.

A strange feeling had started in his fingertips, as if he were holding his hands in a cold flame. The sensation slowly spread to his hands and wrists. He couldn't stretch his body to relieve the pain—though it wasn't pain, exactly. He felt as if his skin were unraveling.

Long seconds passed. Was this the ritual Adrises had mentioned? Maybe, but Jack couldn't remember how he got here. I'm beneath the Shute, *he told himself, yet minutes wore on and his location slipped from his mind.*

Soon after, the ritual made him forget even his dearest memories. The kiss his mother gave him as she'd boarded the ship that went down at sea and took her away forever. His own small hand, flipping open books and savoring the texture of paper in Lillian and Philip Just's library. The first time he had pressed two fingers to the rough trunk of the Dead Tree. Cameron and his walking stick.

Jack's body itched. He was changing.

He was dying, too. His lungs had stopped inflating. He simply didn't need to breathe.

In his emptying mind, Jack envisioned himself in the morning, climbing a creaking gangway up to a chugging, mist-filled boat. His only regret was that there was no one to watch him go. No one to see him onto the ship.

Light materialized at the edge of his vision. It appeared as if underwater, bobbing bodiless through the dark. Footsteps echoed in the massive cave.

Moments later, a figure dropped to its knees before him. A man with a handsome face, holding a burning torch.

He spoke, but Jack couldn't hear properly, and could only watch through strands of his hair as the man's eyes grew round with fright. The torch dropped from his hands and rolled across the cave floor, flame alight. In the semi-darkness, the man lifted Jack's head, stared into his eyes, and passed a finger beneath his nose. Checking for breath.

His touch lessened the burning in Jack's limbs. A scrap of sensation returned. He parted his lips.

Seeing the movement, the man grasped Jack under the arms and hauled him off the stone chair. He laid Jack gently on the cave floor, rubbing a thumb over his cheek.

"Jack." The man's voice came to him muffled. He leaned over Jack, hair falling into his eyes. "Breathe. Come on. Take a breath."

It took all Jack's effort to open his lungs and let air into his body, but still the breath was fresh rain, cooling his prickling skin. With it, knowledge began to return. He knew where he was. He knew who had saved him. He knew who was waiting in the dark.

He wheezed out the name, and Cameron gasped in relief at the sound of his voice. Firelight flickered over a dazzling smile.

"What did you say?"

Jack tried again, forcing his slack tongue to form the three syllables.

Cameron tilted his ear to Jack's mouth, pressing two hands to his chest. "One more time."

"A-dri-ses," Jack moaned. Horror flowed through his paralyzed limbs. They needed to get out. They needed to run, but feeling was returning to his body at a snail's pace.

"Adrises?" Cameron sat back on his heels. "What does that mean? Is it a—"

He never got to finish his sentence. His body jerked as

ghostly fingers clutched him around the neck. Adrises giggled, her voice seeping from the walls.

"Die, interrupter," she said.

Jack tried to yell, but could make no sound. He remained rigid on the cave floor, heart palpitating as Adrises' unseeable hands lifted Cameron clear from the ground, choking him. Cameron's feet kicked, hands scrabbling at his neck. His bulging eyes rose outside the nimbus of firelight, head lost in shadow, and Jack could merely twitch his fingers.

Don't let us die here, *he begged.* Not me. Not him.

But Cameron's arms fell from his neck and dangled, limp. Adrises sighed, and a tearing sound sliced through the silence. Cameron's jacket flopped open aside a long, diagonal cut. Blood soaked his chest. He dropped and lay crumpled on the ground by Jack's feet.

"No," Jack croaked, his legs lurching. He drew on all his strength and rolled over onto his stomach, pushing his elbows beneath him. To Adrises, he said, "I won't let you kill us."

She laughed. "Even if you could escape me and my ritual, Jack Fael, you would return. The change stays with you when incomplete. It draws you. You would never be able to resist finishing what has already begun."

The change. *What had she almost done to him? Jack struggled, attempting to lift himself, and in the torchlight caught a glimpse of his hands. A shock went through him, breath hissing from his lungs.*

His fingers were gone. Hollow. Nothing but outlines of hands filled with distant lights.

Jack blinked, and the effect was gone, as if it had never been. His hands stared back at him. Was it magic? Was he hallucinating?

He rose to his knees, wobbling, and the side of his face

STUNG WITH AN ABRUPT, burning pain. The cavern in the mines resolved around him, his consciousness yanked back into reality.

"Okay, that time I actually had to slap you," Cameron said, "but in my defense, you *were* trying to kill me."

Jack shook his head, clearing the memory's haze. The image of Cameron bleeding on the cave floor vanished, but the terror he felt stayed behind. He was standing inches from Cameron, who was backed onto the glowing Nine Men's Morris, head tipped back.

Jack broke out in a cold sweat. His hand was clutching Cameron's neck.

Die, interrupter.

"Did I hurt you?" Jack asked. He was having trouble catching his breath. He tore his fingers from Cameron as if he'd been burned.

"I'm fine." To Jack's surprise, Cameron grinned. He rubbed a hand over his neck. "I was one second from shoving you into that ravine, actually."

Stars. They had been lucky. Jack stepped backward,

threading his fingers into his hair. More of this and his mind was going to break. What had happened in the House of Matchsticks? He had been dying, sitting on that stone chair. Adrises' ritual had been *transforming* him.

Cameron had saved his life.

The *pull* stabbed an icicle into Jack's chest. He didn't want to believe what Adrises had said—that he would be unable to resist her draw—but it was true. She had known he would return, had promised memories to lure him. Jack had brought himself to her door.

Cameron's smile faded, his gaze wandering the air around Jack's head as if he were bordered by ghosts. "It's her, isn't it? She's controlling you." His voice lowered to a murmur. "She's giving you your memories. In return for what?"

"I ..." Jack's heart had sped to a gallop. He didn't know how to verbalize a response. *In return for her freedom. In return for my life. In return for taking me away from you, and you from me.*

The past was repeating itself. He had left Cameron in the workshop to find the House of Matchsticks. Cameron had come after him. And now, again, Cameron was the only thing keeping Jack from completing the ritual. Adrises was going to kill Cameron. She was going to *use Jack* to kill him.

A deep pain spread through his body. This time, it had nothing to do with the *pull*.

Cameron stared at him, chewing the inside of his top

lip. He stepped closer, repeating his question. "In return for what, Jack?"

Jack couldn't bear to speak what he knew: he was going to die here. Or fight not to die. He had no choice but to leave Cameron behind. He wouldn't let Adrises hurt him, not now that Jack had accepted the truth. It was Cameron who had shaped him, looked after him, kept him safe, all along. Cameron was the reason Jack was determined, and curious, and alive. Cameron was the reason Jack *was*.

A memory nudged him, threatening to surface. He could feel Adrises' touch, the tap of her fingers inside his head. He didn't have much time.

"I shouldn't have left you in the grotto." The words tumbled from Jack's mouth, the first true statement he could find. "I wouldn't, if—if it were today. I wouldn't go."

Cameron seemed taken aback, but then a hint of a smile touched his lips. Adrudian light spilled over his features like water, hugging the contours of his chin, the shadow along his jawline, the strong crease between his brows.

Jack's focus drifted despite his effort to stay conscious. What would happen if he brushed his thumb, just there, in the space at the base of Cameron's throat? In the spot behind his ear, nested in a tangle of hair ...

"Don't go, then." Cameron was close enough for Jack to count his eyelashes. "Don't go."

"I need to."

"No." From the corner of his eye, Jack saw Cameron's fingers flex, as if debating whether to reach for him. He drew closer. "That's Adrises talking. She's influencing you."

The *pull* rested a disembodied hand on the inside of Jack's chest. Cameron's dark eyes widened, catching on the blue veins marking his cheeks.

"That's it," he whispered. "She's hurting you. That's why you Drank."

Jack opened and closed his hands, fighting the spots blooming in his vision. He didn't want to tell Cameron about the *pull.* He was ashamed of it, the vise around his heart, the claws poking inside his mind. Ashamed as he had been the night he tipped his bedside lantern into a cup, trying to understand the *pull,* to dig it out of his body.

Cameron was watching him, watching his eyes, watching his mouth, waiting for Jack to confirm or deny what he had said. But Jack didn't want to talk about the *pull.* He wanted it to stop. He wanted to go through the door to the House of Matchsticks. He wanted to make the discovery that would save him or end him.

"I want to kiss you," Jack said. Even to his own ears, his voice sounded drugged.

Cameron made a noise that was near-tangible, the sound impressing hotly on Jack's skin. He lifted his hands and set them on either side of Jack's face, covering the blue veins. "Promise first."

"Promise what?"

"To come back with me."

The ache in his chest was agonizing. His eyes watered. "I can't."

"You can," Cameron urged. He began to caress Jack's cheekbones, his hairline. His fingers left tingling warmth behind, but not enough to thaw the fear that had iced over Jack's insides. Adrises was approaching again, her hand becoming his hand, his fingers spasming at his weapons belt. At the hilt of his knife.

"You have to get away from me now," Jack said. His breaths rasped. The *pull* pounded in his chest like a drumbeat.

Come, come, come.

Cameron shook his head fiercely, brows knitting. He took Jack's hand and flattened it over his chest. His heartbeat was strong and fast beneath Jack's palm. "Fight it," he said. "I dare you."

Jack shivered at the press of him. He was a gift. How could Jack have thought him any less?

Cameron braced his knee against Jack's, pulling them as close as they could be, as close as they had ever been. His hand moved from the side of Jack's face and wove into his hair, cupping the back of his head.

He whispered against Jack's mouth, "Kiss me. I dare you."

Jack had only to tilt up his chin. He did, and surrendered to the heat of a soft kiss, bringing his hand from his knife and brushing it instead at the hollow of Cameron's throat, the spot behind his earlobe, across the angle of his cheeks. Cameron's breath hitched at Jack's touch, his body going still.

The rest happened in a rush.

Cameron fell back against the Nine Men's Morris, bringing Jack with him, folding him tight against his chest. The blots of memory behind Jack's eyelids grew and shifted as one kiss became two and three, each hungrier than the last, each drawing from him a feeling that was new and intoxicating. The cavern faded until there was only him and Cameron, somewhere between past and present.

Images began to flicker as Adrises' dark, encroaching memory loomed. But these images didn't belong to Adrises; they belonged to Jack. In flashes, they were in the forest, they were standing on the stone plateau, and they were in the creek-lined grotto.

Cameron's hands slid down Jack's back. Jack saw them in Little Space.

As they traveled through the mill, Jack felt the tease of Cameron's eyelashes on his cheek.

When Cameron's lips moved to Jack's jaw, trailing kisses down his neck, they were in the mines.

Finally, an image of the House of Matchsticks rose around them. Jack's hand dipped into Cameron's shirt and grazed knotted flesh. The scar. The injury Adrises had left him. The attack that had almost killed him.

Hot blood wet Jack's fingers.

He broke the kiss, stumbling backward. Were they in the House of Matchsticks? Had Jack's hands opened the scar? Drawn blood from Cameron's skin?

No. Cameron leaned against the glowing Nine Men's Morris, winded, his face flushed. The top three buttons of his shirt were undone, exposing a long strip of scar, but there was no blood. He looked at Jack, dazed, then flicked his eyes to the center of the board. The square of darkness concealing the House of Matchsticks.

Adrises wrapped her fingers around Jack's mind. He had run out of choices. The memory was surfacing, and he was being carried away.

Cameron made a frightened sound, as if anticipating what Jack was going to do before he did it. "No, Jack—"

But Jack had already lunged forward and hauled himself through the hole in the wall. The stone square slammed shut as he drew up his legs, the earth knowing to lock him inside. A tomb, or prison, or both.

The solid wall allowed a muffled sob from the other side. Fists against rock, cries of grief.

Jack was gone

gone

gone.

In the past, Jack raised himself from the cave floor on weakened legs. He took the torch in one hand and shook

Cameron with the other. Cameron's eyes fluttered open, blood seeping through his clothes.

"Am I dead?" he said, red pooling and dripping down his neck.

Jack swung the torch through the dark, looking for Adrises, but saw nothing. Perhaps she feared the fire or the light. No time to guess. He hooked an arm behind Cameron's back and helped him to sit, then kneel, then stand.

Cameron stumbled and sagged against Jack's side, but he could walk. Together, they hobbled unimpeded to the edge of the House of Matchsticks, where they found a tunnel leading out of sight.

"Am I dead?" Cameron asked again as they staggered through the dark, up a passage that would release them near the Dead Tree.

Jack swiped a hand down his jacket, bumping the contents of his pockets and tipping a rock of purpesia onto the ground. He didn't notice, just as he didn't notice the thrum that was born in his chest, a pull *that would bind him until he returned, alone, kissed, and shivering.*

"No. No, I've got you," Jack said. "I've got you."

Time circled, overlapped, and was forgotten. Jack and Cameron climbed and climbed into the light of day.

10

THE PLACE BEYOND THE DOOR

ISALINE

Isaline trailed Donborough and King Faraday through a slender tunnel, determined not to lose her balance.

Rocks were scattered about, as were cracks in the ground, deep crevices, and plunging slants. She kept one shaking hand on the tunnel wall, picking across the tricky path with her toes. Ahead, the light from her headlamp illuminated Faraday's broad, brass neck, rattling with the beat of his engine.

The three of them were traveling slowly. Donborough, at the head of their procession, was having as much difficulty with the terrain as she was. His agonized breaths were in sync with the swing of his flashlight.

"Faster." Faraday prodded him with a metal finger. "Adrises has waited long enough."

"Are we almost there?" Donborough asked. He was

obscured by the bulk of Faraday between them, but she could sense his dread as if they were holding hands.

"Not much longer, now," Faraday replied in his greasy voice.

Soupy, humid air deadened Isaline's footfalls. The unending heat and the smell of rot made her nauseous. Had Jame, Winn, and Neave already taken Faraday's cart upriver and left the mines? She imagined Jame sitting in the cart with the others. Was he angry at her? Did he hate her? Her heart shriveled, but she forced her feet to keep moving. The firework he'd given her was tucked gently inside her pocket.

She couldn't go back, not until she saw the end of this.

At some point, the rock walls bled into soil threaded with black, slimy roots. Tendrils reached and swiped at her shoulders, pulling at her trident and worming their way into her hair. The temperature stabilized, then dropped, affording some relief from the heat. Goosebumps rose on her skin.

"Highness, what are these things?" Donborough said from the front of the line.

At first, Isaline thought he was talking about the black roots, but then Faraday said, "What is left of them. My old pickaxer friends."

Cold descended on Isaline. Faraday took a large step over a pile of something, and her shoulders recoiled. It was a heap of clothes, streaked with dust and blood. Old pickaxer uniforms.

"What did you do to them?" Isaline heard herself ask. She couldn't take her eyes off the dark splatters coating the coats and pants. The remnants of Mining Team 5.

Faraday turned to look at her over his shoulder. His head twisted a little too far on his neck, red-black eyes glinting above his crooked iron grin. "I did what I was asked. The fire took care of the rest."

"The fire?" Isaline's words were muffled beneath the hand she held over her nose and mouth. "You started the mill fire."

"It was necessary."

"Why?"

Faraday took a grumbling breath. For a moment, Isaline thought he wouldn't answer, but then he rolled his shoulders—*clunk, clunk, clunk*—and spoke.

"We discovered the House of Matchsticks by accident, me and Theresa. Adrises spoke to us. We worshiped her, and we brought in the others—Haris, Mio, and Richard. Our friends. But when the ritual was prepared, and we were ready to free Adrises, the others grew afraid. Theresa ..." His voice wavered, a tiny, near-imperceptible tremble. "Theresa's feelings overcame her senses. She didn't want to make her baby the keystone. Neither did Haris, your father. They planned a mutiny in secret and stole you halfway through the ritual."

Haris. She envisioned the dark-haired, athletic man with the striking smile from the photo. He and Theresa had been together.

"Adrises foresaw Haris and Theresa's betrayal," Faraday continued, pushing a giant rock to the side as if it were feather-light. "She warned me. She whispered inside my mind, giving me the plans for Adrudian explosions I could control with a button. I set the mill ablaze while they tried to escape. But still the ritual failed, and you were lost."

Isaline shuffled around a notch in the ground, trying to steady her breaths. If Haris was her father, there wasn't much resemblance between them, except for his dark hair. Her features must have come by Theresa. Isaline still hadn't seen her face, only her long, brown waves. Maybe they had the same nose, or eyes.

"I erased every one of them," Faraday muttered. "Even Richard, in the end."

Isaline could think of no response. She peered at the stretched back of Faraday's suit jacket. This man had killed countless pickaxers and mill workers, including his own friends, to try to release Adrises. What had Adrises given him in return? The ability to forge machines that thought, sensed, and woke with the sound of a voice. The heart-engine that had powered him after his human body's decay.

Her stomach churned. Nothing could be worth such evil—and Isaline had been there during these events. She had survived a ritual and a devastating fire before she was old enough to walk. Where were her memories? She had been an infant, but her memories could have persisted through the pendant's magic. There might have been a flash of light, or a smell, or the feeling of her parents' hands. There had to be something.

"You'll always remember," Nalissa said, leaning against the cold stone of Casret's dormitory.

Flapping noises came from above them. Faraday and Donborough didn't seem to notice, but Isaline craned to look at the ceiling of the tunnel. Her headlamp caught the silhouette of a bird flying overhead, an outline filled with the points of stars.

Help me, she thought desperately. *Even if you're just a hallucination, help me remember.*

The bird turned a circle in the air and seemed to beckon.

After a stretch of walking, the tunnel bent in a series of snake-like curves, then opened onto a dark threshold. Isaline wiped a coat of slime off her eyelids and hovered a few paces behind Donborough and the King, who stopped and stared into the shadows. Donborough's light shone only feet into the darkness. Faraday practically giggled.

"We're here," he breathed.

As if in response, the Adrudian inside Isaline's headlamp flickered, then dimmed. Darkness swallowed them. From somewhere ahead, Donborough moaned; his flashlight had gone dark, too. He tapped the slats against the wall, rattling the bulb.

"What's going on?" he asked.

"It's her," Faraday said. His engine thundered, but his words were hushed, almost reverent. "Your simple Adrudian won't work in the House of Matchsticks. She takes it."

Shivering, Isaline fingered the slats on her headlamp. They were still open. The King was telling the truth.

Faraday's brass hands clanked, then a scrape and fizz cut through the air. The head of a thick match glowed between his fingers, casting them all in a dim halo of light. He brought the head of the match to a white-wax candle he produced from the inside of his pocket.

"Follow me," he said, striding into the space beyond the threshold. Thin light illuminated the edge of what looked like a massive cave. "Touch nothing. This is sacred ground."

Both Donborough and Isaline hesitated, staring as Faraday's light floated into the distance. *Sacred ground.* Faraday really did worship Adrises, and Isaline's mind was too stretched to predict the consequences of freeing her. If what the King said was true, Adrises had orchestrated the murder of innocent people. Even Richard had tried to stop the King from completing the ritual.

If Adrises is freed, tell my—tell my family I tried to stop it.

Donborough glanced at her, shadows skimming over

his ashen face. His long mouth was twisted and anxious, far from the cocksure, menacing expression she'd come to expect from him.

"You're a Watchling, right?" he asked her, breath sweet and steaming. "You haven't taken your oath."

The question surprised her, dulling her nerves. She hadn't been called a Watching for what felt like a lifetime. "What are you talking about?"

"You can stop him." Donborough wrung his hands. His white gloves were filthy with dirt and slime. "You can do something. This isn't right. I—I think the King is ..."

He looked meaningfully at her. Isaline let out a long exhale. Faraday had dragged Donborough thousands of feet beneath the earth, talked of imprisoned gods, mill fires, and murder, and still Donborough was upholding his City Watch oath. Afraid to say a bad word about Johannes Faraday lest he be punished for treason. Isaline could hardly believe that a week ago, she would have blindly taken such an oath and upheld it herself.

"Your oath is meaningless," Isaline said to him, her whispered tone masking none of her conviction. "He's going to kill us if you don't open your eyes."

Donborough's expression folded into a poor imitation of a threat. "Insolent little ..." He pursed his lips. "You've been breathing the air of Quandary Thieves for too long. They've corrupted you."

Isaline laughed bitterly. "Maybe. I've only met two Thieves." She stepped closer to him. He was taller than her, but she glared up into his eyes. "They're the most honorable people I know. Not like you. Now go, before he comes back for us."

Donborough sniffed, shooting her an icy look, but relented and stepped from the tunnel. Isaline followed him inside, a knot clenched in her throat. Had she just told off a City Watchman?

The cavern beyond the tunnel was giant, as cold as winter, and slowly taking shape in the light of the torches Faraday was busy setting aflame with his candle. Ramshackle sconces were hammered into the rough rock walls, holding dense wooden torches Mining Team 5 must have smuggled from Ar. Isaline lifted her gaze. A massive, bare-branched tree sprouted upside down from the ceiling, its roots nestled in a crunch of rock. Stalactites reached like fingers down the blackened trunk.

Her chest grew heavy. It seemed impossible for a tree to grow in a cave. Her memory dug up a moment from her Survival Portion, sitting with Jame across the fire as he planted flowers.

They're Nightblues, I think, he had said the next morning, when the seeds pushed pea-green shoots through the soil. *They grow in the dark.*

She stared through the mass of branches above her, eyes following a long, winding crack that had carved itself into the ceiling, reaching from where the tree's trunk had grown too thick for the rock. Anxiety fluttered in her chest. Whether this tree was possible or not, it didn't look stable.

Isaline was so distracted by the inverted tree that she nearly walked into a stone block situated in the center of the room. There was a line of them—seven—each taller than her and two paces wide. She lurched back, afraid to touch them in case the stone should burn or bite her. This place was alive; it was the only way she could think to describe it. Ancient and awake.

Donborough stood facing her, frozen in place, a hand clapped over his mouth. He looked as if he were going to collapse.

"Who are they?" he asked through his fingers, looking at the side of the blocks Isaline couldn't see.

Faraday blew out his candle. The torches along the walls sizzled, lighting the House of Matchsticks in wavering red light. "A mirror of souls breaks the seal," he said, as if that answered Donborough's question. "Arcane magic."

Donborough's eyes held such horror Isaline was afraid to walk the few steps to see what he was looking at. Still, she did, holding her breath, and as soon as she turned, she realized the stone blocks weren't blocks at all—they were thrones. Each was intricately carved into rock, adorned with letters Isaline didn't recognize, images and glyphs from ages long past. Dust packed the grooves, years of dirt heaped on the seats, alongside what looked like ...

She let off a little groan. Skeletons. Bodies, one sitting on each.

Seven thrones.

Faraday came to stand beside them. The turnover of his engine echoed wall-to-wall. "The engineers that sealed the gods away in this place. These were their seats."

Donborough was standing as close to Isaline as he could get without touching her. "But not their—their bones?"

"Do you think they would have gone on to be the Seven Thrones if they'd died in this place?" Faraday said. "No. These are offerings. Adrises' own attempts to break the seal. Seven is seven; the gods' supernatural laws demand balance."

"A mirror of souls breaks the seal," Isaline murmured, eyes fixed on the throne at the leftmost end of the line. The skeleton that had sat there was old enough to be nothing but a pile of dust. Her mouth soured. These weren't the rituals Jack and Cameron had described in Little Space. This was old magic, dark magic. Winn would never believe it, even if Jack had alluded to it when he was reading from his book in the workshop.

The seal can be broken, too, but that would require too much power for a group of pickaxers.

Isaline's legs tingled, overwhelmed with the urge to run. Before this week, she had never given thought to gods or magic. If she stayed, she didn't know what would happen to her senses. In this cave, it was difficult even to know what was up or down. She felt she was standing on the ceiling.

Donborough gulped, fighting his gag reflex. "Are these the ones ... those clothes ..."

"None of these offerings were pickaxers," Faraday replied. He clicked his fingers together as Isaline's eyes slowly moved down the line of thrones. The second skeleton to the left was crumbling, its jaw wide and hanging. The third still had some semblance of clothing, though it was disintegrating, and Isaline found it impossible to imagine what it might have been wearing when it died.

"Who were they?" Isaline asked, fearing the answer.

"Most were Treasurehunters," Faraday said. "They came looking for the ritual site in the Shute. Adrises lured them herself, one-by-one, long before Theresa and I found the House of Matchsticks. Centuries before." He ran his hand through his oiled hair. "There was one throne empty when we first came here ... the mirror was near-complete."

The fourth and fifth skeletons were shrunken by time and decay, fragmenting clothes pooling around their hip bones. Isaline's eyes stung. They had died alone, all these Treasurehunters. Alone in the dark. Her gaze moved to the next, the sixth. It wore a discolored leather jacket, a small-brimmed hat, and an old weapons belt. Taut and splitting skin stuck fast to its bones. The eyes had long since rotted away, leaving dark holes through which a worm crawled.

"My pickaxer friends and I could have offered ourselves this way, but ..." Faraday gave a low chuckle. "None of us were willing to volunteer."

"And that one?" Donborough asked. "He's still alive."

Isaline's head whipped to the seventh throne. The man slumped there had wild, black hair and pale skin. One hand flopped to the side, open like a wilted flower, a box of matches spilling from his fingers. The other hand held a knife. He had tried to defend himself.

Her heart sank into the floor. "Jack."

"That Blueveins," Donborough said, but Isaline had already rushed forward, dropping to her knees in front of the throne. Jack's face was slack, his eyes half-open, muted blue, and unmoving. Even the veins climbing the sides of his cheeks had gone gray and bloodless.

Isaline bit back a cry. He looked dead—but he wasn't. His chest fluttered weakly up and down. Small, rapid breaths. She reached toward him, but the sound of a pistol being cocked at her back made her freeze.

"Touch nothing," Faraday said. The barrel of the gun nudged her between the shoulders. "Not until our ritual is complete. With you, we will be able to free Adrises before she frees herself. I will reap the reward she promised me."

Jack stared on, responding to nothing. Isaline stood and backed away from him, her palms in the air. The world swam behind a veil of horror. She needed to get him out of here, fast. But binds had wrapped around her heart, impeding an escape as much as the gun at her back.

I'm here for a reason. Fate chose me.

Freeing Adrises was what Isaline had been born to do. Destiny had brought her here. Destiny meant there were no other options—and what if completing the King's ritual was the only way Jack could be saved?

Isaline shuffled backward until Faraday swept the gun aside, clenched a hand in her tattered blazer, and turned her about face.

"Look at it," he said.

She drew her elbows to her sides. The wall of the cave spread before them was teeming with ancient artwork. Thorny vines, lumps of Adrudian, and figures Isaline guessed were gods adorned the rock in great slashes of black paint. Every curl and streak on the wall tumbled and spiraled to one distinct spot straight ahead of them. The image of an entrance, filled fully in black.

"A ... door?" Isaline said.

Faraday pushed her closer. "The door that locked gods, millennia ago, into these walls." He sounded cheerful again, his voice a singsong. "The door that you, our keystone, will walk through tonight to free our new Queen." He snatched Isaline's hand, forced her fingers open, and dropped the pendant into her palm. "Place the first keystone into the door, and the entrance will open."

Isaline closed her fingers around the pendant. The purpesia was heavy and cool in her palm, its keyhole cutout pressing into her skin. How many times had she held it, just like this, and wished? Wished to be significant, somehow extraordinary, to make a mark in Ar or on the world? To have a clear-carved path?

Her feet carried her toward the wall. She ran her free hand down the painted door and discovered a round, shallow hole in the rock, the precise place where a lock should have been. Where it *could* be. All she had to do was return it.

Faraday sensed her hesitation. "Go on, girl. It is predestined. It is your purpose. Just as it is my purpose to rule Benemourne and to wield Adrises' power."

Fate's been stirring. It knows how everything connects, one to the other. It pushed you here.

Isaline didn't want to obey the King, but she couldn't help but be a part of this. Mining Team 5 had given Isaline a role to play here, in the House of Matchsticks. Now she had to walk the route laid out for her sixteen years ago.

You'll always remember, Nalissa said in her head.

No. I don't remember, Isaline countered. *I don't know. But I can't go on pretending like there's an alternative.*

She forced Nalissa's protesting voice away and let her body speak for her. Her hand reached forward and slid the pendant into the hole on the wall.

There was an explosion of light. Isaline was momentarily blinded, her eyes clamping shut on instinct, and when she slid them open again, she saw the cave lit up as if in daylight. The black paint on the walls had transformed into Adrudian orange, shining impossibly bright and setting the ancient artwork aglow. Isaline was reminded of

Neave's Adrudian paint, a line of glowing *X* marks leading them home.

Donborough drew in a sharp gasp, and Faraday clapped his massive hands. Isaline could do nothing but stare. The effect was beautiful.

"Now," Faraday said, placing his fingers on her back again, "walk through the door, so that Adrises may walk out."

The door no longer appeared to be a painted image. It glowed an intense orange. A window at daytime. An Adrudian sun.

"I have to go through?" she whispered, her watering eyes fixed on the door. Jack's book hadn't revealed what her role as a living keystone would be, only that she might not die.

There are things worse than death, a part of herself said, but it was barely noticeable beneath the rushing that had grown in her ears. Buzzing, like a bug burrowing into her skull.

"You are a replacement," Faraday said, sounding far away. "Balance. We don't have the power to break the seal, only alter it. The keystone will be imprisoned while Adrises goes free ... and it must be the original keystone. Then she will reward me with power over Adrudian. Over the world."

For a second, Isaline was utterly numb. She would be imprisoned in Adrises' place? Faraday would have control of Adrudian? The words made that small, distant part of herself shriek—but she couldn't tear her eyes from the glowing door.

"Everything will change, now," Faraday murmured. "Everything will. Everything, everything."

The door had an inexplicable draw, a *pull* that tugged at her ribs, coaxing her forward. The light looked warm and soft, like the comfortable bed she had dreamed of at Casret Academy but never got to sleep in. It looked like her first step into Ar with the City Watch, days after graduating and taking her oath. It looked like a summer day with her best friend, sitting by a salt-smelling sea. It looked like a kiss on the beach at night. It looked like ...

She stepped into the light.

The place beyond the door wasn't warm, as Isaline had imagined. Frosty air enveloped her, burning her skin with cold fire. Her surroundings warped, twisting until she was weightless, suspended in space. She wheezed, terror coating her body like liquid. Orange rotted into black, and the House of Matchsticks disappeared, and—everything stopped.

Isaline opened her eyes. Adrises was floating in front of her.

This woman could only be Adrises. Her skin was waxy and dripping, her mouth sliced open as if cleaved by an ax, and her eyes were obsidian stones. Oil-slick hair cascaded from her pallid scalp, the ends swiping against the fabric of a gossamer, tangerine dress. She stared at Isaline, upside-down and hovering.

"*What a pleasure,*" Adrises said in Isaline's mind. Her strange, divided voice held no joy, only dry disappointment. "*How delightful to meet someone new.*"

Isaline had no idea what expression she made in response. She couldn't feel her face. "You're ..."

"*I have many names.*" Adrises' marble eyes shone. "*But the one you know will do.*"

"Adrises." Isaline cast about in the darkness. There was nothing around them, just swirling black, as if they had been engulfed by a storm cloud. Numb fear spread through her body. "Do you ... do you recognize me?"

Tilting her head, Adrises made a sound that could have been a laugh. "*I should ask you the same. Do you recognize* me?"

Isaline's eyes ran over Adrises' features—the drooping skin, the wide, empty mouth, the tattered orange dress—and she shook her head. She had never seen this woman before. Adrises was as absent in her memory as Faraday's ritual or the House of Matchsticks had been.

"*I must admit, you're a surprise to me, too.*" The disappointment in Adrises' tone sharpened. She sounded uncannily similar to the Headmaster of Casret Academy scolding Isaline for failing her Weeklong Review. "*You're not who I thought you were. I am weakened in my prison ... I must not have seen to the full extent of my power.*"

"What do you mean?"

A strand of Adrises' hair wiggled. "*Poor, inconsequential girl,*" she said. "*You're nothing but an ant.*"

Her tone made Isaline's chest twinge. It didn't make sense. If Isaline was the keystone, Adrises should know her. She had been in the House of Matchsticks before, stolen halfway through Mining Team 5's ritual. Faraday had said so himself.

"I'm the keystone from sixteen years ago," Isaline said. She had to fight to keep her voice from trembling. Why didn't Adrises remember? "I was just a child."

Adrises' mouth stretched into an unpleasant grin. "*You hope to be the keystone, do you? The child born underground, the only child who can alter this seal for Johannes Faraday?*"

"I ..." Isaline's voice hid in the back of her throat. She wanted to say: *I don't hope that I'm the keystone. I don't want any of this*. But the words weren't true. Her heart was a traitor—she *had* hoped for it.

"*Your hope is willing blindness.*" The fine threads of Adrises' dress glimmered, cobwebs spilling up her arms. "*Being a keystone is easier than being nothing, isn't it? Being no one.*"

Isaline swallowed. Again, Adrises reminded her of being at Casret Academy, kneeling in front of Nalissa's body, tears slipping down her cheeks. *I can't stay at the Academy without you,* Isaline had thought. *I can't leave. I'll never make it on my own. Tell me what to do, Nalissa.*

Adrises said, "*You think you were born in the House of Matchsticks, selected by destiny to be part of something extraordinary. You think you were* chosen." She made a scoffing sound. "*Did you stop to think that the real keystone had been touched by magic? That they would be better than you? Brighter?*"

Isaline couldn't speak, only stare. The words were a fist around her spine.

"*You can't think that in the eons I have been alive, your mediocre consciousness impresses me.*" The wax of Adrises' face sagged, then jiggled into position again. Isaline had the abrupt impression she was wearing a mask, hiding her true face. Dread ripped through her. "*I am the source from which all your light flows, Isaline. I am in your lanterns, I am in your machines, I am in your industry. I am in your blood, and now, here, I see your unremarkable heart.*"

She paused, and in the silence Isaline's skin shrank. She wanted to get out of here, to finish the ritual. Even freeing Adrises was better than facing this—whatever this was.

"*You cannot free me,*" Adrises said. "*Leave, now. You are not my keystone. You are an insect in my house. Nothing more.*"

Isaline's knees weakened, her pulse fluttering. Adrises inhaled through her gaping mouth and blew a gust of rotting air with the force of a gale. Reflexively, Isaline dug her heels into the spectral ground, but the wind was too strong—she was pushed and pushed. The darkness transformed into bright, painful light.

She awoke standing in the House of Matchsticks, the tip of her nose inches from the painted, glowing door. It no longer resembled a portal. Rock peeked through the light, solid and unyielding.

Faraday stood at her side, his brass jaw hanging open, orange glinting off his silver tongue. He looked absent, as if in prayer, but when she turned to look at him, his eyes settled on her with astonishment. Donborough was sitting on the ground behind them, arms hugging his knees, staring at nothing. He jerked as Isaline came to herself and stepped back from the wall.

"What is this?" Faraday said. He drew up straight. "Where is Adrises?"

Isaline couldn't form a response. She stared at him. How could she describe what she had seen? What Adrises had said? Faraday was going to kill her. She wasn't the keystone—he wouldn't be able to complete the ritual and secure his power. Isaline and Jack were as good as dead.

Still, the question niggled at her. If Isaline wasn't the keystone, who was? How had she gotten the pendant?

You'll always remember.

She'd been silent for too long. Faraday slammed the wall with his brass fist, knuckles crunching through a layer of rock. Isaline's legs jolted, and she fell to the ground on her backside, breath heaving. Steps away, the branches of the inverted tree shuddered, the vibration from Faraday's punch rippling down the tree's trunk. Chips of dry wood floated into the air. Donborough lifted his head to stare at them.

"Where is Adrises? *Where*?" Faraday took a heavy step toward her. His first was coated in powdered rock and flakes of ancient paint. "Tell me, girl."

Isaline scooted backward, whimpering. Her trident bumped against the nape of her neck. "I don't—I don't know. She said I wasn't ... she said I couldn't ..."

Faraday's bloody eyes flashed, his mouth expanding to show his black teeth. He slid a hand into his suit jacket and dragged out a piece of folded parchment. Tossing it toward her, he said, "Is this not her? Is this not your mother? You were born in Adrises' magic, a carrier of the pendant since infancy. You should remember."

The inverted tree shook, branches scraping in a chilling susurrus. Donborough got slowly to his feet while Isaline caught Faraday's paper with a shivering hand. She unfolded it, smoothing the old, crinkled sheet down on top of her thigh. It was the ripped end of the photograph of Mining Team 5 from the workshop.

On the right was Johannes Faraday, human, with a faint smile curving his upper lip. Next to him was Theresa, her dark brown eyes staring directly into the camera.

Isaline's blood froze.

Theresa had Nalissa's face.

"Is this your mother?" Faraday repeated. Greasy foam

gathered at the edges of his mouth. "Are you Theresa's child, born in this cave, escaped in a rowboat sixteen years ago?"

Isaline gaped at him, and a memory clunked in her mind, a gear falling into place. Images jostled for attention. Her vision fogged.

Nalissa had been standing at the other side of their dorm room when Isaline arrived at Casret Academy for the first time. She had taken Isaline's hand, led her out of the dormitory, and huddled them into a secret spot between shrubs at the base of the building, where they'd sat with cold stone at their backs and their feet resting in a snarl of shiny leaves.

There had never been anyone like Nalissa at the orphanage. Even at eleven years old, she exuded importance, strength, and *magic*; the same magic that would attract legions of admiring students in later years, and the same magic that would cut for her a clear path. She seemed lit by a constant spotlight.

"We're going to be best friends," Nalissa had whispered.

Isaline was too nervous to be convinced. "How do you know?"

"Because you'll have this." Nalissa had reached to the back of her neck, unearthing a bronze chain from within waves of her ash brown hair. A pendant glittered at the end, a red-purple stone adorned with a keyhole cutout. She pressed it between Isaline's palms, covering both Isaline's hands with her own. "You'll always remember."

The memory slid into the jigsaw puzzle of Isaline's mind. She held the photo of Theresa and Faraday between her palms, squeezing her eyes shut. This was the only memory the purpesia had taken from her. She didn't know why. But it was the only memory that mattered.

Nalissa had been the keystone. Not Isaline. She'd given Isaline the pendant as a token of friendship. Isaline had never been to the mines, had never been to the House of Matchsticks. Adrises knew it, and Richard had realized it moments before his death. He had only seen Nalissa in the dark of their dorm room and must not have recognized her. And then, in the river, he had looked at Isaline in the light for the first time.

"*Ah*," he had said. "*Not you ... not you ... not you ...*"

Isaline opened her eyes. The photograph in her lap was blotted with the tears dripping from her chin. She and Nalissa had looked alike. The brown hair, the brown eyes —Nalissa's a warmer tone than Isaline's own, but close enough to be mistaken by anyone but Isaline and Nalissa themselves.

She felt her body was made of glass. A hollow chest, the feeling of nothing. Of being nothing.

I have no destiny. I'm just me.

The truth was a dagger. But, as Isaline lifted her head to stare into King Faraday's eyes, as she felt his Adrudian-laced breath huff against her face, she realized the truth was also a key. It unlocked something inside her, releasing the bonds that had coiled around her heart.

She stood on wobbly legs, clutching the photograph in her fist until it crumpled.

"You're a murderer," she said to the King.

Surprise flickered over Faradays' face, followed by a brutal sneer. "And you're not the keystone. You're just a girl, aren't you?"

Isaline squared her shoulders. Her mind whirred in a familiar way, ideas forming like combustion in an Adrudian engine. She slid her eyes to Jack, sitting immobile on the seventh throne. Donborough was standing near him, looking like he might faint. Neither would be any help. She could only rely on herself.

"The keystone was my best friend," she said, shuffling backward. She dropped the photo and inched her right hand behind her, fingertips brushing the staff of her trident. "Her name was Nalissa, and she's dead now. Because of you."

Faraday took a step, his giant foot pulverizing the ground. "Dead? The keystone is *dead?*"

Taking a deep breath, Isaline flicked her eyes upward. The crack in the rock reaching from the inverted tree soared above them. She estimated the distance between her and the ceiling. Four stories? Five? The same height as a shaky, poorly maintained fire escape she never thought she could climb.

But she *had* climbed it.

Slowly, she wrapped one hand around her trident. With the other, she edged into her pocket, grazing the firework hidden there.

"Nalissa was killed by your monster," Isaline said, "and I came in her place."

Faraday flexed his brass fingers, a clump of shiny hair falling into his eyes. "You've destroyed my ritual." His engine roared, rattling Isaline's eardrums. "I'll rip your head from your body, *girl*."

The threat made Isaline's muscles seize, but she still managed to slip the firework into her hand. The trigger rested against her index finger.

"You're right. I'm not the keystone," she said. Her body was glass and fire, and for the first time, Isaline could truly feel the fabric of her bones, the strength of her stomach, the rhythm of her heart. She was going to destroy this place before it got the chance to hurt anyone else. "But I have something Nalissa never had."

Faraday advanced on her, Adrudian Milk frothing from his lips, coating the collar of his suit jacket in copper. He dwarfed Isaline, nearly twice her height. She braced her feet and held his gaze.

"And what's that?" Faraday growled.

In one swift stroke, Isaline unslung the trident and pressed the button on the middle grip. Three sharp points slid into place. The King's eyes rolled, his chest depressing with the pulse of his engine. His giant mouth widened.

"I have a choice," Isaline said, and shot the firework straight up into the air.

Time seemed to slow. Isaline, the King, and Donborough watched as a line of smoke and brilliant white light climbed, and climbed, until it hung suspended just below the cave ceiling. Then, with a blinding flash, the light exploded into multicolored balls of fire, rocketing in every direction.

Isaline could have sworn she saw the air ripple. A bird was flying beneath.

Split seconds later, the sound of the firework hit with a deafening *crack*. The ceiling shuddered, letting forth a rain of dust. Isaline's breath disappeared as the crack in the ceiling widened, weakened by the explosion, and the inverted tree made a deep, undulating sound. Its branches shook as if in a hurricane.

It worked, said Isaline's mind in an unhinged, jolly tone. This place was coming down.

A rock the size of her head broke from the ceiling and plummeted, landing and splitting into shards near Donborough. He shrieked, jumping away.

"*Run,*" Isaline yelled to him.

He took off sprinting as she bent her knees and faced the King. He was snarling at her, bull-like, his massive hands quivering. A crunching sound came from above. Isaline rushed backward as another rock detached and fell, plunging between them. Faraday batted it out of the air as if it were a fly. The rock sailed into the wall and cracked in half with a burst of dust.

"You're dead," Faraday said to her. "I'll grind your bones."

Isaline gripped the trident with paralyzed hands. The ground was rippling beneath her feet. The House of Matchsticks was collapsing. She was going to fight the King.

She was going to fight the *King*.

Faraday lunged, swiping at her with a brass hand. Panicking, Isaline jumped to the side, falling onto her knees and scrambling up again, one hand hefting the trident. Her heart hammered, turning her blood to acid as a falling rock tumbled and shattered near the King's advancing legs.

Just a clockwork, she told herself. *He's just a clockwork.*

He made another grab for her. Isaline's body reacted automatically. She raised the staff of the trident and blocked his swinging forearm, a chunk of metal as thick as her neck. Brass and silver steel clanged. Her elbows trembled, the force of the impact shaking her teeth. Faraday was *strong*. Powerful enough to crush stone. She couldn't let him get ahold of her.

Faraday's other arm came at her face, fist clenched. She ducked, pulling the trident back across her body and jabbing at his knees with the three blades. They made contact, tearing a hole in the leg of Faraday's trousers, but the points bounced off his brass calf. She dodged his swinging arm and struck again. Nothing—only a dent.

Not good. The trident couldn't pierce him.

Grunting, Faraday reared back, preparing another attack. Isaline darted out of the range of his hands and risked a glance over her shoulder. Donborough had disappeared, leaving the line of thrones behind her, Jack sprawled limply across the seventh seat. Branches swayed and shook above him. The tree whined.

Stop the King. Save Jack. Don't get crushed.

She needed a miracle.

"No child makes a fool out of me," Faraday thundered, stretching his arms wide. Adrudian Milk leaked from his mouth, running off his chin. Some kind of overflow from his engine.

His engine.

An idea popped into Isaline's head.

Wiping a sweaty palm down the leg of her pants, she took three steps backward and reaffirmed her grip on the trident. Jack's limp body was beside her, the dark nest of his hair piled against the back of the throne.

When Faraday loped toward her, she avoided his hands and struck out with the trident, aiming for his chest. The King smoothly evaded her weapon, but he made an effort not to throw himself near the seventh throne, and Isaline noticed.

Flipping the trident, Isaline maneuvered Jack between herself and the King. Faraday wouldn't touch the throne, not if he didn't want to interrupt Adrises' ritual. He reached out for her, eyes glittering with rage, but she crouched and allowed the throne to give her cover. She stabbed at his chest with the trident once more. This time, the points scraped a line down Faraday's shirt, revealing a mass of red-hot gears and cogs chugging at the center of his chest.

Yes. The sight of the engine emboldened her. *Only a machine.*

She thrust the trident over Jack's head, aiming true, but the sound of splintering branches threw her off. Isaline looked up just as a boulder plunged through the tree's upside-down canopy, headed directly for her. She yelled and launched forward, clambering onto the seat of the throne, propping her feet on the armrests.

The rock smashed to bits behind her. She teetered, the tremor shaking her legs, and Faraday released a gurgling laugh. He wrapped his fingers in the front of Isaline's shirt and yanked her like a rag doll up to his face, his sharpened iron teeth glinting in the flickering light.

"You're mine," he said. Flecks of spit and Adrudian Milk spattered Isaline's neck.

She scrabbled and kicked, trident pointlessly waving, throat constricting. One of her thrashing heels made contact with Jack's shoulder. He shifted, and somewhere inside her terror, Isaline registered his body slumping forward, away from the backrest. She kicked her heel again and he slid from the throne, crumpling into a heap on the ground.

Faraday didn't seem to notice. His black, bloodied eyes were trained only on her.

"Die, now." He pressed the side of her head into one huge palm. The metal was hot on her skin, singing the hairs on her cheeks. She screamed. White seeped into the edges of her vision.

Then there was movement. Out of the corner of her eye, Isaline saw a figure charge at Faraday's back, wielding a smoking torch. Donborough. He brought the torch down over Faraday's spine, cracking the wooden board in half.

The King bellowed, dropping Isaline to the ground. He turned on Donborough, then reached behind his back and unholstered his gun. Isaline pulled herself on hands and knees in front of Jack, unable to move her eyes from the pistol's menacing shine.

"*Wait,*" she cried, but Faraday didn't hesitate. He pulled the trigger. There was an air-cracking *boom,* and Donborough fell to the ground.

No. He had helped her—he had saved her instead of running away.

A second boulder fell through the branches above, landing behind the line of thrones with a burst of dust. Isaline coughed. The giant tree groaned and dipped. Roots snapped near the ceiling. Faraday glanced upward, but seemed only mildly distracted by the collapsing tree.

He pinned his gaze on Isaline and Jack. He raised his gun.

Isaline's stomach lurched. "Wait, stop—" she stammered, but her senses descended beneath a haze of fear. The barrel of the gun yawned, smoke billowing from its mouth. Isaline seized Jack around the chest and attempted to push him behind the throne. His pulse fluttered weakly beneath her hand. He was alive, but not for long.

Faraday cocked the pistol. The gunshot split the air.

Isaline stiffened, numbness spreading through her. She waited for pain to bloom somewhere in her body, for her blood to soak the ground—but there was neither pain nor blood. She patted her chest, her legs. Unhurt.

Faraday's attention had been diverted; a bird's silhouette had wrapped its claws in his hair, squawking and tugging at his scalp. Faraday fired the gun again, this time above his own head, but the bullet missed the bird's beating wings by inches. Gears rotated in his exposed chest, letting forth a shimmering light.

Real, was the only word Isaline's mind could conjure. The bird was real. Not a hallucination.

And it was giving her a chance.

Her blood quickened. Leaving Jack on the ground, Isaline flew to her feet, grasping the trident in firm fingers. She pulled the staff up and behind her head. The three razor-sharp blades gleamed in the firelight, bordered by the quaking branches of the ancient tree.

Isaline ran at the King. She released a cry, stabbed

through the air, and rammed the trident straight into his heart.

Gears crunched, the trident's blades embedding into sputtering metal. Faraday roared, a sound muffled by the sudden gush of Adrudian Milk from his mouth. Smoke and steam burst from his chest. The trident's staff was wrested from Isaline's hands, and she stumbled backward, shutting her mouth against the Milk that fountained over her face and hair.

"*What—have—you* ..." Faraday's gaze shifted to the staff sticking out of his chest. His pistol wagged through the air as he wrapped his free hand around the staff and yanked. The trident snapped in half, its blades buried in his thundering engine. He fell to his knees.

Energy tore at Isaline's limbs. She couldn't have killed Faraday, only delayed him. She had no other weapon, and rocks were plummeting in groups, filling the House of Matchsticks with staccato bangs and clouds of dust. The canopy of the tree lurched, dropping a full foot as its roots splintered from the ceiling.

"Time to go," she said to Jack, who was still motionless on the ground. His eyes flicked in her direction.

"You cannot destroy this place." Faraday's voice was a burble beneath the din of the splitting ceiling. He hunched over, shoulders rounded. "The House of Matchsticks will rebuild."

Isaline didn't bother to ask what he meant. Grabbing Jack under the arms, she dragged his limp body from the line of thrones and toward the exit. Her arms screamed, muscles burning. The mouth of a tunnel was in sight, a dark opening in the cave wall. The bird's silhouette raced in circles around her head. *Faster.* If Isaline could just get them into the tunnel, out from under the tree, she could ...

A gunshot whizzed through the air.

Isaline stopped. She felt herself jolt, her body tightening and releasing in the space of a second. The world blurred and glistened, dreamlike, and Jack fell from her arms. She looked down at herself. A flower of blood was opening on the right side of her chest.

"Oh," she murmured, barely breathing. "Oh."

Her legs wobbled, then sagged. The ground came to meet her with a muted *whump.* She sprawled on her back, her heartbeat pounding in her throat. Tangles of branches above her knocked and swayed. Jack's head rested on her calves. The bird screeched, a falling stone passing through its wing. It spiraled to the ground.

Just a little farther, she tried to say to it. *We're almost there.*

But her mouth wouldn't form the words, and her mind wouldn't work. Everything inside her was shivering. Outside, too. The roots on the ceiling gave one final groan before tearing free of the rock.

Isaline lay still, fire licking her chest, as the tree came down.

Darkness. Silence.

She opened her eyes.

The torches had been extinguished by what Isaline could only guess had been a gale of crushed rock and chipped wood. She took a shallow breath. Her shoulder and chest burned. Hot, excruciating, and wet.

Isaline's brain told her to get up, but when she tried to shift, she found that she couldn't move. Her right arm was pinned under a heavy object. A tree branch. The wood creaked when she feebly attempted to extract herself.

It was no use. She wasn't going anywhere. She lay back.

Silence had descended over the House of Matchsticks. Isaline peered into the dark. Where was Faraday? Adrises? A pebble fell from somewhere, clattering off heaps of fallen rocks and branches.

"J-Jack?" Isaline said. Her voice was thin.

There was no response.

Her right side pulsed with a crystalline agony, sharp like the edges of the precious stones on the shelves in Little Space. She moaned. A small sigh came from on top of her chest. Looking down, Isaline saw a bird lying on her breastbone, wings unfurled and motionless. Faint stars shone through the shadow of its body.

"Are you hurt, too?" she whispered to it.

The bird laid its head over her heart and sang a low, weak tune.

Isaline listened until the song faded. She sniffed. Even

breathing was painful, each gasp sending needles of fire through her limbs. But another feeling had grown alongside the pain: a strange *undoing*, as if the buckles of her body were softly coming apart.

I'm dying, she realized.

It wasn't so bad. She closed her eyes and imagined herself in the clearing at Casret Academy. Leaves swished against a cloudless sky. Grass wove between her bare toes. She had been told there was a river, not far away, from which she could drink.

And someone else was there, too. Isaline could feel her. A girl with her hair tied into a knot at the nape of her neck.

Nalissa, Isaline thought. *Nalissa, I'm here.*

She wasn't sure if she said it out loud, but maybe she had. When she opened her eyes, and the blackness of the House of Matchsticks rushed in, Nalissa was there. Walking toward her through the dark.

Nalissa's face shone with the same warmth Isaline remembered, her body radiant with a calm glow. A smile played over her lips. She was wearing an all-weather jacket, as if she were taking the Survival Portion of her Weeklong Review.

Tears filled Isaline's eyes.

I'm sorry. She tried to move again, but her body was frozen. *I miss you.*

It was then that she noticed Nalissa was leading someone by the arm. A second figure, taller than Nalissa was, but walking with the same gait. Ghostly, as if drifting on an ocean of air. A man—he had one hand grasping the brim of his hat, and the other holding Nalissa's leading arm. A lantern hung over his elbow, emitting a gentle, sky-blue light.

Isaline was suddenly certain that her life was over. It was the only logical conclusion. She had to be dying, because this man couldn't be real.

She had to be dying, because this man was made of stars.

11

A PART
THE COLLECTOR

On the surface, after the King's engine had disappeared into the mine shaft, the rain went on until morning. Light crossed a colorless sky. Night swept in again. The Collector remained alone in the shadow of the mill, trying not to breathe.

It had been easy before, the Collector realized. Not breathing. Even when his lungs had withered in the palace in Ar, it had been easier. The urge of three days ago was nothing compared to this.

His throat was a hiss of vapor, the need for air a constant strike of lightning through his bones. The Collector couldn't open his mouth. If he tasted air, he knew he would gulp it as if he were parched. He wouldn't be able to stop. Humanity would flood him, and his world would alter irreparably.

Caladrius is gone. The words repeated over and over in the Collector's mind. *You've abandoned her.*

Fear was the only feeling that eclipsed his need to breathe. The Collector slouched against the concrete retaining wall and watched the sky dim, trapped between suffocation and his own terror. Caladrius was in trouble, but if he went into the mines to find her, he would breathe. If he breathed, he could become human, and if he became human, he might die.

The Collector couldn't go on. He couldn't go back, either.

Instead, he waited.

Hours passed as if days. The ocean waxed and waned, taunting him with its rhythm. When he wasn't thinking about Caladrius, the Collector's mind turned to the memories the air had given him in the palace. He had felt his body skirting the edge of a giant, dead tree. He had looked back to see two others—a woman and a little girl—waving him goodbye. His family.

The Collector hugged his knees to his chest. He had been a father. What had it felt like? Had he been a good dad to his daughter?

Take a breath.

No.

Sea breeze passed through his body like mist. Closing his eyes, the Collector imagined himself dangling off a cliff, trying to keep hold of everything he thought he knew. Wandering Benemourne, collecting souls, watching them travel beyond the clouds. He and Caladrius had spent a century as a gateway. The Collector had never wanted to be the one walking through the gate. The one falling off the cliff.

Then ... he had pushed a rowboat.

At midnight on the second day, the Collector's gaze snagged on twinkling constellations. The canopy of the sky was vast and clear, and he imagined the baby's face, sixteen years ago, looking on with wonder at stars hidden behind smoke. His mind hadn't known how it felt to be human, to see the world come alive with mysteries.

Still, the Collector reasoned, his body had known. His soul had known. *Yes*—there was a soul housed in his chest. He knew that now. His soul had been the one speaking to him, encouraging him to breathe and remember.

The man you were, it said, *guided your hand to the rowboat.*

The man you were would have done anything if it meant that baby could go on living.

The Jar of Lights sat beside him. The Collector played with the wire handle, watching his arm drink the starlight. The souls inside the lantern swirled as if caught in a tiny, microcosmic sea. Lillian and Philip Just floated to face him.

"What good did it do?" the Collector asked them, risking the parting of his lips. "I saved her life. What was it for?"

To his surprise, Lillian and Philip slipped to the back

of the lantern, parting to make way for another soul. A brilliant, daffodil-yellow light came forward. The girl under the blanket at Casret Academy.

The Collector stared, his fingers embedded in the rocky shore. The soul rose from the Jar of Lights and hovered in the air before him.

"Hello." His astonishment lessened the pain in his lungs. "Are you leaving?"

The soul spun in the air, as if replying *no* to his question. Its movement reminded him of Caladrius. His chest twinged. Before the Collector knew what he was doing, he lifted his hand, palm up. The orb of light came to rest between his fingers. He brought it to his face.

"Talk to me," he said. "Please."

Nestled in his hands, the soul quivered. It shone like a minute sun, releasing radiance that rivaled even the Jar of Lights. From its center, a wave of feeling fanned through the Collector. He drew up his shoulders. This was communication without language.

Calm spread through him, and in an instant, he bore the soul's feelings as if they were his own. Warmth and friendship. Closeness.

Gratitude.

The ocean crashed. The Collector's heart began to pound. He suddenly understood; this was the soul of the child he had saved. Memories filled him. He saw sky above sea, and a fisherman, who spotted the rowboat drifting. He saw Nalissa—because that was her name—being taken in by the Quandary of Thieves. He saw her at Casret Academy, laughing with an umber-haired girl the Collector recognized. A girl that had looked so like Nalissa, the Collector hadn't realized his mistake.

His blood grew hot in his veins. "It was you. I saved you that night. Not Isaline."

Nalissa's soul bobbed, as if nodding.

"You lived a good life." The emotion in his voice startled him. "You were happy."

She bobbed again, and a lump appeared in the Collector's throat. Nalissa's memories had flowed through him, leaving only a trace of the love she had felt, but that trace was enough to rattle his bones. To open his eyes.

Moonlight shone as the Collector came to an abrupt realization.

He had done a good thing.

Nalissa's soul watched him closely. As the Collector's focus fell back to her, she twirled, indicating the path behind him. The path to the mill. His hands shook.

"I can't. If I help them, I'll remember who I was," he said. "I helped you, and I started to want to breathe. I'll *change.*"

She huddled against his palms, warmth exuding from her light. Her message was clear: *We all change.*

In the end, all will be Collected.

The Collector pushed his knees beneath him and peeked over the retaining wall. The mill was a mountain of shadow swallowing the black clouds. If he went after

Caladrius now, would it be too late? Would she have breathed enough air to live?

He turned to Nalissa's soul. "I won't be able to find my way."

She danced in the air, as if laughing.

NALISSA'S SOUL led him by the hand down the mine shaft and through a maze of tunnels. The Collector's courage wavered as they traveled deeper, but the urge to breathe had lessened, as if movement restored his energy.

His surroundings were crowded with invisible horrors. The darkness was as impenetrable as it had been on his first visit to the mines, when he had collected the souls of pickaxers burned in the mill fire. Craning his head, the Collector studied the stalactites spiking the ceiling. This place hadn't changed. It crept a hand into his stomach and clenched.

As they came to the entrance of a giant cavern, the Collector spotted two figures hoisting a second over the lip of a gorge. He came to a stop, watching as Winn, Neave, and Jame collapsed on the flat ground, breaths ragged.

"We can't—just—*leave her here,*" Jame rasped. His chest rose and fell at a rapid pace.

Winn had already risen to her feet. She had one wrist wrapped in a bandage, the other clutched tightly in her tool belt. "She made her choice."

"Only because the King threatened us."

The Collector's stomach dropped. Faraday had found them. He stepped closer, examining their dirt-streaked faces. Exhausted lines bunched at the corner of Winn's mouth, Neave's makeup was running, and Jame's eyes were wide and scared. If the Collector didn't know they were the same party from Little Space, he might not recognize them.

Winn used the tip of a knife to dig a rock from the sole of her boot. "Isaline lied. She told us she was a Quandary Thief ... our whole expedition could have been compromised."

Neave stood, rubbing her shoulder. "It's already been compromised, Princess. We need to get out of here."

"But she's alone," Jame insisted. "There has to be something else we can do for her, and Jack, and Cameron."

The Collector drummed his fingers on the Jar of Lights. Isaline had split from the rest of the group—but where had she gone? Had the King kidnapped her?

Winn said, "Our best option is to go to the surface and come up with a plan. We'll come back."

"*Come back?*" Jame flew to his feet. "She'll be dead by then!"

"If we follow Neave's marks—" She gestured to the tunnel entrance, no doubt referring to the glowing orange Xs the Collector had passed on his way here. "—we can get back to the surface quickly. We can return with reinforcements before anything happens. I don't want Isaline to get hurt, either."

"But—"

"Stop, please, both of you." Neave dropped her head into her hands. "Just ... let's breathe for a second. We can't help Isaline right now. The King will kill us if we try anything ... but I've seen her fight. She can take care of herself, and Jack and Cameron will make sure she's safe. They were all headed to the same place."

Jame's frown deepened. "We're just going to hope, then? And what about Adrises?"

The Collector had been drifting toward the gorge, making to look over the side, but now he stopped. *Adrises.* The name was an insect in his ear. Where had he heard it before?

Take a breath.

"We don't know enough," Winn said. "We can't stop the ritual, but Cameron and Jack will. And Isaline knows what she's doing." She checked her watch. "If we hurry, we can get to the surface by sunrise. Come on."

The three of them jogged into the tunnels, their headlamps shrinking into the pitch-black.

The Collector looked at Nalissa's soul floating on his upturned palm. "Isaline." The soul bobbed, light shining a nimbus over his fingers. "Caladrius will be with her—that's where we need to go."

She steered him down a steep, zig-zagging passageway that spit them out at the bottom of the gorge. From there, they skimmed over a roaring river and entered another tunnel. Sweltering air vented from cracks in the rock and poked at the Collector's mouth, trying to enter his lungs. He bit his lips closed.

They had been traveling downriver for some time when they came across the Head Inspector.

Cameron was wading against the current, holding his weapons belt above his head. His cheeks shone wetly in the blue glow from the Jar of Lights. The Collector stood at the tunnel's edge and watched him as he passed out of sight.

"He's going back to the surface, too." The Collector glanced at Nalissa's soul. "That leaves Isaline and Jack down here."

She made no answer, only led him deeper into the mines.

Faraday's workshop came next. With anxious hands, the Collector inspected a destroyed mining cart for bodies, but there were none. He climbed into a dark hole in the floor of the workshop and followed a round passage beneath. Finally, he stood before a glowing wall.

The Collector let his eyes roam over the illuminated design, his mouth going dry. Three squares overlaid on each other, lines intersecting the pattern at top and bottom, left and right. The same symbol he had seen tattooed on Theresa's neck sixteen years earlier.

He had forgotten about the tattoo, but now the

memory shone clear in his mind, punctuated by Johannes Faraday's oily voice.

You chose this ... but she *chose* me. *In the cave. In the House of Matchsticks.*

The Collector set down the Jar of Lights and smoothed his hand over the symbol. The rock was freezing cold. This was it. The entrance to the House of Matchsticks, the ritual site Isaline's group had been looking for.

Nalissa's soul shone with shimmering light. The Collector looked at her.

"They're in there, aren't they?"

She bobbed—*come*—and pulled him through the wall and into the House of Matchsticks.

The threshold behind the wall was narrow and short, no bigger than a crawlspace. The Collector melted through the rock and faced the massive cave on the other side.

The silence here was as oppressive as the dark. A great hush blanketed the House of Matchsticks, as if time was caught in the moment after a dying exhale. The Collector lifted the Jar of Lights. Blue slanted over rough-hewn walls streaked with black paint. At his feet, a giant pile of rocks and debris stretched outside his light. Interspersed with the rocks were the black, splintered limbs of tree branches.

Tree branches? In a cave?

The Collector took a hesitant step inside. "Caladrius?"

No answer.

Nalissa's soul tugged with a renewed vigor at his hand. The Collector allowed her to lead him over heaps of shattered rocks toward the center of the room, where he was met with a strange sight: Johannes Faraday, lying prone on the ground beneath a felled tree's giant trunk.

The Collector approached with cautious steps. The King's face was pressed to the side, Adrudian Milk puddling beneath one brass cheek. His eyes were open and blank. The rest of him was crushed beneath the black trunk, bits of brass scattered underfoot.

Despite all this, Johannes was alive. Unconscious, but somehow breathing, air leaking from his nostrils. Just as he had been on the dock sixteen years ago. The Collector shook his head. Time had bitten its own tail, the night of the mill fire resolving in front of him like a mirror.

Beyond the King were seven stone thrones, sitting in a row and topped with skeletons.

The Collector touched the brim of his hat. A shiver trickled down his spine. Something about the thrones and bodies pulled a wire taut in his mind. The feeling before remembering.

Take a breath. Take a breath. Take a breath.

No. No. No.

He dragged his gaze from the bones and studied the ground, where boulders had amassed in a circle around the thrones. No falling rocks or branches had disturbed the skeletons. It was as if the rocks had simply bounced off, or some unknowable magic had warded them away.

Nalissa's soul twirled on his palm, drawing him to the right. The Collector stepped back from the thrones and surveyed the spread of rocks and branches at the back of the cave. Something caught his eye: a glint within a thick nest of boughs.

"Cal?" The Collector said, but he already knew it was her. A pile of silhouetted feathers peeked from within the branches, daubed with points of dim light.

A faint tweet responded. The Collector's heart seemed to vanish. He rushed toward her, leaving Nalissa's soul in the air to follow. The Jar of Lights rolled from his arm and clattered to the ground. He had eyes only for that little body folded, those wings outstretched, those black eyes half-closed.

"Caladrius." He kneeled next to her. She was lying on the chest of someone buried beneath a ribcage of boughs. The face was wrapped in shadows, but he knew those clothes—Isaline. "I'm here."

Caladrius made a weak sound. The Collector reached between the branches, but his fingers stilled, hovering in mid-air. He was afraid to touch her. She was lying as if injured, but he couldn't see where she had been hurt.

"What happened, Cal?"

Her beak opened, and to the Collector's horror, a hint of yellow appeared. A starling's beak. *Changing*. Panic rooted itself in his stomach. The tips of her wings were unraveling, as if spooling off into space, and the barbs of a starling's feather protruded.

"Oh, Caladrius," the Collector whispered. Without thinking—without considering the consequences—he shoved the branches away from Isaline's body. They cracked and fragmented at his touch, the spectral ink of his hands spreading over the wood, then receding when he released them.

Isaline lay on the ground on her back, her arms resting to either side, limp. Dark blood soaked her shoulder and pooled beneath her head, smearing her hair. Her right elbow had been crushed by a heavy bough. Her eyes were closed.

The Collector bit back a groan. Dead? No—she had fainted. Isaline's chest pulsed weakly. Caladrius lifted and fell with her breaths.

He sat back on his heels, following the line of Isaline's body to her legs. A second person was draped over her feet, tangled black hair spilling over a blue-lined face. Jack.

The Collector stared as Jack's eyes shifted in the dark, pupils swallowing his blue irises. He was uninjured, but he couldn't seem to move. His fingers twitched and wiggled. Rocks were piled around him as they were around the thrones, as if a magic had wicked them from his body.

What *was* this place?

"Cal ..." The Collector turned back to Caladrius and

gently slid a shaking hand beneath her, cupping her in his palm. Her weight, so light before this, rested like a stone in his hand. "I'm here now."

She twittered quietly. The Collector's chest heaved. He needed to breathe, and he couldn't. He needed to save her, and he couldn't. She was coming alive.

"Of all the visitors I've had today," a voice said, *"I had never guessed you would come, Collector."*

The Collector startled. He whirled, searching for the source of the voice, but there was nothing. Only darkness. Nalissa's soul had returned to the Jar of Lights, leaving him alone with Caladrius and the humans.

"Who—who's there?" he said, holding Caladrius protectively to his chest. Her breaths puffed against his neck.

"Someone who knew you, long ago. You can call me Adrises. What brings you back to my house?"

Adrises. This time, the name rattled something deep in the Collector's brain, something he'd never known was there. He shuddered, his spine rocking.

"How can you see me?"

"I see many things. Now I'll ask you again: what brings you back to my house?"

The Collector stood, holding Caladrius gently in one hand. He retrieved the Jar of Lights and swung the light in a circle. Rocks sent warped shadows over the walls.

"I'm here to ..." He hesitated. He didn't want to explain the urge to breathe that had brought him here, or the warmth that Nalissa had given him. After a pause, he asked, "What happened to this place?"

"Something extraordinary, Collector. A single ant has felled my tree. Without the tree, the source of my magic, I weakened even further ... I couldn't reach from these walls. I could merely watch as she interrupted my ritual."

The words meant nothing to the Collector. He drew Caladrius even closer to him and looked down at Isaline. Her skin was deathly gray. She didn't have long before she lost too much blood to wake up.

Adrises seemed to know what he was thinking. *"The House of Matchsticks will rebuild, Collector, but they will not. They will rot in this place like the others."* Her tone was low and dangerous, the sound of someone who's patience had worn to its last thread. *"Take your bird, if you must, but leave the humans. They deserve their suffering."*

Caladrius released a soft coo. The Collector brought his hand to his face and stroked a gentle finger down her feathers. He could carry her back to the surface and try to convince her to close her lungs, stop the change before she was lost. But what would happen then? She would be caught between two worlds, and she had never wanted that. She had chased the change, had accepted it.

And if Isaline and Jack died here, Caladrius would be lost to the Collector for nothing. She would have tried to help for nothing.

She would one day die, for nothing.

Adrises said, *"If you deign to save these humans,*

Collector, they will return to my house. Without my tree, I may not be able to lure my final Treasurehunter back here with magic, but ..." Her voice crawled into the Collector's ears. "*I will choke their Adrudian until the world bleeds.*"

The Adrudian shortage. Adrises was behind it—and she could make it worse. The Collector's stomach churned. Benemourne without Adrudian was a dead world. There would be nothing to power their machines.

His eyes fell to Isaline's drooping body, and Jack twitching on the ground. Surely two human lives couldn't be worth ...

But the memories Nalissa had given him rang in his heart, a bell's toll. If the Collector left them here, of what life would Isaline and Jack be deprived? What moments of joy or sorrow? Moments with their friends and those they loved? Moments the Collector had called *wonder*?

His spirit filled him and abated. The rhythm of a breath.

The man you were, it said, *would never leave them to die. He would save them and help them find another way.*

The Collector felt the words were referring to someone else. He didn't know the man he had been. He hadn't walked in a human body in a hundred years. His century had been spent skimming above the footprints of that man's buried dreams.

Was it too late to recover himself? He was terrified to discover what he had forgotten. Terrified of ending.

Maybe not today, or tomorrow, but one day in the future, when his existence was used up.

"I can't do this," he murmured. "I can't do this."

Caladrius stirred. She rested her soft head on the inside of his knuckles. The content of her body had changed even in the short time he'd held her. The stars in her wings had soared into the distance, her feathers, beak, and even the top of her head edging into reality.

She had been brave. The Collector imagined her flitting against a moonlit sky, drawing him toward a bright spot of flame on the horizon. Cal had always known where to go.

And, the Collector realized, the only feeling stronger than fear was his desire to follow her. To let her lead him.

He was going to do a good thing.

Swallowing, he tucked Caladrius into the breast pocket of his coat, where she lay close to his beating heart. A heart that had somehow endured in space, inside the stars, all this time. She went with a short song, an understanding.

"*Do not think of this, Collector,*" Adrises said from the walls. "*I know the transformation you underwent. I know what will happen to you if you interfere with humans.*"

The Collector didn't respond. He hooked the Jar of Lights around his elbow. Then he kneeled on one knee and pressed a tentative hand to Isaline's chest. The darkness of his body spread onto hers, slowly encompassing her in a starry, hollow shadow.

It was painless, he thought, for things he touched to enter his unreality. Maybe it would be just as painless for him to be human.

He slid his arms beneath Isaline's back and knees and lifted her to his chest, careful not to bump Caladrius in his pocket. Isaline's head rested in the crook of his neck, lolling unconsciously onto his collar. She was warm, but cooling fast.

"*She's just a girl.*" Adrises' anger rippled through him. "*She is insignificant. You are willing to forfeit your existence for* her?"

The Collector lifted his chin and studied the black void of the ceiling. If he retraced his steps through the mines, Isaline would die before he made it to the surface. The only way out was straight up. He prayed he had the energy to ascend through miles of rock and ocean without falling down again, and without losing his nerve.

"*Her existence is nothing.*"

"It might be nothing," the Collector said, glancing down at the Jar of Lights, "but I know now what she will miss."

Adrises growled, the foundations of the House of Matchsticks trembling. The Collector eased his gaze to Jack, who, to the Collector's amazement, was looking straight at him.

"I can only carry one of you at a time," the Collector said. Jack's eyes widened. "I'll come back for you."

"*Listen to me,*" Adrises said. Her voice had become an

earthquake, loud enough to make the buried tree branches rustle and sway. *"If you save her, Collector, you will change. One day, you will die."*

The Collector felt air graze his lips. It pushed him, the untold past, the potential of what he could be, and what he had been. He summoned his courage into armor. Unflinching. *Real.*

"Then I will die," he said.

He kicked off the ground and rose into the air.

Solid rock left his feet and he ascended through the House of Matchsticks, up into darkness.

The wind ruffled the ends of the Collector's coat and the curls of Isaline's hair. She was bathed in stars, as if she had become a part of him, an extension of his body. The Collector tightened his grip on her and focused on the ceiling, getting closer now, stalactites emerging into the halo of blue from the Jar of Lights.

A second later, they melted through the stalactites and into the bones of the Earth. Firm rock enveloped the Collector. He pushed, flying upward with all the strength he had, the Jar of Lights dangling from his elbow, Isaline held flush to his chest.

What am I doing? What am I doing? his panicked mind repeated, but aloud he said, "Keep going."

He rose higher, faster.

A change registered as the rock became a tunnel. Then, in a split-second, he was through another ceiling and into the rock again. Around him, the Jar of Lights illuminated multicolored stripes in the stone, sediment that had compressed and fused with eons. Layers of time winked in rapid succession as he climbed. A moment later, the skeleton of a giant, unrecognizable animal flew past. A fossil encased in the ground it had once walked on.

The Collector watched the fossil disappear below his feet. This place was old, older than him by eternities. He felt very small in its hold, like a speck of dust. His heart pounded.

What good did it do? I saved her life. What was it for?

Fear wracked his body and screamed for him to stop. His body burned with the effort of carrying both himself and Isaline upward.

"Don't stop," he told himself. "Keep going."

Rock turned into tunnel, into rock, into tunnel. The Collector tried to envision himself as a bird gliding up the trunk of an enormous tree. If he could get to the top, if he could get to the canopy, he could break free into the sweet, fresh air.

But the more he flew, the more the reserves of his energy drained. Fire set his limbs ablaze, overwhelming, blinding. The rate of his climb began to lessen. Isaline's breaths against his neck weakened, dying. Her blood dripped down the back of his coat.

"No." He tried to pull higher. "*No!*"

But it was no use. He couldn't go any further. He slowed, and slowed, until he was hovering in place. Then he quickly couldn't do even that, and he began to fall, his insides jumping into his throat. He tried to change his composition so he could stand, but stand on what? They were in the center of a great, solid crust of earth.

They plunged. The Collector's body jolted uncontrollably, his arms clutching Isaline with the only power he had left. Air buffeted his clothes. He kicked with his feet but found no purchase. He gripped the brim of his hat to keep it from flying into the abyss.

Down, and down, and down. A yell pulled from his mouth. They were plummeting too fast; they would shoot all the way past the House of Matchsticks and fall into the deep, unplumbed chasms below. Freezing air brought tears to his eyes. He closed them.

I tried. I'm sorry. I wasn't strong enough.

Then a light flared outside his eyelids, followed by a heart-shaking wrench, and his movement stalled.

He hung, suspended, in silence. A twitter met his ears.

The sound made his heart tremble. The Collector opened his eyes. Stone surrounded him—he was still inside the mines, but he had stopped falling. A bird fluttered in front of his face, wings outstretched, sparkling feathers.

Caladrius.

She had wriggled from his pocket. She flew in a circle

around his head, singing, nudging him with her claws. Her song was joyous and alive.

"You're ..." Words failed him. Had she been restored by his movement? Had she been saving the last for this?

Caladrius dipped and dove, buoyed by a phantom breeze inside the rock. Pinpricks of light twinkled through the shadow of her body, obscuring the yellow beak and bird's feathers poking from her silhouette.

The Collector stretched out his hand to her, a gesture as natural as thought. She landed in the cup of his palm, and the contact lit an ember between them. *Magic.*

His mouth fell open as light so vivid it was almost liquid bubbled from his hand, connecting his palm and Caladrius' claws. Their surroundings shone bright gold and resplendent. The two of them were still for an instant, tucked in a pocket of light deep underground. His hand grew warm.

Caladrius sang, as if to say, *Follow me.*

She leaped from his hand and flew upward. The light vanished, but miraculously, inexplicably, the Collector felt himself elevate. Slowly, at first, but then gaining speed, hurtling through the rock. Gravity's force pressed his hat to the top of his head, and he laughed at the sensation of being lifted, boosted from underneath.

Rock soared past, twinkling minerals and mica melding into a kaleidoscope beneath the Jar of Lights. The Collector didn't need to kick or use his energy, this time—

he found that his body was light. His strength had gone, but he flew upward as if caught in a current. An updraft.

Despite his fear, despite his caution, the Collector's heart soared. He fixed his eyes on Caladrius above. She surged on wings of glittering starlight, darting and twirling and dancing through the cold rock, singing a tune of exaltation the likes of which the Collector had never heard. She pulled him. Her movement was *his* movement. A chain had linked them, and as he pressed Isaline to his chest the way he might have once done with his own daughter, the Collector understood.

This was what it meant to make waves with the push of a hand, to be a part of a world where life rippled and evolved with every small choice. To be linked to everything around him, everything breathing and alive. To exist.

To Caladrius, the Collector thought, *I will always follow where you lead.*

He did follow her. He followed her until they were rising so fast the tunnels passing by were like the sputtering flickers of a candle flame. He followed her when the rock gradually gave over to sand, and then again to a churning, emerald sea. He followed her up through an enormous crevasse deep in the water, where the headlights of strange creatures swarmed and swam. He followed her into a glimmering cloud of silver, a school of fish, and when he waved out his arm the fish waved with him, caught in the Collector's murmuration as he was in theirs, shimmering scales like constellations leading to the next, and the next, and the next.

The Collector followed Caladrius until the surface of the sea came to meet them.

He squeezed his eyes shut, holding onto Isaline's still-breathing body. They burst from the water. Ocean spray fell and scattered at his feet, evanescing into the foamy waves. A blanket of dawn stars stretched across the sky, made light by the new sun from the east. He changed his composition, letting the ocean soak his clothes all the way through, and his fear dispersed into the waiting air.

The Collector opened his mouth and took one long, gasping, salt-scented breath.

12

WORLD INSIDE

ISALINE

On the morning she was carried from the mines, Isaline returned to consciousness to find that she had been having a mysterious dream.

Her eyelids fluttered, her fragmented mind recalling the events in the House of Matchsticks. Nalissa had been walking toward her through the destroyed cave, gliding over rocks and tree branches. She had been leading someone by the arm—but who? A starry man with a long coat, a hat, and a blue lantern. As he approached, a bird had lain on Isaline's chest and sang.

Then there was a peculiar feeling, like her limbs had evaporated into fog. She didn't understand why she felt that way, and it wasn't a feeling she could conjure now. It just was.

Strangest of all, she dreamed she was flying. A

moment of pure confusion swam back to her. She had opened her eyes to see a multicolored world rushing by at an impossible speed. She had been held by someone strong and intangible at once. The pain in her chest and arm had disappeared. The moment just *was*, and then she had fainted.

Now Isaline was here, soaking wet, freezing, and drifting with the tide on a rocky shore. She floated on her back in shallow water, salt stinging the gunshot wound on the right side of her chest. Her elbow had been dipped in fire. Morning sky stretched above, rose pink and butter yellow. Her eyes had trouble focusing, but she caught the edge of a flashlight beam pointed at her from a distance.

"It's her!" a voice cried.

Splashing footsteps approached. Someone kneeled over her, knees dunking in the water at her side. A gentle hand brushed her cheek. There were metal bands over the fingers. Rings.

"Isaline." The voice was familiar, but had never said her name before. Warmth spread into her belly despite the agony slicing her chest. "Stay with me, come on." The person lifted his head and called across the shore. "Isaline's here! She's hurt, we need help!"

Isaline tried to sharpen her focus. Her brain wouldn't obey. The face above her remained blurry, a splotch of dark hair and freckles. She lifted her hand from the water and a trickle of droplets fell from her wrist.

"Where am I?" she mumbled.

The boy rubbed water away from her cheek with the pad of his thumb. "Outside the mill—you made it out. We're going to get you help. It'll be okay."

The comforting tone of his voice sparked recognition.

"Jame," she said.

He picked a curl of wet hair from her forehead. "Hey."

Isaline released a rattling breath, her muscles tensing and relaxing. Jame drew her floating body closer to him, the small of her back resting on the tops of his thighs. Seawater washed into her ears, and vaguely she heard a *crack* from another part of the island. The streak of a flare signaled for rescue across the dawn sky.

I'm back on the surface, she thought, but her relief mingled with remorse. She gazed up at Jame and recalled the stories she had told, the tapestries of lies she had sewn him. If she lived, she was going to undo those tapestries knot by knot.

"I stole your fire," she murmured. It was an old lie, but the one that had begun all of this. "In the forest. I lit my fire with yours."

Jame laughed and stroked her temple. She could feel his smile on his fingertips.

"I know. I know you stole my fire," Jame said. He sounded far away. "You still have it, Watchling."

THE NEXT THING she knew was soft sheets. Her head balanced on a thin pillow. Afternoon sun was slanting through a round window above her, casting dusty light on smooth wooden walls, an old-looking wardrobe, and a desk.

Isaline blinked, knowing the room was familiar, but unable to place it. When she tried to move her arm, she found that it was bound tight to her chest in thick bandages. Her shoulder throbbed with a dull pain. She groaned.

Something across the room shifted, and the heel of a boot tapped on the floorboards.

"You're awake."

Isaline lifted her head. It was Cameron, sitting in a wooden chair beside the cracked-open door. His legs were stretched in front of him, ankles crossed, the ash gray of a fashionable sock peeking from beneath his hems. The folds of his Head Inspector's coat had been draped tidily over the back of his chair.

"You've been asleep," he said. "Do you know where you are?"

Pushing her hair from her eyes, Isaline looked around. The space was coming back to her—she had spent a restless night here a lifetime ago. "The Harper and Cup."

Relief washed over Cameron's face. "Thank the stars. I was worried whatever brew Minna gave you might have been too strong. You were out for a week."

"What—what happened?" Isaline sat up, bending

gingerly at the waist. She winced at her smarting shoulder. Her limbs felt heavy as lead.

"We found you outside the mill." He sat forward, tugging at his sleeves. "You and Jack. Both of you alive."

An image came to her: Jack, limp on the seventh throne in the House of Matchsticks. Her hands under his arms, trying to drag him toward the exit. They had made it out. Adrises hadn't killed them. The King hadn't caught them. She sighed as the memories settled on her chest.

"Faraday attacked me," she murmured. "Adrises ... I spoke to her. I wasn't the keystone. It was my friend who—"

Cameron stood and lifted his palms, stopping her. "Jack filled us in. He heard and saw everything. He said you saved him. Us. Everyone. You knew what to do."

Isaline envisioned the firework exploding on the cracked ceiling of the cave, the ancient tree's groan, the crunch of the trident in Faraday's engine. Her hand flew to her neck, touching her empty collarbones. The pendant had been left underground, slotted into the door of Adrises' prison.

"The King ..." she said, looking at Cameron.

"Disappeared. His clockworks are guarding the palace, and he almost never went outside, before ... there'll be some time before anyone notices. One advantage to having clockworks do his bidding, I guess." He passed a hand over his clean-shaven face. "We think he's still down there. Probably not dead, but we have a head start in finding a way to kill him, now. Neave's been in Ar's library archives all week, trying to find information on Adrises' power and how to stop it."

"The archives?" Isaline gawked at him. "There could be information on Adrises in the library?"

Cameron's teeth flashed white. "We were hoping she'd find stories no one had paid attention to before. Stories no one knew were real."

Real. Isaline opened her palm on her lap. Had any of it been real? The bird, the man with the lantern, the *flying*? Or had those moments been mere images summoned by her dying brain?

Her mouth was dry as sand. Maybe it didn't matter what was real. What mattered was that she was alive, Adrises hadn't been freed, and she had bought them time. She knew the truth about the pendant and Nalissa. She knew who she was, and who she wasn't.

With effort, Isaline swung her legs from the bed and let her feet dangle over the hardwood floor. Despite her exhaustion, a balloon expanded in her chest. Her identity had been revealed to her friends at last. Once she touched her feet to the ground, she could start being whoever she wanted to be. Not Nalissa—just Isaline.

"I'm sorry I ..." She locked eyes with Cameron, determined not to shy away from his friendly gaze. "I'm sorry I lied to you. I wish I hadn't."

He grinned. "You were forgiven the moment you saved our entire expedition, I think." Slipping a hand into his pocket, he retrieved a crumpled envelope. "Besides, we might have thought you were Nalissa but ... Isaline isn't exactly a stranger."

"What do you mean?"

Cameron tossed her the envelope. She caught it clumsily with one hand and shook out a leaf of folded parchment. When it furled open, she bit back another gasp. The letter was in Nalissa's handwriting.

The bulk of the message was addressed to Cameron. Isaline skimmed the paragraphs—Nalissa had been making arrangements to fail her Weeklong Review, travel to Ar with Neave, and stay at the Harper and Cup—but a short postscript at the end of the letter caught her attention.

P.S., Nalissa had written.

You mentioned this expedition will require a team. If you have space for one more, I'd like you to meet my best friend, Isaline. She's the best fighter at our school. She's smart and loyal, and she wants to see Ar more than anything. I would love for her to come with me.

Isaline pressed the letter to her chest. In another world, maybe she and Nalissa could have traveled together over the sea. The two of them: a girl who had been chosen by destiny, and a girl who had been chosen by her friend. For Isaline, it would have been enough. It still was.

"Thank you," she said to Cameron, blinking tears from her eyes.

"Keep it." He lifted his coat from the chair and threw

it in a black furl over his shoulders. Winking, he said, "I have enough adoring letters to last me a lifetime."

Before Isaline could respond, the door flew open and Winn Just came hurrying into the room, her blue skirts cinched at the waist by her tool belt.

"I thought I heard voices," she said. She took Isaline's free hand in both of hers, gentle on her own still-healing wrist. "You're awake, finally. How do you feel?"

Grease-streaked gloves hung from Winn's belt, and she had a pair of goggles pushed up onto her forehead, the black coils of her hair loose and bouncing. Isaline wondered what machine she had been tinkering with moments before.

"I feel ... good," Isaline said, and it was true. Her shoulder ached, but it was tolerable, and her arm was tight and warm in her bandages, but not painful.

"Great." Winn squeezed her hand and Isaline felt she might float from the bed. She *was* forgiven, at least for now. It was more than she could ask for. "I've been dying for you to wake up."

This brought Isaline up short. "Really?"

"Really. Our group was minus one."

The floating feeling grew and spread inside Isaline. A flush crept into her cheeks.

Over Winn's shoulder, Cameron smirked. "Don't be fooled. She's got another reason."

"There's always another reason, Cameron," Winn tutted. She sounded so much like Neave, Isaline had to smile. Reaching for her tools, Winn unclipped a pair of long, steel scissors. The blades glinted in the light from the window. "Can you stand?"

Isaline nodded, but she wasn't sure. Her muscles were weak from days lying in bed. Winn stepped back and Isaline pressed the soles of her bare feet to the floor. The wood was cool beneath her toes. She pushed to stand, her legs like tubes of rubber, but she teetered until she found her balance.

"Excellent," Winn said, eyes sparkling. "Now off come the bandages."

She took the scissors and snipped the wrappings holding Isaline's broken arm to her chest. Isaline started to protest, but her voice died as the gauze fell away and her arm extended painlessly from its sling. She tried to roll her shoulder. Hot needles stuck into her chest.

"The gunshot will hurt for a few days." Winn gathered the gauze and threw it in a ball to Cameron, who caught it awkwardly, surprised. "Minna said the wound was clean. She gave you medicine to speed up the healing, but it'll be a while until you can practice with your trident and—"

"I don't have a trident anymore."

"—you'll have to change your bandages. But your elbow ..."

Both Cameron and Winn watched as Isaline's eyes slid to her uncovered elbow. Her eyebrows shot up. A brass cuff had been braced into her joint, an ornate piece of metalwork that reached from the center of her forearm to the peak of her bicep. She gave her arm an experimental bend and the cuff folded with her, its shiny components interlocking in a smooth motion.

Winn gave her a satisfied smile. "Your elbow was crushed in the House of Matchsticks. Fusing your bones with brass was the only way to save your arm."

Isaline could do nothing but stare at it. The design was beautiful, swirling metal tendrils reaching over her skin. The detail reminded her of the branches of an oak tree. She hinged her elbow in a series of easy, rapid bends.

"Not bad," Cameron said. His Head Inspector's badge glittered in the sun.

"Of course it's *not bad*." Winn clipped the scissors back into her toolbelt, retrieved a match, and stuck it between her teeth. "I built it."

CHANGING into new clothes was one obstacle, walking was another, and getting down the stairs that led to the Harper and Cup's tavern was another still. The steps creaked beneath Isaline's fumbling feet, but Winn took her arm and helped her to the bottom. By the time they had walked into the tavern, Isaline's confidence had grown.

The tavern was bustling with people she didn't recognize, but the crowd didn't seem as alien to her as they had the night she first arrived. Tables of friends clinked their tankards together, groups of Treasurehunters pored over maps, and Thieves leaned nimbly back in their chairs. There were even a few City Watch sitting in the corner. Isaline recognized the two members of the Watch that had been with Donborough the night Jame had stolen his flask. With a pang, she wondered if they were discussing where Donborough had gone.

Behind the bar, Minna was accepting a coin with one hand and pouring a drink with the other. She nodded at Isaline, a warm look playing over her face, and Isaline nodded back.

Winn pushed through the double doors behind the bar and led them through the Harper and Cup's small kitchen. The door to Little Space was propped open, sunlight spilling onto the kitchen floor. Isaline lurched down Little Space's single tall step and was met with the smell of spices, bread, and the ocean. The long table at the center of the room was spread with papers and books, flanked by shelves of glittering stones. Deep green wallpaper shone clover in the light from the row of windows, curtains flung wide.

Neave sat at the end of the table, hunched over what looked like a worn map. Her braid was tied into a neat bun behind one ear, and she had one hand picking dried fruit from a plate piled high with food. Seeing Isaline, she broke into a broad grin.

"Looks like you decided to wake up," she said, tossing

a compass to the tabletop. Fresh ink covered the map—she'd been drawing a path. "How'd you sleep?"

"Okay." Isaline sank into a cushioned chair, minding the fresh gauze beneath the collar of her new top. She'd opened the wardrobe in her room to find it full of clothes: sleek black trousers, leather boots, and even a long fur coat that had made her heart leap. "I guess I have you to thank for my outfit."

Neave chewed and passed a hand over the top of her own knee-high boot. "Don't thank me. It was a simple necessity. I couldn't let you live in those horrible Casret Academy clothes forever."

"Neave was carting boxes from boutiques in Ar the moment we got back to land," Cameron said, tucking into a seat across the table. "I don't think she slept for two nights."

"We all have our strengths," Neave replied. "Mine just happens to be—" She passed a hand in front of Isaline, indicating her outfit from head to foot. "—this."

As Winn pulled out a seat next to Cameron, Isaline leaned forward to examine the map Neave had been studying. The parchment was yellowed at the edges, torn in one corner, and faded, but she could still make out the title emblazoned across the top in decorative letters: *The Shute.* Neave had drawn an ink line through clusters of trees and the curving bends of rivers. In the southwest, she had written *History?* by a mountain.

"A new expedition?" Isaline asked. The map had a

curious gravity; she couldn't tear her eyes from the path Neave had drawn.

"A side project." Neave leaned back in her chair. Her smile turned impish. "Speaking of which ... settle a bet, Princess. The Head Inspector doesn't think you'll want to come with us on this little foray."

Cameron bit noisily into a piece of bread from Neave's plate. "The Princess has better things to do than—"

'What is it?" Winn asked, chewing on the end of her match.

Neave popped her knuckles, shooting a sly look at Cameron. "I've been researching Ancient Benemournian deities, trying to learn everything I can about the gods' imprisonment. I couldn't find any documents that reference Adrises, or how Adrudian was discovered. A shame, considering that's exactly what we need to know to stop the world from going dark." She looked across the table at Cameron. "But then Jack and Cameron told me there's a place in the Shute with a mural—an image depicting Adrises and the gods."

"It's a grotto," Cameron said around his bread. "The mural's on a big rock."

"Right. Well, I have reason to believe it's going to help us figure out what to do."

"The grotto's going to help?" Winn said, at the same time as Isaline guessed, "The ... rock?"

One side of Neave's mouth tugged up. "The mural." She turned to Isaline. "Jack said there were glyphs on the thrones in the House of Matchsticks. Did you see them, too? Bunch of fancy chairs with writing on them."

Isaline had been preoccupied with the six Treasure-hunter skeletons sitting on the thrones, but she *had* noticed the writing. There were words and images carved into the ancient stone, letters she had never seen before. "Yes, I remember."

Cameron said, "There's glyphs on the mural in the grotto, too. We didn't recognize them at the time, of course, but Jack confirmed it was the same language as on the thrones in the House of Matchsticks."

Winn planted her elbows on the table, making a pensive noise. "You think the mural in the grotto tells Adrises' history."

"Precisely." Neave set a newly-polished fingernail on the map, over her scribbled *History?* "If we decode the glyphs on the mural, we can discover more about Adrises. We can use the information to stop her from keeping Adrudian from us. We can keep the King from coming back and using her power. Winn can rebuild the Seven Thrones."

There was a pause while Winn and Isaline stared at the map. Isaline's tired body was suddenly buzzing with energy. Countless murals had been painted on the walls of the House of Matchsticks, but the only language she'd seen had been on the thrones. If they could figure out how to decipher it, what secrets would be revealed to them?

"What does this have to do with your side project?" Winn asked.

Cameron scraped a hand through his hair. "There are a few ancient language experts in Benemourne, but we'd need to travel, and time with them doesn't come cheap. We need funds, so—"

"So I found us a little cash," Neave finished. She traced the line on her map of the Shute. "This will lead us to a diamond deposit. Nothing huge, but enough to cover this expedition, and another."

Cameron's eyes twinkled. "And another ... and another ..."

"That's the gist." Neave patted the map with an open palm and popped a square of cheese in her mouth. "So, Princess? Will you come with us?"

Winn looked around at each of them. Her lips pressed in an expression somewhere between a smile and a frown. She rolled her match between her fingers. The moment drew long, but Isaline felt no unease. Whatever Winn decided, it would be honest. There would be no lies among them again.

Wear your truths, Winn had said only days ago. *Everything else is just clothes.*

"I'll come," Winn declared after a minute. "Faraday's clockworks are guarding the palace, and the old password doesn't work. I can't get inside while they're enforcing his rule. Besides ..." She flashed them the widest grin Isaline had ever seen from her. "There were only three or four times where you all nearly got me killed."

"Excellent." Neave clapped, delighted. "Here's to more."

Cameron flicked a shiny gold coin to Neave with little hesitation. "Here's to more."

"And more," Isaline said. Her throat was thick.

Footsteps emerged from the kitchen behind them. Isaline glanced over her shoulder as Jame stepped into Little Space backward, calling a greeting to the cooks behind their chopping blocks. He was wearing his dark green coat, his hair mussed at the nape of his neck.

"There's Watch in the tavern causing trouble again," Jame said as he turned to face the room. "I told Minna I'd send you, Neave ..." He trailed off, gaze landing on Isaline at the table. "Oh, hi. You're up."

Isaline returned his tentative smile. She hoped her face didn't betray the sudden hurricane in her stomach. "Yeah, I'm—I'm awake."

Jame's eyes made a fleeting trip down to her shoes. "New clothes?"

She fought a blush, but only half-succeeded. "Yes."

"You look great." He slipped his hand into his pocket, retrieved a small envelope, and held it out to Cameron. "This came for you. It was waiting at the bar. Hard to read the address—looks like it's from him."

The legs of Cameron's chair squealed as he leaped to take the letter from Jame. He ripped open the envelope and flopped down again, eyes moving quickly back and forth across the crisp paper inside. Isaline wrung her fingers, watching as Cameron's lips thinned, his posture deflating beneath his Watchman's coat.

"Well?" Winn prompted.

Cameron heaved a sigh. "He's gone north."

"*North?*" Neave said. "Why?"

"He didn't say."

Cameron's voice was so small none of them could find the words to fill the silence that followed. Isaline shifted uncomfortably in her seat. Why would Jack go north without telling anyone? She knew nothing of northern Benemourne, just that it was full of ice and fish. Of the maps they had studied at Casret Academy, the single place she could recall was the small, gray city of Sneld. She couldn't imagine why Jack would want to travel there.

Stuffing the letter into his pocket, Cameron pushed back from the table. "I'll deal with those Watch," he said, voice flat.

"He'll come back." Neave gave Cameron a halfhearted smile, but it faltered as he ducked under the doorframe and into the kitchen. "Not in time for my side project," she muttered, "but he'll come back."

When a rough plan had been laid out, Neave and Winn went to join Cameron in the tavern. Neave shuffled her papers into a pile and bid Winn ahead of her as they left the room. Isaline stood, finding her balance with only slight wobbling, and she was about to follow them when Jame touched her hand. A little shockwave buzzed over her skin.

"Want to go for a walk?" he asked.

She looked down at her weakened legs.

"Just out to the beach, maybe," Jame amended with a grin. "I'll walk, and you shuffle."

He led her through the rowdy tavern, where Cameron was speaking sternly with the Watch in the corner, and Winn and Neave laughed with Minna at the bar. Isaline's feet were trembling. She couldn't take her eyes from the green door of the Harper and Cup. The thought of stepping onto the huge beach beyond made her stomach twist; she'd been underground for a handful of nights, unconscious for more, and the world had expanded around her, giant and impending.

One step after the other, she thought. *Focus on what's in front of you.*

Jame pushed the Harper and Cup's door open and Isaline eased into the warm seaside air.

Outside the inn, ripples of sand bordered a long, boat-scattered stretch of sea. Splashes of mist on the horizon divided the water from a striking, azure sky. Lines of people lumbered across the docks, shading their eyes as they disembarked from airships and ferries—none of which, Isaline noted, belonged to Captain Knots—and flooded into Ar beneath the arches of the Watch Wall.

Isaline and Jame strode slowly over the sand, silently watching the beach unfold. Craning, Isaline squinted at the top of the Wall, where ant-sized City Watch roamed up and down iron staircases. Beyond them, the great tiers of Ar stood waiting.

She cast a glance at Jame, who was regarding her with curiosity, his hands stuck into his pockets.

"What are you thinking?" he asked her.

Isaline took a deep breath. "I'm thinking that I've been to the House of Matchsticks and back, but I still haven't seen inside the walls of this city."

Jame looked over his shoulder at the nearest archway. The crowd from the ferries had thinned, travelers spreading into Ar and moving on to their destinations. A steep cobblestone street wound off and out of sight.

"Well," he said, taking a few steps backward, "we have time."

Her heart stuttered. "Now?"

"Why not?"

Isaline opened her mouth, but closed it again just as fast. Her body was gaining strength, and they didn't have anywhere to be. She couldn't find a reason not to walk into Ar that wasn't her own nerves.

Jame cataloged the anxious look on her face. "Don't worry." He hooked a finger under his sleeve and checked his watch. "I have an idea."

They retraced their steps past the Harper and Cup, up to one of the soaring archways funneling people into the city. There, Jame took her arm and led her beneath the archway and onto a narrow, sloping road. The crowd streamed on every side—box-laden merchants, tourists in elaborate hats, hooded Adrudian Drinkers, even a group of Quandary Thieves who acknowledged Jame as they passed. The heavy odor of roasting vegetables, burning Adrudian, and close-packed bodies made Isaline's nose scrunch.

I've smelled better places, Jame had said when Isaline long-ago asked him about Ar. Now she understood what he'd meant.

Ahead, a row of trolleys lined the street in front of a large, weathered station with a red tile roof. People climbed into the trolleys left and right, hauling trunks or packages or children with them. Jame ushered Isaline to the trolley at the far end, which had a smattering of open seats inside.

She reflexively moved toward the trolley's steps, but Jame pulled on her arm again, shaking his head. He brought her around the trolley, where he took hold of the back window's edge and clambered onto the trolley's roof, sitting so his legs dangled over the side.

"Have you forgotten I was in a coma two hours ago?" Isaline said, looking up at him.

"I highly doubt that will stop you." He leaned down and offered her his hand.

Isaline raised to tiptoes, grasping Jame's hand with her left arm. She braced her feet on the trolley, grit her teeth against the sting in her right shoulder, and pushed herself up with her feet. The pain was deep, but fleeting; moments later, she comfortably oriented to sit on the trolley's roof, her knee bumping Jame's.

"Not bad," he said, echoing Cameron's earlier sentiment.

"Are we allowed to be up here?" she asked him. People milled about the trolley, paying no attention to the soles of Jame and Isaline's boots waving above their heads.

Jame gave her a wicked grin. "Wouldn't you like to know, City Watchling?"

She laughed, softness spreading through her. *City Watchling*. That wasn't Isaline anymore, but it was how Jame knew her: not Nalissa, not a Quandary Thief, just a Watchling he'd met in a forest.

A moment later, the trolley lurched to life, climbing steadily up the sloping cobblestones and away from the Watch Wall. The crowd parted to let them through as the trolley gained speed, rumbling on its rails into the city.

Isaline clutched the roof's edge, insides dancing as the trolley station rolled out of sight and was replaced by a procession of buildings with iron-latticed windows and colorful clothes lines drawn across rooftops. She tried to look everywhere at once, drinking in the unfamiliar surroundings.

"So," Jame said. They were sitting close enough for his

voice to be audible over the din of the trolley. "How'd you make it back from the mines? Jack said he couldn't remember ... just closed his eyes and he was on the surface."

Isaline had the abrupt image of the world speeding by her half-lidded eyes, her body folded against someone's chest. A rescuer.

But that couldn't be real.

"I don't know. I think I was ... carried. I was in the House of Matchsticks, and I could feel myself dying. I thought I saw ..." She shook her head, unsure of how to describe the man with the lantern without sounding insane. "I thought I saw something. Then I was on the shore, face up in the water. Maybe it was magic."

Isaline added that last part as a joke, but Jame just nodded, watching the street slip by beneath them. "Maybe it was."

The trolley turned, making its way further up the mountain. Sunlight cast a wet-looking sheen over tall buildings and the shadowed entrances of alleyways. Wispy clouds drifted across the sky, and Isaline caught the distant, white balloon of an airship carving a path through the air. She tapped her fingertips on the brass under her sleeve.

Jame pulled up his knee and hugged it to his chest, heel resting on the edge of the trolley's roof. "Busy, isn't it?" He gestured at their surroundings with his chin. "What do you think?"

Isaline gazed at the city rolling past, speechless. Tiers of buildings soared from the mountain, jumbled like a giant, unsolvable puzzle. People roamed on either side of the trolley, talking with each other, calling farewells, sliding onto side streets. Ar was alive in every direction. The city was too massive for her mind to comprehend, but she *felt* it: the lives existing through and among each other, entwined like threads. Ar's heartbeat echoed through the mountain and harmonized with her own.

Their trolley rumbled past an open corridor between two wide, terraced buildings, and the sea shone through for the space of a breath. Isaline folded her hands. "It's ..." She hunted for the right word. Jame waited, his smile fading, as if nervous about what she was going to say. "Mesmerizing."

Jame chuckled, but the anticipation didn't leave his face. He said, "Do you think ..." He took a deep breath. Isaline's heart thumped—he *was* nervous. "Do you think you might stay? After Neave's expedition?"

The wind blew his hair into his eyes. Gently, without thinking, Isaline brushed the strands away from his brow, tucking them behind his ear. His breath caught, and she drew away, afraid the gesture might have been too familiar. They didn't know each other, not really, and she had so much to apologize for.

But then he captured her hand and pressed her palm to the side of his face, leaning into her touch. Relaxing, she smiled, her heart aglow with things to tell him, her voice untethered.

The trolley climbed. The city hummed. Isaline and Jame sat together for a long time.

"I think I will," she said, and the words came easy. "I think I'll stay."

13

THE PULL

THE COLLECTOR

North of the mountains, clouds roiled in a steely sky, threatening rain. The Collector stared into the brewing storm's depths, holding the brim of his hat and suppressing a shiver. Days ago, when the Collector and Caladrius had saved Isaline and Jack from the House of Matchsticks, it had seemed summer had finally arrived. He and Caladrius had spent long hours in Lower Village, sunlight bathing Caladrius' black, iridescent starling's wings. Now, at a docking port on the edge of the sea, she huddled close to his collar to stave off a chill.

The Collector stroked her feathers, wondering if his warmth affected her as it used to. Her stars were nearly gone—but he pushed the observation away. He didn't need to think about that yet.

Ahead, an undulating crowd of people inched up a wide, wooden gangway. The Collector and Caladrius lingered behind the crowd, paces to the right of the bench that held Jack Fael.

Jack had made the day's travel from Lower Village, coming to a stop at an airship port overhanging a steep bluff. The Collector had followed him at a distance. Caladrius, in her emerging bird's body, had no interest in collecting the dead—and the Collector had no interest in leaving her until it was necessary—so they trailed Jack up the coastline, to where the departure of his airship had been delayed.

The gangway was packed with travelers wearing their best fashion, lining up to climb aboard the enormous ship hovering before them. The Collector had never seen so much silk and shoe polish in one place. The passengers looked like people going to a ball, rather than boarding an airship.

"This is no expedition," the Collector said, eyeing Jack slouched on the bench. "This is luxury."

A passing woman in a magenta peacoat spotted Jack sitting at the edge of the crowd. He wore an old, gray jacket, leather gloves, and a thin pack over one shoulder. The woman gave him a long, perplexed stare, no doubt marking the blue veins on his face, but Jack didn't return the stare, or any of the crowd's confused looks—he was busy studying the side of the airship, where the words

AFS Gloriosa were displayed in perfect midnight-blue paint.

The Collector followed his gaze. The ship was a colossus of aluminum and coated steel hanging mid-air off the bluff. Lustrous, unblemished sheets of metal had been fused to form the pointed hull, which resembled an ocean liner's hull, not the gondolas of the airships the Collector had seen in Ar. Two towering smokestacks thrust out of the body of the ship, releasing clouds of Adrudian-laced steam.

With a series of smooth *clunks*, a hatch lifted on the back of the *Gloriosa* and a second gangway lowered, thumping against the edge of the bluff. Passengers gathered against the railings to watch as teams of workers jogged onto the bluff and began pushing sizable tubs of Adrudian up the gangway, stocking fuel for the journey ahead.

"That explains the delay." The Collector glanced at Caladrius, who twittered. "Late arrival from the mill."

I will choke their Adrudian until the world bleeds.

Dread crept into the Collector's chest, at odds with the crowd's excited murmurs. Passengers pointed at the tubs as workers shoved them through the hatch and into the back of the airship. Gripping the Jar of Lights, the Collector drifted closer to listen to their chatter.

"The ship is beautiful," the woman in the peacoat who had stared at Jack said. Her husband, a tall man with a mustache, held her arm. "It looks so new."

"Good," he replied gruffly. "We're paying out the nose for this tour."

"It'll be worth it. We'll have an unmatched view from the skies, and besides, we only have to suffer through one stop."

"One stop in *Sneld*."

She arranged her fire-red hair, which she had piled on top of her head with a gold pin. "You hardly have to get off the ship, Sterling."

The Collector looked at Jack, who was fiddling with the cuffs of his gloves. The *Gloriosa* was a luxury airliner departing on a vacationer's cruise. Why was Jack flying on this ship?

The ground vibrated beneath the Collector's feet. He peered to the top of the passengers' gangway, where the line was finally starting to move. Steam flowed with a fresh vigor from the ship's smokestacks. The captain must have ordered a start to the ship's Adrudian engine, warming the *Gloriosa* for takeoff.

Jack stood from the bench, hitching his pack over his shoulder. The crowd milled before him, for once paying no attention to the Adrudian Drinker lingering at the back of the line. Pursing his lips, Jack tightened the knot of hair at the crown of his head and, casting around to ensure he was unnoticed, pushed a thumb beneath the cuff of his right glove.

The Collector stepped closer as Jack lifted the leather

glove from his skin. But *skin* wasn't the right word; where Jack's hand should have been, there was only a cutout in the air shaped like a hand. His fingers were glittering shadows filled with the winks of faraway stars.

Caladrius cooed in recognition. This was the same as their bodies: the same silhouette, the same distant galaxies. Jack stared at his no-hand for a moment, then opened his mouth and quietly inhaled. The starry darkness receded with his breath, the skin of his hand appearing as if a curtain had been swept aside.

The Collector's stomach shrank. Jack's hand disappeared when he held his breath.

"That's interesting," the Collector said to Caladrius. He lifted his own hand, examining the vacancy of its outline, the pinpricks of light shining through. Steeling himself, he inhaled. The tips of his fingers solidified into skin. Fingerprints and nails carved themselves out of air, pale in overcast light.

No memories had come from his breaths, after the House of Matchsticks. Instead, he was *changing,* his human body appearing gradually each time he breathed. Like Caladrius, the Collector would soon occupy a corporeal form.

Stopping his breath, fingertips disappearing back into shadow, the Collector glanced up at Jack, who had returned his glove to his hand. Fear and curiosity rushed through the Collector in equal measure. Both he and Jack had been marked by the events in the House of Matchsticks—both of them changing into something new. The Collector couldn't fathom what the transformation meant or if it could be stopped.

Jack trudged up the gangway behind the last of the passengers, headed for the *Gloriosa* and the skies. The Collector watched, ruminating on the next time he would see Jack or Isaline, and knowing it would be soon. The three of them were linked, existences tied together, and the Collector guessed he would be drawn back to them as easily as a magnet to its twin.

As easily as a bird to her flock.

Caladrius squeezed her claws in his coat. He gazed at her, eyes running over the flecks of white adorning her black feathers. The patterning was new. He was going to have to memorize it before the next leg of his journey began.

As Jack disappeared into the mouth of the *Gloriosa,* the Collector adjusted his hold on the Jar of Lights. His middle squeezed at what was to come.

"Let's go," he said to Caladrius. "Let's get you home."

The Collector and Caladrius arrived at Casret Academy as day rolled into night. They passed the dormitory, the cafeteria, and the training center, each building shrouded in cool twilight. Students roamed the grounds, discussing the beginning of summer and the excitement of graduation. Caladrius drew him away from them and into the forest at the Academy's outskirts, where the air chorused with nocturnal insects.

As night deepened, the Jar of Lights lit his path, blue mingling with glistening green. The souls inside the lantern's bulb swirled as if caught in a spectral whirlpool. The Collector flexed the fingers of his right hand on the brim of his hat, trying to calm his pounding heart.

His shoulder was empty. Caladrius flew ahead, darting between trees, leading the way.

I will have to get used to being alone, the Collector told himself. A pang went through him, so he repeated the prayer until it felt true. *I can get used to being alone. I can get used to being alone.*

Clusters of powder-blue flowers poked from the forest floor, blooming heads bobbing on long stems. The Collector slowed to run his fingers over the soft petals. Nightblues. They were close.

Minutes later, the Collector passed through a tight-knit line of trees and into Isaline and Jame's clearing. In the weeks past, the clearing had been transformed into a meadow, Nightblues waving in the warm breeze. Ash from the two fire pits had been mixed into the soil by rain, and Nightblues grew even there, the ground healing over and beginning afresh. At the edge of the meadow, a twist-rooted oak tree swayed, its branches laden with birds.

The sight of the tree made the Collector's stomach

bottom out. Still, he drifted into the meadow after Caladrius, ignoring his shaking legs.

Caladrius fluttered into the canopy of the oak tree, gliding within the labyrinth of leaves. The Collector stood beneath her, craning as she flitted between branches, mapping the tree and its hundreds of sleepy starlings, who stirred at the sight and sound of her. He smiled, wondering if Caladrius felt familiar to the starlings, a kinship forged weeks ago when they flew together above the forest.

When she had explored every inch of the tree, Caladrius fell through the air to perch on the Collector's outstretched hand. She tugged at his fingers, as if to carry him into the canopy with her.

He shook his head, his arms heavy. "You'll be safe here."

She twittered, stretching her sleek wings, and pulling him harder.

"I have to finish what you started. I have to see where I fit." The Collector looked above them in an arc. Fireflies had appeared, hovering among leaves and starlings. The tree's canopy resembled the night sky. "This is where you fit."

Caladrius stared at him, lights reflected in her black eyes. She made a low, mournful sound, and he brushed her with the pad of his thumb.

"I'll see you again," he whispered, "one day."

Don't forget me, he wanted to add, but his voice had failed him.

She stared for a moment longer, then leaped into the air and soared on every side of him, nudging his shoulders, his neck, the underside of his chin, the top of his head. Her song was bittersweet, but still it enlivened him, spreading love through to his every corner. The Collector fanned his arms and let her spiral around them before she lifted and joined the starlings in the oak tree. He raised the Jar of Lights. Caladrius perched among her family, looking so like the others the Collector's knees gave up and buckled.

He sank to the grass, letting his spine round. His heart was breaking, and this was only the beginning. There was a place for him, as there was for her, but finding it without Caladrius to guide him seemed impossible.

Still, he knew he belonged somewhere. He knew it as readily as he knew his own heart. His hands. His soul.

A light blossomed beside him.

The Collector turned, half-expecting a swarm of fireflies. What he saw instead was a brilliant light emerging from the Jar of Lights, and the souls inside the lantern rising from the top. They ascended, floating in the air like balls of smoke.

He swallowed the dry lump in his throat. "You're leaving, too. It's your time."

The souls of Lillian and Philip Just came forward, grazing the skin of his hands with their light. Nalissa joined them, followed by the sea captain and the mill warden. Their brightness hurt his eyes, but he dared not close them for fear of missing their farewell.

"Thank you," the Collector said, and he meant it with his whole heart. "I will look after them. The people you leave behind."

They circled him, alighting on his cheeks, his elbows, the edge of his jaw, just as Caladrius had done. Despite the storm inside him, the unknown world before him, he laughed. These human souls knew his long, mysterious road, and still they celebrated it: where he had been, what he had done, and what he was going to learn.

"Goodbye," he said to them.

The souls made one last orbit of his body and rose into the air as one, flying toward the branches of the oak tree. Their glow cast the canopy of leaves in a rainbow of color. Soon they were hidden beyond the branches, ascending for the stars.

Seeing them disappear, the Collector's despair and joy merged, sparking a fire that stood him from the grass, threaded his arm through the Jar of Lights, and turned him to face the tree's trunk. He couldn't miss their flight.

Grasping the lowest branch of the oak tree, he hauled himself up until he sat at the top, nestled at the zenith of its canopy, and had a clear view of the sky. Hundreds of birds surrounded him, starlings murmuring as the moon rose, full and radiant. Branches shook as the birds took to the air. Caladrius was among them.

Above him, the souls soared into boundless space, flying to wherever the souls of humans went. The

Collector sat, huddled in the leaves of Cal's tree, and looked up.

He watched them go.

THE ADVENTURE CONTINUES IN ...

PART FOUR OF THE HOUSE OF MATCHSTICKS SERIES

Coming soon! Sign up for updates at elisadowning.com/newsletter.

WANT FREE HOUSE OF MATCHSTICKS CONTENT?

Hi! Elisa here.

I hope you enjoyed *Tree of Matchsticks* (Part 3). If you did, I'd love to hear from you in a review. Reviews help readers take notice of books—and even a sentence or two can mean the world to indie authors like myself. Thank you so much!

If you're itching to read more House of Matchsticks content, join my newsletter to receive your free House of Matchsticks Reader Bundle. You'll get a novelette starring Jack and Cameron, map downloads, and more. Find out more at my website: elisadowning.com.

As always, thank you for reading. And see you in the House of Matchsticks.

Elisa Downing

THE HOUSE OF MATCHSTICKS SERIES

House of Matchsticks
Night of Matchsticks
Tree of Matchsticks

ALSO BY ELISA DOWNING

Josie and the Scary Snapper

ABOUT THE AUTHOR

Elisa Downing is an author of strange stories about brave kids, teens, and new adults. An MA Children's Literature graduate, she's spent years climbing through the windows of books to better see the world beyond. She enjoys writing fantastical adventures full of ancient mysteries, slow-burn romance, and lots of monsters. When she's not writing, you can find Elisa reading under a tree somewhere, playing video games on easy mode, waxing poetic over cult cinema, or watching horror movies.

www.ingramcontent.com/pod-product-compliance
Lightning Source LLC
Chambersburg PA
CBHW030340310726
48979CB00001B/113
9781777885700